FLAG ON THE SUMMIT

APRILISH. CH. SANGMA.

iUniverse, Inc.
Bloomington

FLAG ON THE SUMMIT

Copyright © 2011 by Aprilish. Ch. Sangma.

All rights reserved. No part of this book may be used or reproduced by any means, graphic, electronic, or mechanical, including photocopying, recording, taping or by any information storage retrieval system without the written permission of the publisher except in the case of brief quotations embodied in critical articles and reviews.

This is a work of fiction. All of the characters, names, incidents, organizations, and dialogue in this novel are either the products of the author's imagination or are used fictitiously.

iUniverse books may be ordered through booksellers or by contacting:

iUniverse
1663 Liberty Drive
Bloomington, IN 47403
www.iuniverse.com
1-800-Authors (1-800-288-4677)

Because of the dynamic nature of the Internet, any web addresses or links contained in this book may have changed since publication and may no longer be valid. The views expressed in this work are solely those of the author and do not necessarily reflect the views of the publisher, and the publisher hereby disclaims any responsibility for them.

Any people depicted in stock imagery provided by Thinkstock are models, and such images are being used for illustrative purposes only.
Certain stock imagery © Thinkstock.

ISBN: 978-1-4620-7196-8 (sc)
ISBN: 978-1-4620-7197-5 (ebk)

Printed in the United States of America

iUniverse rev. date: 01/18/2012

CHAPTER 1

BOLCHUGRI WITH ITS QUEEN AND THE YOUNG PRINCESSESS.

It was early nineteen eighties, at Bolchugri, a non descript place of a non descript town; the name itself was derived from the giant cotton tree that stood in the middle looking majestic and imposing like a king, regally; it was surrounded on all sides by few numbers of decent thatch houses of lives so simple; its four corners were totally blocked by Ranggira range where superstition reigned supreme; there the simple lives began; the lives of innocent children. The life people led there was next near to primitive; their lives were ordinary yet meaningful; their lives are simple but enchanting, boring yet beautiful in mixture with rampant gossip more of destructive than constructive tinged with jealousy green began. For Palmina and her friends giant cotton tree had lots to give. They played hide and seek around it, house—house, watched the cartoon box shows and waited for the season when it give both the red flowers and the white cotton. When Palmina was novice in doll making, Jentilla taught her the art of making dolls out of thrown rags and earned the latter's friendship. Palmina's parents are the one among fifteen families settled first in Bolchugri, a dense forested land none dared to break into with their hearts thundering at the howl of a wolf at night. Jentilla's parents settled earlier. She came to her house, a shy little girl, two years older to her five years and offered her friendship with all embracing welcoming smile. When her parents brought her here, they saw first the leopard below the giant cotton tree and giant snake coiled into a high backless sofa where none dared to sit but stayed awake the night. She saw too, the long nest of a bird in a little tree out of big leaves. It was low below the small tree. Palmina called

Jentilla and showed her the nest near their house. Jentilla came, shrieked, peered inside the nest and saw four newly hatched chicken and watched them grow everyday. They both searched for grasshoppers, the tiny ones and fed the hungry chicks. Now, they had neighbors in plenty and more still came Palmina joyously watched them building houses with Jentilla sharing her happiness; a new colony in a small town. She had a friend in Chinche too, few years older to them both, had advance knowledge of everything. At Bolchugri, slander had its reign freely and people are of more religious than God-fearing, going ritually to church every Sunday in the best clean clothes possible, even if their hearts hidden well from the naked eyes were as black as the coal. The children were innocent, pure and untouched by the blackness of their thoughts. The men with their pant, white shirts, well oiled hair combed with side parting looking sleek, the women in their best *dakmanda* but worn repeatedly and blouses with the round knotted hair behind their heads on top and the girls in their frilled frocks with elastic above their waist, a little below their small pointed nipples and their hairs in two plaits with red ribbon at the bottom are regular church goers. The elders with Hymn books in their hands, singing hymns, praying solemnly yet doing nothing good but bad only are regular church goers. They knew nothing about their sins but only about others whom they condemned later when the church service was over and earned the sinner's wrath. Holier than thou, that was how they thought of themselves. The preachers preached in the church about something his neighbor had weakness for but not the one he had weakness of unaware of his own very malicious intent of a malicious heart. Chinche, Palmina and Jentilla went to church, unwillingly, to the urge of their parents. Chinche had none to urge her but she went along only to accompany them. She lost her mother just few years back. PHE water was unheard of, but the pond water was used, both for drinking, bathing as well for washing, tax free Palmina thought to be blessed to have it. For children, it was fun to bathe in the pond water, shrieking, laughing and throwing water at each other their mothers had tough time shouting at them to stop at with no success. In the public pond, Jentilla's father dug with the help of few young male neighbors Jentilla was proud of Palmina had the privilege to bathe. When they fought, "don't bathe in the pond my father made" were Jentilla's words to Palmina. She had other reasons to be proud of; the pond water had in the nearby three big trees towering; the trees offered a colony for many sparrow families; long straw nests hanging from each branch then swaying from side to side when the wind blew. They made much noises fighting both in the morning and in the evening. When Chinche came to bathe in the pond, early well before the class she fluttered her long lashes at the boys with only some returning her flutter. They fluttered back when Benta-ma and Tochi-ma are not around, too worried of the stretchable mouth they had and tarnishing their names. She often brought her brothers along too, bathed them, scrubbed them hard, slapped their clothes hard on the flat rock. Milche had her mother for chaperone, stuck to her like a limpet and never enjoyed the friendship they enjoyed. Jentilla's father poured bucketful of red potassium monthly purifying the water or a bucketful of overnight soaked white lime and with it dried in the dry season Ringrey stream was a blessing—for bathing and for washing clothes and for washing kitchen utensils as well. Palmina hardly could go to Ringrey stream; her mother forbidden it, strictly; she said the stream brought the waste materials from upstream settlers but Palmina heeded not. The water was crystal clean, ran over clean sand and moss strewn rocks and sneaked out to bathe only to get the severe beating from her angry mother. In the very early eighties, Bio gas was unheard of. Most people had not seen it and it instilled fear with the word spreading that it burst and killed people, a good excuse for wanting but unable to buy; the firewood was used all the year round. The people not bought it but cut down from the jungle nearby, depleting it and moving to next leaving the jungle naked then dried the raw green trees for two three months, stocked it for the Summer and for the rainy season when still in the winter. Palmina-ma had a tough time with the firewood during summer. It rained and wet the firewood. Then it gave much smoke than the flame hurting her eyes and the whole family. He father complained much of smoke. For Palmina, Jentilla, Chinche and Milche winter was a blessing. They had the winter holiday they used fully to explore the nearby jungles where only the hunters dared to tread and loved the exotic beauty of nature, the singing of the birds, of all varieties, the serenity, the streams. Electricity has entered the small heart of the town but Bolchugri and the elders still fought with the local member of legislative assembly for its entry with no success for five years yet with a promise unending given to them for which they waited for him to fulfill, patiently, anxiously, who asked in return for the next term to vote for him, stretchable for two terms but at the end of ten years, they still used the kerosene lamp. Palmina had her reading till late night with the kerosene lamp, its chimney black with soot till it gave dim

3

light straining her eyes in the late of the night. She was the most hardworker. Television was heard of by the people and it came to the heart of the town when Delhi hosted Asian Games. It was first seen in a house far in the main town, in a house of a doctor, lucky enough to win it in lottery in Gauhati. The children heard of it and went literally to look at the wonder box they so much heard about and returned disappointed when they saw nothing in the screen but the woman in a *saree* cutting fishes. Motor cars are much luxury and are privately owned with only the ministers in the government were the lucky few to ride in them. With the red light on the top that shone golden bright inside, they drove swiftly in fleet with the policemen in jeep ahead waving red flag to anyone interested to look and demanding to make way signaling 'look who is coming.' They came once in every five years from Shillong, crowded with the flags waving and the symbols printed on the flags—rose, drum, sickle, hand, kettle, lamp, water lily in the middle; but the children knew not what a government was. The parents laughed, pointed at them then circled their fingers towards themselves and said "we and you", still they opened their mouths, unintelligibly dumb. The buses they saw, everyday, came from Garobada, its head protruding, nose with long slit holes like that of a pig snorting its nose, jammed packed. On the roof of it too people sat packed, and the poor bus groaned, whine, complained with the load too heavy to bear and at snail's pace it came with the weight above and behind pulling it back rather than pushing forward and moaning of pain not pleasure. Black pitch road ran in the main town road with pot holes with muddle water filling it in summer with rain, some even wide enough for a swimming pool. But life was peaceful, serene, carefree and gay. A narrow foot path ran for a long playfield for the children. In it the evening brought shrieks, screams, laughter, cries in between houses on each side, all thatch and the tin sloppy roofs only very few could afford, handed down by the rich grandparents with acres of paddy fields in the village. The life began always with children, childhood days a major part of everyone's life, memorable, unforgetful, the beginning.

Palmina looked at the giant cotton tree as she often did wondering all the time calculating at the same about its age and always ended shaking her head with failure. It was indeed huge, unimaginably so. Nobody knew its age. Somebody roughly guessed it must be few hundred years old. Another calculated its age thousand years old. Palmina innocently asked her father the age of the tree and got the answer 'as old as Adam himself' and she believed it missing the twinkle in his eyes. But nonetheless her life revolved round it. She grew around here with Jentilla and other children from Bolchugri—Milche and Chinche. She knew the season it gave both the red flowers and white cotton and waited for both. Now, stood below its huge bottom she looked up at the top and leafless branches with the red flower burst opened and the white cotton came out matured, ready for use. Some lay at its massive feet, motionless, waited for a pick yet with none interested except children who picked it and played with its pure white flower and let the thin shreds fly in the air and spread their film of whiteness; some on the sloppy roof of the L-shaped house, below the tree on the left side of the road. The tree had the curse, the curse as the leafless tree no one missed out but an open display for anyone looking. Yet it stood proudly erect for the fruit it bore and the cotton. Bolchugri, the name was apt for the place, named after the tree "Bolchu" in a local dialect. It stood majestic in the middle, only for the power it lacked otherwise he looked like a king with queen sadly missing but the locality in the town corner had its own. She reigned like a queen, with the mouth like a loudspeaker, that exuded power over her husband, neighbors, children and grown up alike, judging rightly and wrongly with no complain but always wrongly and no one righted the wrong. Not that they knew not of but terrified of the mouthful of abuse she sure was to bestow on anyone dared to invite. Her words crossed boundaries; her voice untamed; her temper volcanic no one missed of and ran in miles if given a chance. Both Palmina and Jentilla hated her. Chinche squirmed at her sight. Milche liked her, not much but more lot than them. She had a reason too; she was sweet to her.

"I know who did it. Jealous woman."

Tochi—ma fumed breathing raggedly, her eyes angrily glittering larger with dilated pupils than on normal days. She stood on a narrow road above the house, where all gathered for the evening meet after dinner, before dark, mostly to catch gossip, criticize and to condemn. Her maid servant left her house the night before and tiptoed her feet out of her tyrannical mistress. It was not her first nor her second attempt but the third. She failed miserably in the first and second attempt. In the first she ran as far as Palmina-ma's house but dragged bodily back home heaping abuses at Palmina—ma. In the second attempt she tried another tactic and left home early morning but missing the early morning bus she waited for the eight thirty bus and sealed her doom again. Her mistress charged all the way to the bus station and dragged her back again. Everyone knew the timing of her bus—Both the times she showed badly beaten black bruises to Palmina and Jentilla. Jentilla helped her flight, was terrified when caught by her mistress and made her swear not to mention her name. The servant girl honoured her promise and never breathed her name much to the relief of Jentilla. She later massaged the bruises and swelling with the cloth dipped in a hot water and cringed when she squirmed. Later she smuggled boroline her mother brought home and applied in the darkness. Palmina gave her a word of advice—not to pull any stunts for few months but to remain docile and quiet. Her mistress was taking no chance and was alert all the time round and was not letting her guard down. She had the eyes of a hawk. The months saw her crying endlessly with cruel touch of her mistress rendering two of her friends. She showed them many red lines on her back brought with the thin strips of a bamboo. Her tears and pain angered the two children. They made a plan. The third time was a lucky attempt and had her mistress' blood pressure shot high up. Tochi—ma seemed blaming everyone around for her get-away but gave the hint of her suspect. Deep within Palmina was elated and secretly shared the happiness of the servant girl and enjoyed the rage of a fat bad tempered woman with tolerance almost nil. Tochi—ma struggled with her breathing in rage. She was an asthma patient no one had sympathy for. She was a hard worker, the servant girl, left bed with the touch of dawn and kept the kettle filled tea ready for her mistress, she enjoyed no end. But Tochi—ma saw nothing good to speak of her. Palmina saw her in joyous mood and it made her day. It ignited joy in her too. She danced all the way to the pond with an empty basin in hand she threw from side to side stopping only when in the sight of her mistress jealous of her happiness who let the smoke out through her nostrils like an angry bull. Her joy gladdened the hearts of two children. She sang when she worked and never left the works undone with no complain. It ignited jealousy. The neighbors itched hard. They worked themselves, slogging from morning till evening with no extra hand to help. Tochi—ma had an upper hand—a hard working servant. She never left the work undone with no appreciation to the service rendered.

"Someone injected poison in her ears."

Tochi—ma said repeatedly with suspicion breathing fire but with restrained anger. She still withheld the name and the culprit still escaped and was at large. Total silence reigned among the women; they were all standing near their houses, gathered to catch the latest gossip. The other women looked at each other in silent query and suspicion. Jentilla ran behind Chinche with a cloth-ball in hand and hit her with it. Inside, her heart beat quickened and looked at Palmina who gave her stern look, telling "don't give away." All the children shrieked and laughed for the former's laxity in failing to hit. It narrowly missed the mark. But the elder women all are beset with anxiety.

"Who could it be?" she said talking more to herself than to others standing, looking at her with mixed confusion. Then they looked at each other for the outward sign of guilt. Palmina—ma narrowed her eyes, probing indepth. All remained curiously puzzled.

"That wretched old woman with her big mouth. Jealous always of others"

She continued relentlessly. It dawned slowly. The others got the hint of her suspect slowly. Their eyes smirked. Their mouths twitched.

"Last week also, she threw the stinking bag full of dirt to our compound. The throwing of the waste is everyday happening."

With these words she confirmed their suspicion. It must be close neighborhood woman. All looked at one but she remained unperturbed with no betray of emotion. She showed no show of inner turmoil and her eyes remained unperturbed. Cool and calm.

"Her pig set free came and destroy all my yum, right from the root."

It revealed the person without being named and somebody swiveled to her side instantly. Her words sparked off instant reaction.

"*Hare* . . . am I the one to send your servant away? To inject poison into her? You always say this and that about me but I kept quiet."

Jentilla-ma took the hint and reacted angrily with the accusation. She was fuming with the smoke seemed ready to emit out of her ears, nose and eyes with her lips tightly sealed in boiling rage. Both stood on the road above glaring at one another charging like an angry bull to the red cloth waving. She was older, a bit wiser but raised to the bait and ignited for the lightning like strike of verbal duel. She was younger and cantankerous. A pompous; boastful; proud; an irritant; mean. Lastly, a big shrew with foul mouth, all are scared of. The accusation flowed like a water flowing, non stop. The counter accusation strengthened. Everyone around looked at the duo with their mouths opened. They listened, unable to side and merely watched. Palmina heard her own hearts drumming loudly. She had a reason too but fought bravely to show her calmness. The verbal duel heated and sparked off fire and turned physical. The younger had the husband watching with his right thumb in the left palm, kneading Bandar tobacco, well mixing it with the lime and put it inside his lips. He stood restless and shifted his short plump body from side to side. He saw the trouble brewing and expectation of him. He knew his role—water to douse the fire raging wildly. Everyone knew he was the water engulfed by the fire. Palmina was no exception. She too knew of her—The fire of a fishwife, like a fiery dragon breathing fire and charring the victims till they heaped in ash. The older stood alone with no husband watching yet remained undaunted. Bolchugri saw the women fighting, their hands on each others hair, pulling. Both women attempted to prove their strength with none winning but both fought with equal strength, the one with a husband behind strictly supporting and the other without one but on her own, dauntless. The children stopped playing. Their shrieking stopped. Palmina, Jentilla, Chinche, Milche and Salmina stood rooted, their mouths opened, gaped at the two women. It took time but they registered in the end. It was a fight—the women's fight. The elder male and female were mute spectators too, watching, amused at first and not knowing what to do. Benta-ma stood; her thin hair coiled, the little bun supported by long hairpin, perched on her tiny head, sided with Tochi-ma. She had her reason for siding. For everyone standing it was well defined. Palmina-ma knew now; Palmina too, Milche-ma, Jentilla, Milche, Chinche, the headman, his wife, the village male elders and the young men enjoying the fighting with a suppressed laughter shared in between much hidden from their elders with respect or disrespect. There were shared words in between all who stood. They talked. They opined. They criticized. They even jested. They had a suspect with all fingers pointing at one—culprit was someone else. They whispered on each others' ears dreading their voice would carry. It must be someone with a motive, selfish or with ulterior they could hardly put their finger on it. The innocent was suspected. The culprit was overlooked. Nobody saw the stark fear in nine year old girl's eyes. Jentilla breathed raggedly and heaped abuses at the younger woman siding clearly with her mother. She ran forward and bit at the hand clasping her mother's hair bun but thrashed mercilessly and went backwards and fell with her buttock hitting a pointed stone and sat there writhing with pain followed by few drops of tears she wiped with the back of her hand. Palmina rushed forward and sat squatted asking her repeatedly whether she was alright. Palmina was a child but understood it was unbecoming for the elders to fight. She thought it was not right but kept her voices well hidden. She had no voice to raise. The children never did that. The grown ups never listen. It was for the children only to listen what they spoke; whether right or wrong. The fight lasted several minutes, their hair buns out open, splaying the hairs, covering both the faces and the other, elder resident left with just white petti-coat, her *gana* on the ground below at her feet in a heap. The men lowered their eyes embarrassed but nothing embarrassed her. Rage overwhelmed her not the embarrassment. There was no stronger, no weaker of the two but both fought and none was a winner. Both of them fought in the heat and their emotion unwrapped but not to win. The headman interrupted, lately so yet with the urging, asked the husband of one to separate them. He went and pulled her to one side not hard and pushed another forward with manly strength, who fell backwards and her back hit the tree. Palmina watched him closely and saw his instant guilt. The hit narrowly miss the head. But she sat there for few minutes. "Ahhh . . . ahhh . . . aaahhh" she moaned, her face writhed in pain with her hand touching her own back. Jentilla rushed forward, sat squatted by her side, closely surveyed the few nail scratches in her hand, then insolently at the other woman retreating. The husband did his part, dragged his better half home, still looking back and threatening the older other still sat writhing at the foot of the tree. She avenged the innocent for her lose. The servant girl already home, a three and half hours of bus journey from here, in the village where she hailed from, happily reunited with her poor but loving parents oblivious of the brawl her stealth departure had made. Her mother made an effort to get up. With her two small hands in her mother's right arm she tried to lift her mother up and succeeded. She led her towards home with her mother still her one hand in the back and writhing in pain. The husband sided his wife. He feared her; her foul mouth, her vicious temper he never had mastered over feared him. Whisperings showered on their back. All wondered the fate of the husband at home. The deep scar on his forehead, the bald patch on his left side head foretold them. The dented pot and the deformed silver mug in their kitchen spoke well ahead. No one told them but their kitchen maid in the bathing place spilled beans of the family affair everyone listened to with rapt attention and the virus carried forward to anyone susceptible to listen. The evening had a topic. Bzzzzzzbzzzbzzzzbzzzzbzzzzzzbzzzzzzbzzzzzzbzzzzzzbzzzzzzbzzzzzz bzzzzzbzzzzbzzzz. It was buzzing like bees. The other topics are forgotten. The topic zeroed only on the fight and the reason. Their hands were in their mouths, covering one corner of their own mouths, protecting the words from spreading but with futile effort. They were trying their damnedest to protect the words from spreading but the words escaped from the corners of their own mouths. They are the messengers themselves. The cause of fight was queried. The late comers asked curiously and those that witnessed did the explaining. The servant girl had the sympathy of all those who listened. Now the whole story came out. Tochi-ma's servant girl was the instigator of the fight. She had bruises all over her body, the servant girl, on her back, on her legs, on her arms and had a sleep outside the house in the kitchen floor. The ooohs and ahhs and "poor thing" dominated the conversation. The mat she slept in was bare saved for the *gana* she wore and spread on and curled her big body small into a little bundle and warmed the body the night over. No one heard her pitiful sobs and heartfelt cry. But she cried, cried the night out, relieved when the cock crowed twice. She left the early morning with no money for bus fare but it was known she met a good fairy. Tochi-ma had a one year old baby, someone who needed constant attention, and an extra help was her utmost need, without one she'd gone crazy, wild and frenzy. Palmina had a reason for guilty; she gave the money for the girl, out of pure compassion, nothing else, thus this ugly episode occurred yet she felt no regret. Her year's coin savings in an empty coconut oil tin was depleted. The small narrow opening became wide the night before. She saw the servant girl sat sobbing alone in the dark on her way back from Jentilla and felt her need. She returned to Jentilla and plotted her escape. Jentilla too gave the half of her year's saving. Together they paid her bus fare. She smiled with triumph. Their compassion succeeded and they were not caught. The topic lasted for two weeks then died down. The culprit was never caught. The guilty was never punished.

The month later another servant girl came. It was evening. Palmina after the school had been playing house—house with her friends. The mammoth feet of the giant cotton tree offered haven for the children shading them from the fading yet bright evening sun. Palmina wore a slim white frock with two pockets on her breasts and two below above her knees. An old frock of her aunty. She put a wire around her neck. She told her friends she was a doctor. She called Chinche, brought her forward and made her sit on the giant root crawling towards the beaten footpath and lifted the end of the wire and examined her heartbeat. Malaria, she declared in straight face of her feigned sickness and given the name of the only medicine she knew. Paracetamol.

"I will be a doctor when I grew up."

Palmina declared loudly. Her desire vividly written in her serious eyes.

'I will be a Magistrate.'

Chirped Jentilla excitedly. She saw one alumni of her school came to grace the occasion and the exuberant way their head mistress announced her students; it was a proud moment for the school with their past pupil for a magistrate. She had challenged her students for more of her kind and Jentilla took it in her heart; an unspoken decision only told to Palmina. Palmina already had decided to become a doctor and waived it. Two flags atop the summit; too far into the future; dreams of two young girls.

'I will marry a rich husband and stay at home.'

Chinche rolled her eyes upwards in wishful thinking. She had her both palms rested in the mid of her heart. It was then they noticed two strangers treading slowly on the footpath—a young girl and an elderly man. They watched her curiously. With her limp hair, red, coarse and wavy, tied with a loose orange rubber band, her scalp seen through the sparse well oiled thin hair above, her body lean and lanky stiff with muscles of hard physical work she trailed an elderly man like a smitten puppy. Like a slow loris she lowered her eyes then glanced away to other side under their curious scrutiny. Like all village girl, her calf below the hem of her old frock was tightened like the chicken leg, its flesh all pushed tight up slimming right above her ankle. Her old frock was dirty not it was unwashed of but of stains like juices of those of young raw mangoes or of jackfruit and the man with bundle on his back walked a little ahead, leading the way; the bundle was small, all wrapped in a single white cloth, tied at the mouth; Palmina imagined the contents—perhaps a pair of *gana*, a blouse, or a frock and no knickers. The man, his hair graying, tall and little stooping asked of her of Tochi—ma's house—the father and the daughter. Palmina pointed at the house with the L-shaped sloppy roof and glanced at her friends in askance.

"Perhaps a poor country relative."

Chinche, the oldest suggested with assumption they neither agreed nor disagreed but they all shrugged off—Jentilla, Milche, Chinche. They all hate the woman. But the evening carried the neighborhood grapevine and her assumption turned wrong. It was the complete story altogether. Tochi-ma had a new kitchen help, someone from Gasuapara, a little place near Bangladesh border. Benta—ma found her for her neighbor. Everyone felt sorry and pity for the latest victim. The father left the daughter and left the morning next with his hopes high. With his ears full of sweet words Tochi—ma fed like regular salary his daughter could send home with his daughter needing not a rupee with them tending her every need; he went floating in the cloud. Palmina wondered how she was lured and why she came but she knew she certainly forgot to do homework before she came. She felt pity for the latest victim. The skeptics wondered for her lasting and she waited for it actually to happen. Perhaps she'd wait for long or short, it remained to be seen. With the nightfall, the children departed and left the feet of the mammoth cotton tree.

CHAPTER 2

RICH NEIGHBOUR.

Hundred meters from their house group of laborers swarmed. They camped there with a triangular green tent to cover. They cooked outside. Twin triangular, three even level stones each makeshift stove erected outside. Like three sisters in two families. Palmina asked the labourers the new comer in Bolchugri. The labourers shook their head failing with the name but replied shortly he was a doctor. The new soon to be new neighbor excited Palmina and Jentilla jumped in ecstasy, clapped her hands in happiness. She baby-sat her brother Jonan there and her friends joined, Chinche, Jentilla and Milche. Together they all slide the slope where the new loose soil was thrown. Jonan entered the tent, their bedroom in the evening and lay for few minutes and blessed the next morning with two circles of tiny dots of flesh he scratched till it bled. It widened its size and spread in his whole thigh. His mother brought a derobin tube and spread around it at night. The next day it all turned red. Palmina got beating for insincere in her work but cried not. The laborers dug since morning till evening and let the loose soil rolled down more below. After a week, Palmina, Jentilla, Chinche and Milche sloshed down it and enjoyed the thrill. They went home with red loose soil stuck hard at their frocks and their Hawaii sandals an inch thicker much to the chagrin of their parents. Her mother shook her head, her unsmiling face spelled anger and Palmina squirmed within and said nothing when heaped with an earful of lectures on where to play and where not to play with all the words escaped through the other ear. She asked nothing about her friends. Chinche had no one of to face the wrath of. Palmina thought of her and envied. One evening the owner came. He stood, a tall bulky man in blue jeans and blue shirt with white sneakers with black zebra stripes across and with his one hand on his hip he seemed pointing every corner, an authoritative figure in complete control over the house building. Domineering. Imposing. Stern. Two weeks later, dozen posts were erected. Rusted brown long iron rods stood looking above and towering over. Sand mounted aside and gravel chips scaled the rocky stairs from the Ringrey stream sat inside the bamboo baskets of the women laborers. Their heads thickly covered easing the weight. Everyone curiously waited for the house to finish. Everyone in Bolchugri stood every evening and watched the construction in the neighborhood and its progress. The laborers brought shovels and mixed cement, sand, chips and water. They sloshed down in between four posts of rusted uneven iron rods covered by four planks from all sides. They made posts out of these; solid hard posts in each corner. Orange red bricks came all the way from Damalgre, deposited in haphazard heap two kilometers away and brought in rows by the women day laborers in bamboo baskets, their strength all pushed forward carrying the weight; the sweat glistened on their faces and trickled down from the covered head down their neck; their dirty old shirts sweat and dirt streak. Their bare shoeless feet dry cracked stepping into pebbled rough *kutcha* road. Like the dry rice fields when the rain failed; and they widened. Their chests heaving rhythmically fast with every heart beat. They removed their load, sat in the tree shade, took out tobacco rolled in a paper, lighted the top of it and took long mouthful of smoke and let it out through their nostrils. They relaxed, wordlessly, each in their own thoughts. Their fast heaving chests slowed. The sweat evaporated. They stood and resumed the work, a real hard work. Palmina watched it all intently and felt the added weight of the woman labourer. She had on her back a brickful of basket with a strip of bark balancing from her head. On her breasts an infant swayed his head a little when she walked heavily. She had heavy burden both at the backside and the front Palmina really felt the compassion for her. Long strip of cloth carried an infant's weight; the both ends of cloth strip are tied together on her neck. An infant closed his eyes fast shut; shielding his tiny eyes from the strong midday sun or dreaming a hard future and the strategy to fight; the curse of poverty. He opened his eyes slowly, flippant at first when his mother sat in the tree shade and fastened his tiny mouth in eager hunger. His small round fair face red roasted in the sun.

"Oh, my God. What a life?" exclaimed Jentilla.

"I'd hate to live that life."

"No, we won't. You will be doctor. I will be magistrate."
"We will live luxurious life."

They made walls, the workers, of the bricks and stuck hard with cement later. The neighborhood houses saw the new house and watched with admiration and envy. They had houses of thatch but for Tochi—ma's. Weeks later, innumerable wooden posts took the weight of cemented plaster above darkening the inside of the windowless, doorless RCC building. The house spoke of wealth, the money and something they never imagined but later discovered—the class. It took three months and the house was completed—the doors, the high arched windows are fitted with fine teak wood, sleekly furnished. The doors and windows shone—sleek shine like wooden mirrors. Deep ash colour, the colour of an ash when mixed with water was painted on the cemented walls. Two days later, wooden folding beds arrived. Their compartments separated, carried by clean clothed men labourers. A set of cane chairs were brought—wide in breadth and low in height even shorter than a dwarf; Two one seater and one long three seater. They hid the faces of the carriers covering their half the bodies. The three seater sat on the three shoulders like a palanquin with no queen. Yet she came later with her bodyguard of a husband leading the way, tall and bulky, his body doubled of hers. She walked straight tall for woman but short for the man walking ahead, reaching just below his shoulder, her pace slower than his. Her hair skimming her neck had the bob cut, straight and silky. Their two off shoots, a small boy younger than the lean and lanky tall girl with horse mane in blue jeans with bell bottom wore with red short tee shirt walked along with them—his hand into hers and she freed from both pairs of hands. New neighbor had come, Jentilla announced, bouncing by, flailing her hands, her long brown silky hair swaying below her thin neck. Her childlike excitement made her small childlike eyes lit fully, shining and her face creased in dimpled smile. The reason, the new neighbor had a daughter of their age. She was pretty and a new playmate was added for them.

"New girl?"
Palmina shrieked, her eyes full of smiles. Her excitement surpassed her friend. It broadened her wide round face. She jumped higher than normal ordinary days. She was happy and exuberantly so. She had only one thought—A new friend had been added.

"How does she look?"

She asked breathless, anxiously curious like a child should be.

"Ohh.She is pretty, very pretty. She came in jeans, had a short hair, fair face and she smiled at me."

Jentilla went on and on excited about the new friend.

"They are rich people."

She added with twinkling eyes—sparkling eyes of pure excitement. Palmina yelped with joy. Her eyes evenly sparkled and twinkled. Palmina went flying too eager to pass the information so vital to her other friends. Her friends all had faces with broad grin from ear to ear. The next day they all went. Milche called Chinche, older in age by three to Jentilla to come. Chinche hesitated at first shyly but crumbled much after the persuasion of her friends and slowly scaled the stone steps, to the house above the rows of houses. It was elevated above all theirs. They all went in a simple courtesy call of the children and to introduce themselves to their new friend.

"Come up. Come up."

She smiled from the edge of the spacious lawn, stood behind bamboo fence, waving, urging them all to come, her smiles of welcoming, all too eager to please and happy. The trio too eager to befriend in her castle, rushed forward attempting the stone steps in two strides; they needed no second urging, scurried forward, unhesitant and eager with no word at first but the smiles on their faces were their pleasantries—a password to friendship. They came closer, put their feet on the top bottom step and met her face to face, girl to girl. Their bond of friendship was sealed with the frowning two pairs of eyes on their back, sore with the friendship yet conceded in the friendless place their daughter badly wanted. She wore long pant, red with black patches on both the knees with white tee shirt, bell shaped at the leg bottom, they were impressed with. They envied her dress. Their parents disallowed them with the words that the longpant was meant for boys and not girls, strict words put into their ears. The girl with a pant on was branded as bad character and frowned upon. It was forbidden in Bolchugri girls and they owned none but longed for one desperately with no luck. Palmina wished for one too but was vehemently denied by her mother. They saw her parents, a tall burly man with short curly hair and a dark grim face, forever unsmiling, a young beautiful woman, smiling permanently for none in particular, just for everyone with fair and short hair on a heart shaped face, holding a little boy in her hand who simply looked totally bored with her mother's interest, licking a round chocolate on top of a slim plastic stick. He had disinterest in his mother inspecting newly potted plants from the verandah, hanging from the ceiling, some on the three steps on each sides, two green leaves drying, dead, above the dry soil, unfed, unquenched, thirsty and frowned her face. As she did so she creased her face in worry concerned with the drying withering flowers than their maid. With the pond water in a far distance from where their lone servant brought the water in an aluminum pot in one hand and small steel bucketful of water in the other hand she watered her flowers every morning and gave them life. But she chose the maid, a sturdy woman with much strength than a woman who struggled with the household chores since the dawn till dusk pouting from half the day with the workload she found too heavy and removed the slender girl her husband preferred. Yet she met their unending needs demanding of her—cooking, washing utensils, sweeping each room in the early morning, washing clothes left her worn out but with no mercy drew water from the well and filled the barrel full, grumbling yet with no escape. When she came to the pond early morning to draw water she had nothing good to speak of her mistress, her husband and their two children and complained endlessly to much younger Palmina. The maid then eyed her and swore her to secrecy Palmina maintained. Palmina cocked her ears to her words and missed the chapel of the class later in the morning. Then she turned, the lady with her soft face, smiled briefly at them but sweetly that seemed compelled than spontaneous while the man remained grim, cocked his arrogant head to one side then turned to their daughter and called her inside.

"Hilla . . . Hilla . . . Hilla . . . "

A shrill voice interrupted, not from her mother, not a man's voice either and certainly not the maid girl busy throwing dirty water out, her lower thick lips in open pouting, angrily and mumbling something unintelligibly. In the corner hanged a cage; the caller perched precariously on a small slim stick lay parallel, a little above the cage—floor inside, with the water full in a cup and a mixture of rice and its waste strewn all over. Hilla, they knew her name, they haven't asked her yet.

"Come in . . . come in . . . " the myna invited, looking neither at them but darted its beak, left, right and centre not literally meaning but just empty words, imitating the words her parents had often called her. It shifted its legs, two bony yellow legs, from one side to another with ten skinny toes and long curling toe nails. Palmina went towards it fascinated with it and moved it a little too hard and watched. The wooden cage oscillated a little wildly. Myna fought hard to stay in the small wooden railing, shifting its legs from one side to another; it achieved. The children stood hesitated outside the door, unsure of the welcome, not of her but of her parents they never have met but seen from far and felt the distance they drew. Hilla stood on the two steps, one leg on each and waited. The house was good, befitting rich, four roomed—a master bedroom, a son's, Hilla's and a guest room. The servant's quarter was a tin sloppy roof, still gleaming, unpainted, stark silver with two rooms detached from the main rcc building that housed the kitchen cum dining room and a small single room. The children went inside. Their eyes and mind impressed with a small room with a single bed, covered with white cotton bed sheet with the painting in black. Mickey Mouse dominated the single bed with a thick mattress underneath. She had books, lined on top of the square table, mostly comic books—Phantom, Tarzan, Bahadur, Batman and Mandrake that drew instant attention of Palmina, an ardent lover of books. The children loved all the things she owned and envied too shamelessly Hilla had the pride in showing off. Her long and short exercise books were all neatly covered with brown paper that the four small girls were impressed with when she said with pride her father did the wrapping, a gesture that told them she was pampered unlike them. They returned completely impressed riding in the cloud to a wall of women, their eyes narrowed grimly spelling danger for the girls. They needed not be told. They needed not be shouted but the scorn and scowl in their faces were dead give away. The mothers stood aground, on the narrow footpath, all three, with Tochi-ma, leaned on the bamboo fencing, wired with sweet potato stems, its green leaves stuck outside, talking non stop. Palmina saw her mouth twitched, then stopped at their sight, their eyes intently angry, accusing them of crime; atleast one of them, displayed pure anger. Palmina dared not close at the gathering four. She saw her mother among them, her dry face cracking and her dry lips too where she applied nothing with little lines at both the corners of her eyes that came not with age but with dryness and uncared face with nothing applied, her both hands on each sides of her hips and nodded her head two times, calling her wordlessly but with an action, and understandably grim and angry.

The harsh query began why they went. It was the only question, "why?". For the children there was no answer but remained terrified with silence and muted, ready for punishment. The barrage of words poured upon them and the girls learnt from the scolding words uttered the reason of their anger; they were rich, unwelcoming the poor new neighbors, a gap marked shown by them and they had breached that, unabashedly too, a social crime committed and cheapened the parents; a messenger was there but the truth was not proved nor could a finger pointed at one but decided it was a malign perhaps; The children thought of nothing and they didn't mind. Hilla, their friend was nice and sweet, they already befriended with no regrets. Though her parents too talk less, asked about their studies and thawed the cold uneasiness they felt in the beginning and sweetened their mouths with red gulab jamun and the children asked no more of but were innocently satisfied.

A television show, announced Jingo, two years younger of Milche's eleven years of age, who saw the magic box in the house packed, seat less in the main town where lived the crème and the rich of the society. It was the one among three, won by lottery in Gauhati, the first prize for the ticket of one rupee and a waste if lost for another and the idea strike out of it for him to make, a cartoon box television. The children ran excitedly unseen yet heard of the magic box. They heard too of the pictures it gave and stood at the foot of an ancient giant cotton tree. The massive leafless tree stood ramrod straight, its top nearly touching the sky and nobody knew of its age. Palmina tried once to measure its breadth and ran twenty steps to circle it around. She looked at the top height of it, a hollow branch. It was the home of an owl, unseen at day but heard hooted at peak midnight. It had the regular visitor too. Every evening woodpecker flew in and pecked in the middle with its pointed long beak failing in attempt. It gave white pure cotton once in a year in between March and April and was a fascinating sight to look at then Palmina so much loved looking. Its giant roots crawled on every side—north, south, east, west and in the midst of the small columns where the children in pair made home—playing house-house. Jingo chose the shade it gave to display his cartoon magic box and Palmina was ecstatic. Jingo was strict; he made them sit patiently on the stone stools; his voice was commanding and demanding to be obedient and brought the magic box out ordering all to obey and threatened anyone disobeyed to leave the show. It was a square box with the outer cover of it was nothing but a brown cartoon box, the front of it with white paper screen. He put it on the flattened stone with careful precision with the ground in front raised, high above them all and like the meek lambs, they dared not disobeyed the owner, the director and the producer of the show. Everyone wondered, curious how, when he rolled, his hands on the short stick on the left side, Z-shape outside with two ropes attached to it, one from the screen top and one from the below and when the Z stick outside went in circles with the fingers, there came pictures, first of Mandrake, his magic show with a rabbit popping out of his black magic hat, the people around him watched with wide eyes and mouths, awe-struck at the trick and a red cloak over his blue dress made him look as magician as he tried to show, fascinating the audiences; Lottar, a bald and tall burly Negro and his superhuman strength; he fought with the evil men; a punch to one with a flat face the man fell came next dominating the screen in front.

"T H U M P", the force of his punch is shown in big bold letters; it dominated the picture, so also the "A A A R R R R R R G G G H H H H H" of the man received it, flying off backwards, his feet off the ground; half nude bodies of their wives, waiting by the swimming pool for their husbands, one white and other black, their briefs scanty, embarrassed the viewers. Palmina looked sideways, her discomfiture plain obvious, shared by her friends too who smiled, covered their mouths for brief moments, stifling embarrassed giggle then relaxed; with its end Tarzan came with an animal skin as his bare brief, a dagger dangling from his waist, grappling a giant croc, forced opened its jaws, red blood dripping both of the jungle man and of an animal, earning sympathy by the man but wrath by the animal with his muscular body half naked; with the fought over, he went swinging on the hanging roots, then changing into another, a means of his transportation in the jungle then began shouting.

"Ahahaahaaaaaaaaaaaaaaaaaaaaaaaaaa." An open palm on the corner of his mouth, he forced the letters out, the voice directed at something or someone that he alone knew but his voice unheard of even in the magic box, muted; the elephant, its huge body emerged, the lion too and the chimpanzees and the children knew to whom he called out later but gleefully watched, fascinated.

Then came a rider, a masked man from the bottom of his toes right to the tip of his head in purple mask, a pistol in his waist side from a black holster, a black boot and his eyes well hidden too. The ghost who walks, the pygmies called him and the children are fascinated no end. He rode a horse that galloped wildly amidst the forest; a wolf ran alongside keeping pace as he spurred on. Palmina loved it most. It had the romantic side too. The mask rider galloped swiftly coming after the helicopter that the pygmies called it "man bird" with not seeing it in the jungle with four rough looking men kidnapping a beautiful woman, a loved of his life. She had the yellow hair, the bottom curl of it skimming her neck. He rescued with the help of jungle African men and their chieftains, their tiny huts like a group of mushrooms and their naked bodies glistened with pure dark skins. The men covered their groins with the leopards skin leaving their muscled torso bare and the shapelessly fat women covered not their upper body exposing much valued part and devaluing, covering at the same their swollen fat thighs with the animal skins. They kissed in the end, the mask rider and his loved with a giant skull in the back drop. The tiny small faces below watched it, fascinated, in rapt attention, asking for more when it ended in the last roll but replied one word firmly, "tomorrow" that brooked no argument. He got paid, Jingo, ten paisa each from the viewers parting willingly for the show, their faces contented; he collected one rupee from ten, then smiled at the collected coins in his palm and muttered, something like enough for tomorrow with his favourite lime juice sweet in mind on the way back home from the school the next day.

"Little children . . . my grannies . . ."

An old frail voice trailed shrilly; they all turned, their eyes towards the voice and saw, then recoiled at the sight. No word but the looks exchanged in between the children, fear and terror in each; the belief was stark naked in each eyes and the call went unanswered. Jentilla recoiled at her side and shuddered. Palmina closed her two hands in her heart, fear stark naked in her eyes. Chinche looked at them all and laughed loudly. Milche too showed some fear that left instantly the way it came. The woman crossed, her steps non stopped, slowed with the age with a long stick in her hand, a support to a frail body, her cracked feet bare, a sparse hair tied in a little bun at the nape, graying with little strand of black barely seen her small lean body bending, eyesight weak with films of white covered and her face just of drooping loose skin, hanging. When she spoke her toothless mouth was opened and her uneven black stained side teeth were shown with the front four teeth missing from both upper and lower part. A dual life she led, they the elders said that imprinted deep in the children's mind with the tiger in spirit and that of a human in form; she scratched the bamboo walls at night in her sleep; the neighbors' piglets and chicken were her dinner with her spirit animal home in the nearby jungle. With her crossed, it was a huge relief. The deafening roar above thundered and scattered the children; the elders looked up to watch, their full eyes above; their necks longer than the days ordinary; the little ones wailed of stark fear; they ran towards their sisters and clutched them tightly, on their waists; while a tail of the machine bird flew above them and the rotor above it whirled, carelessly but on its way; it disappeared, much to the relief of the wailing children who now sat comfortably on the crook of their sisters' arms encircling them protectively while their tiny heads buried in their sisters' breasts. The sun dropped below the cloud in the West; they said it sank in Brahmaputra, kissing the edge of the cloud while the sparrows ran helter skater, quarreling and fighting like a group of refugees with their neighbors for a bucket of water, searched for their place where they slept last but not finding it, on the branches of the tree, hidden by the thick leaves, accusing one of another of switching places, when the other too answered back, unabashedly not listening to one another, disrespecting shown to each other; the children too retired for the night, at home, resigned from the hectic day. Palmina wailed, refusing but the woman, mercilessly stood her ground, stubborn till the hilt; with her one hand on her hip she ordered her; her voice was firm, and the daughter obliged grudgingly, seeing the wagging finger and the glittering angry eyes pointed towards the barrel but above all the fear of empty stomach, she was threatened with scurried her, screaming when the cool water touched the naked body, washing the dirt and sweat of the day. The dinner was good, yellow dhal with steamed young tapioca leaves, wrapped in the plantain leaves with the few slices of onions and green chilies slit open half steamed and dry fish chutney along with the white plain rice. It was a treat or rather it was because her stomach was empty. She had her stomach filled, enjoyed. Later in the evening, something fluttered below the kitchen on the banana tree with the green fruits upside down, the bottom of its fruits light yellow, ripening half, uncut, the dinner for the hairy winged night visitor; one half of it was finished the night before. She threw a stone, chasing the night visitors, jealous of the ripe banana; for a call for a halt from her mother she restrained herself and stopped her action; it could be her grandmother, her mother informed her, tartly; her life existed in the animal and killing it meant her end she said tartly. She obliged, believed it to be true, yet still amazed at the story.

"Granny . . . granny . . . granny . . ."

The boys shouted; she too followed suit but the night visitor made no reply with the dinner as its sole interest and then flew off with loud flapping of its wings, disappearing into the dark night with its stomach full. She lay in bed for three months, her grandmother, in the year last in the second month of the year, the month of forest burning, clearing for cultivation in the village where she lived was sick, unable to get up. Somebody from the village came and informed her parents. Her father was the first to react. Her parents took the children with the thought it could be their last to see her. She saw her; her body was mere bones, her eyes sunken deep, her aging skin loose, her hands black burnt, her short graying sparse hair left her bald exposing the white skull then asked for her grandchildren with the thought the end came near to her only to be recovered later. It was a burnt; her aunty informed, brusquely, a bat in the hollow tree where she lived and her animal body burnt in the forest fire that brought her fate on human. But they are rich, she added, of those leading a dual life with bat in spirit, proudly pointed at the two big barns behind the house—grain-full—a fortune brought by her grandmother. She kept in the barn bottom, below the mounted bags a golden teeth of an elephant for good luck with a believe the barn never got empty, her father told her once. It was added with a proof. They never saw the year their barn empty nor short of rice nor stopped helping poor relatives and cousins. Her mother had a different story to tell. They had vast rice fields, hundreds of acres yielding hundreds of *maunds*, much enough to feed the whole village. Bamboo covering below, on the bed, creaked with her weight above it but she turned to the other side, on the corner where her mother lay, feeding her brother, an infant, beside her five years old brother and pleaded for the third that she obliged willingly, one thing she never said "No" for her children; a bed time story, lullaby, without which a wink refused for entry; with her mind intent on it, she opened her eyes with her pair of ears tuned towards her mother for another story and nagged her till she regaled her with one. The night went older, an infant in her breast closed his eyes, yet his tiny mouth still stuck sucking, like a cow in sleep, while the footsteps above on the narrow footpath sounded loud, clear; they were familiar clucking sound of the oversized shoes loosely worn when her mother cried out, pained, then cringed; she hit the tiny figure lightly, unharmed and began her bedtime routine. Nil Kumar, Nal Kumar are brothers, princes of a certain kingdom; both fell in love with the same princess, they saw on out for hunting. Nil Kumar won her love and married the princess; the other striped with jealousy wickedly sent her somewhere with the help of a witch, whom the husband searched for seven years, totally haggard, worn out with the voice that was barely audible and found her with the help of a good fairy; the story was heard of in times several but still unquenched, she nagged her mother to tell it again but half-way interrupted rudely by the song sung loudly slurred.

"Mujhe . . . duniya . . . walo . . . . . . saraa . . . bi . . . na . . . sam. jo . . ."

It was from the film saraabi. Palmina heard the sound of the loose pebbles slipping on the road above; the voice was too familiar, not unusual, his midnight routine disruption. He was a real pest an itch everyone wished to scratch away but folded their fingers and their palms inside refraining from doing; they showed human kindness; they thought of his children; His children bore the brunt with his drunken tantrum; his drunken tantrum was a midnight spectacle, throwing food, utensils, shouting, hitting at his children. Chinche above all suffered silently, powerless, after feeding her brothers. She was both a cook and a mother to her motherless brothers, left orphan; she was a family dhobi too at the same when their tears she wiped. Her palms were always open, ready with their each demand she met with unselfishness. She found joy in their happiness and still smile the next day, unaffected after a tortuous night. Perhaps a façade, Jentilla remarked one day to Palmina. She masked her in depth feeling, Palmina retorted. They both wondered why. A handmade blanket, light for winter, heavy for summer, precise for early summer morning, several of old *gana,* her mother had thrown, discarded sewn together, creating a multi colored flag, left her legs. She was left at the mercy of the cold biting her naked legs. It was pulled to the other side, tight balled and awoke her from her sleep. The fought took her few brief minutes with Salmina too holding it tight, loosened the blanket after sometime; with it won, the foxes cried out in the nearby jungle with the cold as their enemy at night they screamed at pleading for mercy but with no mercy shown they cried the next night only to be unheard by all who heard. Palmina turned to her side, lay, merciless for the wailing pitifully animals. The folk lore story was heard, several times, in the school and at home too; her grandparents too told her several times when she went for visit in Winter break. The foxes were lazy. In the cold night they remembered the need for warm cover then waited for the day for the task but the daytime heat, bask in its heat, in the warm they lazed; they forgot and remembered in the night again only under merciless cold; then they decided for the next day to make the cover for cold; it carried on stretchable, unending. The wait for tomorrow but the tomorrow when comes they sent it back packing; their decision and the work remained incomplete till the summer came; then they dismissed the thought, completely. The story lulled her to sleep, a sleep inducing potion her mother was adept at and smeared at them; she went into dreamless sleep and awoke the morning next; her mother saw to it she got up early, shook her bodily. The morning chore began with both mother and daughter. The cook and the dishwasher.

'cluck . . . cluck . . . cluck . . . cluck . . . cluck . . . cluck . . . cluck . . . cluck . . . cluck . . . cluck . . .' Her mother clucked her tongue; it was an effort to call the chicken from the coop already out. The mother hen came prancing slowly; nine chicken trailed her from behind. Her mother sprayed rice outside; she counted the chicken. One, two, three, four, five, six, seven, eight, nine and she widened her eyes in anger at the lost. 'It had to be ten' she said then narrowed her eyes with assumption and said' I saw the bloody hawk hovering. It must have had one', cursed it; the mother hen and her children with their brothers and sisters all enjoyed the morning meal. Her mother then set out with the left over food stocked in an old neck-less pot and fed the piglet in a sty. Palmina rushed out to the pond afar off, to collect water and filled the kitchen pots. She then dashed to wash herself before the school.

CHAPTER 3

HEAD MASTER FATHER AND HOUSE WIFE MOTHER.

Her parents had the desire, to educate their children well and be a well—known respected person in the society; often than once, in fact every day her father repeated the words for many years altogether.

'Study. Don't be like others."

'We don't have paddy fields to bequeath you" he repeatedly said then added,

'Your studies, degrees are your properties I can give"

Her father added seriously, she kept in mind.

"As long as I am alive, I will slog day and night for your studies."

She knew well, his was a rich family; his parents had invested in his studies well, but half way after his matriculation, he met her mother; he became love-struck and sentimental without being practical. He failed in the exam lying sick on bed when her mother showed disinterest; he wooed her later, her mother told the story, gave the best attention a woman could ask for; he treated her like a queen and made her feel like one; he won her love again. He dragged her eloping much against the wishes of his parents grooming him for his maternal uncle's daughter. It was a custom none broke in the family but him. Palmina found the story daring and romantic. His mother never forgave him for that but vented not on him. Her mother was the easy target for snatching her favourite son. Later, love alone hardly brought them joy. When penniless hard time came love flew through the lone window of the rented small room; he struggled to keep their love alive. It was not easy. There was tension; they fought when tensed without money. But they stuck. He got the job easily with number of job

26

seekers with qualification on less. She was open—her mother, told her the way they met in the house of a common friend; it was a chase, a one sided chase she told her daughter when cleaning rice. They were segregating stones from the rice and often threw the rice with her mind too engrossed in the story into the mouth of the prancing hen proudly; it was her home but the red cockerel of the neighborhood strutted around nearby; her blue and red tail straightened up with the tip of it stooping, eyeing the chance; he saw it, chased her away, stuffed them well into his stomach rapidly. She shooed him away, well intent on fattening her hen and resumed with the story; he had a pair of brown shocks he wore always, covering his ankle up to his calf when he courted her. She later discovered, he hid his skin disease well under it after the marriage—a very late discovery she smiled in a jest. She laughed. Palmina laughed. She teased him later about the hiding.

'Your mother lied.'

He cheekily answered that betrayed his words.

"Love is blind."

She finished her story, smilingly in a light hearted bantering.

Her father had a different version to tell. He often twisted the story from the truth.

'Your mother spoiled my life. She disturbed my studies.'

He often said relaxing, in light hearted teasing way, playfully but angering her. He was spoiling for a fight. The words aroused her anger and a provocation indeed. Her ego disallowed his side of story to be told. He resigned to hers when she picked the fight. Palmina laughed with her sister, Salmina on the background for his whacky sense of humor. It was just that balanced their relationship of two different personalities—one that of hot temper and him making a jest out of all and lightening it; pouring water on the flame. The watery father and the fiery mother, their children are proud of. The story of her mother was altogether different. The village where she came from had a school only up to its middle section; the desire for higher studies, to pursue came with a price; a servant in a house of a rich man, few hours journeys away from her village; she pounded rice, a bag of it in the morning, evening, before and after going to school. Saturdays and holidays had no spare for her. She pounded with the strength sapped.

"Ohh . . I worked hard, real hard with one ambition in mind, Study. I was a good student." She reminisced with pride in her eyes. Then turned to Palmina, her eyes beseeching in total seriousness.

"You should achieve what I never could do."

'I could have passed my matriculation.'

Sadly then her eyes turned narrowed with anger and looked at him vilely.

'Your father spoiled my studies.'

She pointed angrily but had her father laughing sheepishly unashamed. Someone from her past came, from the village where she studied, near Dhubri; someone who knew the family her mother stayed, studied. The man told the children her mother had omitted to tell. She did it purposely; perhaps she did it with a thought. She didn't want her children to know it. She fought, that someone said, the unwanted advances of the son of the house owner where she stayed. She hit him with something blunt, got him bleeding and ran away. She then tried in weaving school for stipend in Tura. She holed up with a relative of her father, paid for her food and lodging by washing utensils, cooking, washing clothes, pounding rice like before. There she met her father and fell in love with. It must be fate, she finished later. Her father cut off her studies, smitten with her and kept her locked up in the room rented then impregnated her, the reason her mother seemed unable to forgive her father at times;

"I had a job. Your father robbed it of me."

Her mother sadly reminisced looked at something afar unseeingly, then lowered her eyes back to where checking for the stones from the rice. Palmina muted her mouth. She respected the secrecy of her parents and never asked about it, either from her father or from her mother; Tightly shut, locked up. She saw what she wished, her sights into her incomplete desire; to complete what she left incomplete, to continue what she discontinued was what her story invoked.

The next evening, her father came for the weekend; his once in a month visit in the week first; sometimes he came twice in a month but never four times. He had a reason; the only bus that brought him home came from Mankachar, jam packed, whining and groaning and often with flat tyres half way came with the over weight passengers both inside and above on the open roof. Her mother looked forward to it agog, darting her eyes up towards the road every few seconds, expecting his arrival. Even when cleaning rice she kept her eyes fixed not on the rice below but on the stone steps leading down from the main road. Palmina noticed it miserably; she felt sorry for her when disappointed. When feeding pigs she stood awhile beside the pig in the sty. With both her hands holding the neck-less pot with floating husks her eyes reflected the longing heart for his arrival. The pot heavy with immersed rotten rice jerked her back to reality. She resumed her work when the pig grunted loudly below her demanding her attention; her eyes dimmed miserably sad. She spoke less as if the painful heart pulled her words back from outing. Palmina and Salmina too looked forward to the evening, eagerly, missing him. His sense of humour and his tales—bedtime stories are hard to miss. They asked her in the class 'Who loved you most? Your father or your mother?' and Palmina remained mute, unable to answer. She knew both loved her and shared the loved evenly with her sister. When he came on the week first, on the Friday evening with his and both hands full, one with an old air-gun of her grandfather her mother was busy with in the sty feeding the two young pigs. He looked complete haggard and harassed. The air gun was long and single barrel. He prided on its good target.

"I have killed several wild boars with this" he boasted.

It was vouched by her grandfather when he came to visit his grandchildren; the deer too he killed them in several he added; its horns in open display in the sitting room, below the framed picture of Gandhi. Gandhi had white loin cloth as his only garb. He stood with a long stick in his hand with a pair of round rimmed spectacles; they had in the sitting room that of antler too, below the framed photograph of Nehru; he was in his white suit and a red rose on the lapel; he had a passion for them. Her father was the hunter till the hilt; his passion. His Other hand had a bag—cauliflower, spring onions, cabbage, green chilies in it; he brought from the place where he work. They were not bought he told his mother but charitable acts of the villagers; it was also love and respect shown for the good service he gave and handed it to her mother. She was beaming; eagerness shone in her eyes; her hands stained with husks and rotten rice with one hand holding a neck-less old pot where the young pig had his meal stocked. Her dimmed eyes sparked with joy and her smile showed of pure happiness. Like a little child she laughed loudly, happily for nothing but simply for his act of tenderness and care. Palmina and Salmina laughed with pure joy; their wish was fulfilled; their desire was whetted, just to be with their father. They ran forward and hugged their father. He stroked their heads simply and asked one of them for a *moorah*, had the eldest obliged. The moorah had the cow hide for cover.

'Drat this bus, jam packed. I have no place to put my feet and stood with conductor near the door, leaning on it, almost fell when the door opened.'

He sat on the *moorah,* sighed, complained of overload bus he came to his wife not for sympathy but for knowledge she lacked. She stood beside like the maid in waiting ready to do his bidding or for order. Indeed he did, for the water to immerse his parched throat.

"Bring me glass of water."

Hurriedly she went inside and came with a glass of cool water. She watched his Adam's apple moved up and down when the water sloshed down his throat, enjoying it. He told his daughters then he stood squeezed in between sea of people, got in only after twelve kilometers of walk; the narrow path across the mid jungle; the wild animals were the only pedestrians, he told them and of the elephants mostly he evaded in the morning. Salmina squirmed; goose bumps merrily danced out in her hands. Palmina was fascinated no end; thrilled excitingly with the story. He told them he waited for three hours in the main road waiting for the line bus, reeking of slime, dirt with the mixture of bad body odour and stood for nearly one and one and half hour near the door and got down every few seconds for every passenger getting down.

'Pity the bus.'

He said, his eyes on the feet where his hand massaged the cramped leg.

'Why?'

Her mother was curious expecting something unusual happening to the bus or perhaps the news for flat tyre.

'It whined, groaned, complained and screamed of its burden when climbing Damalgre up like an old woman.'

He had sympathetic voice. It brought out the laughter out of her mother, a free pure laughter of joy, something she did few times in a month.

'Check the vegetables properly. They got much squeezed in between like me but less harassed.'

He informed his wife. His eyes worn out; he was dead tired.

"They must have dried or withered."

He finished. Her mother gave a close inspection, holding the vegetables and knew they were as much damaged as he pointed out and conceded, then thought they well can fill the stomach. A cup of strong milk tea in a tray arrived sooner than was expected. A small plateful of purple boiled sweet potato roots lay along with it in the tray. She had the intuition, her mother, about his arrival and kept them isolated for him. Or perhaps she missed him and expected him so much and kept for him with the thought her expectation would be met. It may well be she kept like that on the days she expected and was never disappointed. Perhaps telepathy and he knew when she expected him, the longing-ness of her heart. A hookah was brought, laid in front; he took a deep breath in from the end of a long pipe; the charcoal in a container flared up ember and he let it out, the white films of mist like smoke; with the twin nostrils as his chimney he relaxed; a kerosene lamp stood low before him on the ground, lighting dimly. The other side of the chimney was black with soot he put it aside. He was tired, his eyes worn out but he waved at her to come forward. Palmina went like a pampered puppy and sat on his lap; he drew her closer, put an arms around her and let her back rested against his body and began,

"You must study well and be someone in life" his favourite phrase and added

"I passed my matric in first division".

A twinkle in his eyes was well visible as she looked up but she let it rested where it was. The footsteps coming down the stone steps alerted of new arrival. The loosely worn shoes sounded strange, abnormal than usual but not unfamiliar; the owner was not a stranger, easily recognized, not by the sight but by the sound. Her father opened his eyes, responding, expecting. A tall lean man appeared, his grey half sweater worn above light blue shirt, long sleeve, tucked inside a light grey trouser, a pair of grey socks worn with a pair of loose fitting black leather shoes, his hair turned grey not of age but of pressure, tension, stress and hard work. Her mother came instantly with *moorah* in hand and offered him; it was brought by a generous village relative, its round cover of cow-hide; slices of raw betel nut, green leaves along with it, white lime in the small container with a small stick stuck out was laid before him by her mother; a respect, an honour for the guest, for the man the oldest in the area around was shown; with slow precision she slide off her father's lap and darted off towards the kitchen and helped her mother in the kitchen. Then he started, a slow spoken man, non smoker, his eyes serious, his voice too—the need of the electricity, the water, the pitch road for the locality, the primary school and attracted an instant reaction from the other. Her father stopped his smoking on an instant; his ears tuned, taken in his talk that he joined too;

31

Both became serious for the cause both fought for years several, relentless in their pursue. Their plead and efforts turned futile; Both lose no hope but pulled one another; when one faltered, another pulled up—the one a fighter and the another a supporter. A local member of the assembly, a minister, he approached the day before after the school where he taught, he informed him coolly; the member he said coolly was rude, sent him out with a reply that the locality never voted for him in the election last but for his nearest rival whom he defeated by a threadbare margin. He paused for a brief moment then shook his head in defeat. Her father, angry and disillusioned said, he would stand the next election in the Constituency where he work with an instant reaction from her mother who in no uncertain terms made it clear she would not entertain the voters and gave endless lecture on what happened to other politicians house—the voters spat inside the house, they stole things, they asked for money—for bus fares, for school admission they never needed any in the village school, for rice, blanket and quilts given to them as guests they carried off, the endless cooking—with their family just a mute spectators and with a word for their action meant a lost of election. He seemed considering all these, then kept quiet accepting the truth and she knew she won. Palmina sat silent listening at the same thought with the brain of seven years old, how respected her father was in the village where he worked as Middle school Head Master, his paltry salary not enough for family maintenance but for each and every writing work he did for the villagers in and around and instigated at times for him to stand election. The sitting MLA was threatened, he told them, of his popularity and decided to throw him off from the village somewhere far flung; he saved his transfer only by his vehement assurance of not interested in politics. The talk, ended in the midnight, touched the ring-well, the lone battle for it for five years, the demand, the promise in the election campaign, the relentless pursue—the victory. Her mother brought tea for them; both of them sipped tea slowly, looked at each other yet thoughtful. Tapioca boiled was given, freshly dug out from the garden from below the house and had the two stomachs full. The sisters watched the two men, listened to their talk and said nothing. They just filled their stomachs with early dinner and no inclination for the tapioca. The night went older; the talk became intense; her father got heated not with him or his daughters or of his wife but with the politicians; their failed promises; their absent mindedness—saying something before election and forgetting after their win. He knew the timing when to leave;

off he went, quietly, unnoticed in his silent way but for the loosely worn clucking sound of his oversized shoes that sounded loud even after he left. The story, the boys demanded from their father and nagged him till he relent; she too relentlessly pursued; the father pleaded fatigue but they showed no mercy and he gave in, put up his palm in defeat when all chorused with a word, "story". Then he began, the real story encountered, happened somewhere in mid-sixties, of a class picnic beyond Tura peak, a real thick jungle at that time with many stories attached to it; they climbed for nearly three hours he began when the Summer sun beat down but for the protection of thick trees, still unable to stop the sweat trickling with the monkeys all around making fun, scratching their bottom, then teasing them and scaring the girls who screamed to the delight of the monkeys; the girls were cooking, the boys in split works, some piecing pork, beef and skinning chicken; he collecting firewood and the mischievous two with the guitar—the one playing and the other more of goat bleating than singing.

'ughhhhhhhhhhhh . . .' He imitated the voice they heard in the deep jungle.

'ughhhhhhhhhhhhhhh . . .' The singer stopped his singing and responded, unthinking, on an impulse.

'Ughhhhhhhh . . . ughhhhhhh . . . ughhhhh . . . ughhhhhhh . . . . . ughhhh . . .' The shouting increased, non stop; closer and closer the sound came towards them; the shouting became louder and louder and all stopped, tuned in their ears towards the sound; their eyes became larger with complete alarm; they saw nothing but the ancient big trees moving, their big branches bowed; the leaves shook wildly when the birds flew away in hundred dozens upwards, disturbed, flapping their wings, noisily with the body unseen but the moving of the tree branches and their swaying in sight sent a warning for them all. All saw the red, danger signal before them. They sprint for their dear lives with their intuition spelt danger with no word uttered; a lucky escape he added but lost the utensils, the half cooked rice, a *karahi* of pumpkin and four kilos of pork with white soda mixed, two kilos of chicken with a kilo of potato in a *karahi*, three kilos of beef with a kilo of yum, a kilo of uncooked fish on a plate marinated yellow, turmeric powder, masala, salt mixed in it and returned empty stomach, grateful to the One above. With their narrow escape realized and they brought out gratitude unlike other days they could not careless but the man earned a black eye, all six strings of his hollow guitar left hanging that belonged not to him but his friend, far too busy gasping for breath, one inch of his black cowboy shoe, a heel of his left pair pointedly missing; her father stopped half way with unfinished story yet relieved with the sight of the three pairs of eyes closed, their mouths opened, roaring unashamed but Palmina with her imagination too vivid enjoyed till the last adventure rather than a picnic and slept fitfully awakened when the mother hen began prancing with the *chic, chic, chic, chic, chic, chic*, ten chicken behind trailing her. The morning next, the trio trailed their father with her two brothers behind. Their hero father walked a little ahead with his licensed air gun, stopping at every sound, silencing them with a finger at the sight of birds, aiming; in every aim his eyes rested on the backside U with his one eye closed; he was an amateur, but a man with good shot that was how an ex army—man praised him. He aimed with backside U straight to the target, left out the foresight tip even at night, halting his breath for few seconds gently squeezed the trigger without a miss; but now intent on one, a dove with its back sat in the middle of the road ahead, he crept on silently aiming but missed with its flown away with its intuition spelled danger and the single pellet hit the branch of the tree stood beside the road spilling the green leaves below on the ground; a blue cotton tee shirt he wore sweat streak, the grey *gana*, he wore of her mother swishing he walked swiftly with his anger well shown in his face at his missing the dove he well thought of in advance of good lunch. The ankle length *gana* he wore of his wife earned him teasing from all neighbors along the way held him back a little, slowing him yet still made Palmina to run after. The dreary silence of the stream they tread sent her scurrying behind—sent off a hawk he aimed next earning a scowl. The four returned home after a half a day's hunting. She was well worn out and her eyes nearly closed, a short slim somber body with long bushy tail in her brother's hand with their pride shown in their lit up eyes that he held up at every interval for the neighbors to see with her father who smiled no end taking pride in the kill. The evening next he went for hunting, this time with Tochi-pa and Benta-pa; the place was well selected ahead where spotted the few droppings of a barking deer the day before, below a tree with its fruits well in the season the animal had appetite for; Palmina heard the knocking in the middle of the night and awoke for a commotion; her mother opened the door and she rubbed her eyes awoke and saw her father and his friends with a big burden in their shoulders and arms, struggling. The poor animal lay motionless, its body soaked in a pool of blood, the brown hairs matted with the blood clotting, the blood oozing from the stomach where she took the shot, her eyes permanently closed. Their faces had the satisfaction and they smiled with joy of their own achievement. The midnight brought Tochi-ma and Benta-ma and some others too, stood towering over and looking at the dead deer. A gleaming axe, a dagger well—sharpened were brought, began severing of the legs and limbs for the hunters; the hunters chosen some best parts of the body too with lion's share their wives' had taken but two kilos each for the neighbors that found their way the morning next and the neighborhood enjoyed the kill. Her mother slept when the cock crow second, cut the share into long slices and some into big slices that she boiled in the big aluminum pot in the twin hearths; the long slices she hanged in long row above the hearths for drying. The next morning children enjoyed the meat cooked in a large *karahi*. Her father went back on Monday morning; her mother got up on the third cock crow and steamed sticky rice in an earthen pot placed above a boiling water pot. She fed him with that for early morning breakfast, wrapped some in a plantain leave and handed it to him. "Have it on the way' she told him—a pure caring and affectionate gesture. He said nothing and left when the dawn began, well racing for the time and for the bus.

Three months, a very long months, his salary was stalled and the school had no sanction from the government, her father dropped the words with sadness tinged with hookah pipe in his mouth, inhaling through the mouth and then exhaling the white smoke through his nostrils, staring into a far distance, unseeing; for people with money nothing felt but without money, it was a total netherworld; everything chose to disappear like a spirit from a bottle opened, evaporated—salt, sugar, tea leaves, oil, turmeric powder, onion from the kitchen but the chili grew in the garden behind the kitchen, a pet project her mother carried out the year round, its green lean bodies hanging; the bottle gourd too hanged green, crawled onto every tree around the compound, bulldozing its way up, then spreading into all the branches in the tree; on a huge acres of land, few acres of land occupied that housed their tiny home with other two and half with nothing but with something green—the huge family of bamboos on the boundary, square with four corners, little gap in between the bamboos, its shoots sprout in mid summer, a good dish her mother made of season round were blessing in crisis; sweet potato leaves crawled all around, covered the ground green, underneath with white plump roots with tapioca at every intervals for company, both underneath and over-ground; rice, her grandparents sent fifty kilos each for the month, their expansive paddy field in the village with two big barns full, 300 maunds they harvested in a year, unconsumed within, left for the year next but the year too harvested the same, thus their wealth accumulated with their wealth im measured, dominated the little village they resided; of her grandmother, her mother spoke well for once. Schools had reopened. Palmina lay the list down—uniform first with skirt, shirt, shoe, socks, books, bag—Her mother sat heavy, her thought deep, her mind too heavy, breathed hard and fast, she felt the guilt but kept the unvoiced feeling intact.

"Palmina's school had reopened."

She gave the list. He fell silent, unmoved, unaffected for long, then slowly stirred and began.

'From where will I get." Then he suggested.

She went, Palmina tagged along like a smitten puppy, hanging onto the hem, nearly pulling the *gana* she wore, her mother angry furious with pulled it away rudely. They headed to the L—style house with smooth wooden floor raised well above the ground with big posts below lifting the weight. Headman's house. He was named so with respect for the wealth he displayed. He had behind the house, huge collection of fine wooden planks ready to remove to those with enough money to pay and still with logs piled to be sawn into planks. He married to a wealthy family too, to the youngest daughter, the sole custodian of the family property. He was the only graduate in Bolchugri with job in district magistrate's office. A sly man.

"Money doesn't grow on trees."

He let out the puff, not looking, a sly scornful smile on his face, sat on the arm chair, plumply cushioned, stroked the slightly receding head in front and gestured out. Her mother came back, her frail body slumped, and head hanged in shame, eyes with tears brimmed. Palmina sank. School reopened; she wore the worn out faded skirt, old white shirt of Hilla still new, black shoe torn but the barber stuck the thick motor tyre, sew it nice, old hand—woven bag, with two three exercise books with no text book and paid her school fees three months later when her mother had her fattened pig sold; she was left with nothing of it for her kitchen but said nothing.

Her mother won a loom, a subsidy from the weaving School, an old wood she fitted in behind the kitchen with the roof over it yet left wall—less. She loved weaving, had the experience of it with the training she undergone and desired to utilize it; their family income was uttermost in her mind and the educational costs her children brought. She brought the big two rolls of thread from the bazaar, put them in a charka and rolled them into small rolls; her fingers had the colours of green and red where the thread ran. It nearly cut her fingers. When she pulled, the shuttle ran from left to right and right to left; she pulled it real fast, tirelessly with a target set and her mind fixed on it; at the end of the day a meter of cloth spread in the loom; after three or four days she made three or four meters, well enough for one *gana,* severed it and folded it for the sell. Saturday had a day off for Palmina, she well spent it in sitting with her mother and pulling the shuttle not as fast as her mother but well enough to make half a meter, a gift of time she spent in the kitchen garden. The *gana* she made had no flowers or embroideries in them; they were just plain waist wears covering from waist down till the ankle, modestly. It sold well in the neighborhood and found ready market in the office where Milche-ma sat. She got the money at the end of the month, in the week first when all got their salaries. The neighborhood paid her late; sometimes very late and often forgot their due to her she let off. The profit at times was less and hard to cover the amount spent. She asked only when Palmina and Salmina needed new shoes or uniform and got the dues from grudging givers and heard the mutterings on her back she tuned her ears off. Her mother had other way of making a towel too; she tied the straight bunch of thread tied to a bamboo attached to the wall, and tied the ropes at the other end to her waist and sat on the stool; she pushed the roll of thread in between two lines of thread and made three or four meters into a towel. Her father had many; the neighborhood men too. She later discarded the old style for the loom and the men wore wives' old *ganas.*

Milche sat perched, her thin legs hanging from the low twin branches of a tree, near touching the ground below but evading with intent, enjoying when the music class began with her as the teacher.

'Laaaa . . . . . .Cuckaburra . . la . . ' in high pitch voice, she led the song taught in the Sacred Heart private school with exorbitant tuition fees only her mother could afford, with the barn behind the main house filled, widow but a teacher in the government school; the rice from the barn cooked in the kitchen with no money spent for the rice and left over rice of the year's harvest she sold for her neighbors; the neighborhood enjoyed her grain, preferred for the supply rice from the market with the white powder for preserving; her salary she spent only for the two children, she doted blindly, almost to the point of obsession,—their tuition fees and the kitchen stuff. Milche sang triumphantly and proud of being the lone knowledge of the song. The other children too followed; they all perched on the neighbouring trees delightedly, proud to learn the song they had unheard of. It was English song and new to their ears. They had revering thoughts for the teacher of the song; the same thoughts they all shared. She was the only one who knew the song and not them. She was held in high esteem, higher in the children's social strung. The dusk set in; the parents craned their necks, each on look out for their children, still sat below acacia tree, learning the same lines, repeatedly, unprogressive with their music teacher hammering for better with she herself missing few lines of lyrics but humming the tune, or of croaking than singing with no fruitful result; a small beautiful green bird flew by, sat precariously on the tree top; Jonan took a small stone, marble-size, aimed and pelted only to hit Jingo on his finger; he let out a yelp then a scream of pain. Hollering from all sides, each house began, intimidating, threatening with no result till one came running with a long bamboo stick in her hand, aggressive, threatening but Palmina escaped without even a brush of it with Jonan, his ear gripped in between her two fingers, crying. A little later, commotion began, the widow came, her younger sister in tow, stood on the steps leading down, shouted down, accused her of shielding the guilty, accused Jonan as criminal, accused Palmina—ma too as pampering blindly, encouraging crimes with only the women's voices breaking the silence, one voice shrilly shouting and said he'd be criminal once grow up and called her names too—failure as mother, un-exemplary, unfit mother—Palmina saw tears streaming down and with the words choked, she answered not for the whole half an hour of episode, stupefied with words robbed but her palm on top of her son, clinging, stroking his head, comforting, protecting from the harsh words but none for her; her father saw none; he felt no pain. Pain stabbed her deeply and ingrained, the pain of her mother felt. The tears of the brother she sheltered. She cried deep in the night no one saw of, felt of.

He was treated in Bolchugri, like a disease, a dreaded disease, an epidemic everyone wanted to do without, evaded in marriage parties, funerals, elders meeting, much to the embarrassment of Chinche, the only daughter he was blessed to have that he seemed unaware of but of his drinking. So he lived alone, untouched by all but in the world he created for himself where barged in children, two sons and a daughter, enduring all—shouting, screaming, beating, vomiting on the floor. She removed, water poured for cleaning the floor in the morning and night too with the water from the well below the house that she brought up and filled the barrel kept outside the house. His eyes were red and his curly hair kept unkempt that he combed perhaps in a month. Even in the morning, his mouth smell of the night's drink, everyone avoided the words with simply for with his mouth opening the smell was out. In marriage parties and funerals, he sat with the butchers, killing pigs for guests, had them sliced for he was good at that, saved the big slice in the corner and had it with his night drink, not alone of course but with someone or the other. The intestines and other inner parts were never shown and it was always understood where they disappeared. The younger ones are his friends, entertained with his stories, laughable stories, funny stories, acted as the comedian with the comic stories he collected, stored them in his brain, then recounted and regaled his friends, entertained them and let them out with a guffaw. In headman's sister in law's wedding, he told them of a story, of a man, sick violently and went to meet the doctor in civil hospital, advised for a urine test. The man lay sick in bed at night he said. His wife was heavily pregnant in sixth month, only three months ready for labour. He had his urine kept in a small empty dettol bottle in the corner, ready for test. The wife made the bed in the morning next he told the circle around. She went to the corner and blindly moved her feet. It hit the urine he kept for test. His bottled urine fell splashed on the floor. The wife was much afraid of the husband; he had a violent nature; his anger was intolerable. She had the bottle replaced. The urine was hers. The urine was taken, had tested in the laboratory in the hospital. It came out a week later, to the much in tense waiting man with the result.

The man was numbed.

Shocked.

Flabbergasted.

The hospital sheet said on the top. Dr. C.K. Chowdhury, MBBS. Gauhati Medical College.

The name of the patient, age, sex, the sickness and the symptom.

Below the result was in three lettered words.

SIX MONTHS PREGNANT.

CHAPTER 4

THE WOMEN OF BOLCHUGRI.

Bolchugri, without Benta-ma lost its sheen. Her stories or fables told to others to be aptly put had takers in women's circle. Chinche hated her most, rightly so. She had the best information network none had in the locality. She relayed those stories, exaggerated them and threw them to the uttermost corner to the consternation of Chinche; a taint in her character. She snubbed her every time she met her and turned her face to the other side. Jentilla seconded her. Thirdly, Palmina. She told other tales too to those interested in listening; the cheap tales for reason known to her, then to the others later and often get what she aimed in return. Palmina—ma had given her name *Chukli*. For the name given everybody put their right fingers up in acceptance had indeed had its bearing and stood rightly for her. She never talked what happened in her house; everyone did. Amidst her peer, neighborhood, children, everyone was her victim and preyed unannounced upon others no one cared anymore. They no longer felt the interest to listen, well knew her need and the reason for her stories. Though she no longer had the buyer in yet still she sold her stories forcefully and earned snapping and ridicules at many times yet remained relentless. Her earning solely defended on it. She had the best of friend in Tochi—ma. She often bought her stories and spread them too. Palmina asked her mother the meaning of *chukli* and had her mother let out a guffaw with her stomach in her hands, loudly freely chortling with laugher she stared at with open mouth, saw the tears in her eyes, tried a word with her mouth open the meaning but ended with another round. She got the answer, much later. The stretchable mouth. Cheap mouth, flitting here and there, carrying the word from here to there, there to here, to and fro, fro and to with no telephone line needed, Bolchugri had a 'tele-woman'. In her wake she left a trail of fighting she could not careless but of her stomach she felt the need to fill and her family at anybody's cost. Today, she felt the urge to clean the house, something she neglected for months and demanding her urgent attention and knew the old crumbling house they were gifted with would raze sooner or later with long tunnel roads the ants are making. The white ants made a long tunnel road, the wet soil dried on the wooden pillar where it stood in the inside corner. The house was decade old. It was decrepit; the bottom of its bamboo woven walls shortened with ants making home, perhaps even meal but bulldozing mainly for a road, insensitive to the owners. The tin above rusted, leaky, haphazardly thrown, not properly fitted but squeezed in between the bamboo poles above and below with the tar tied the poles together. A roof over the house of three rooms. Small rooms with only a single bed fitted in each—the master bedroom, the two sons and a daughter separately—with the makeshift kitchen separated. The kitchen with the size of half of the room, slanting to the left with the plastic roofs lapping with the wind—blue, red and green but the two gleaming aluminum mugs. Three old tea cups bought from the weekly market its mouths eaten off rested hanging on the main post of, firmly pinned by the steel nails, rusted brown. Two brown earthen vessels on top of rounded straw woven on the mud floor, kept the water cool against the summer heat seen from outside to inside like a see through glass. The mud floor was smooth. Benta—ma saw to it once in a week. A single storm and the whole family would fly off. A stack of cards with no foundation and flown off backwards with the single rush of wind.

"Drat these ants . . " She fumed removing the earthen tunnel road they made and the white labourers scattered.

'Ai. We have no more rice for dinner.'

On the threshold Benta, her daughter stood, her long hair wet open, her dark face fairer than her luscious dark lips, sexy by no means in her shy twelve years of age, full ripe breasts shook beneath a thin blouse she wore, braless. The mother stared at her for long, her thoughts with trepidation; her fear too real to speak off—hidden underneath.

'Ok. I'll do something about it.'

The white ants earned freedom and she left to the neighborhood, her mind scheming—to extract not to give—her children were her concern.

Palmina removed the betel nut skin with her hands and eyes on it; but had her ears cocked on the two women; they sat on the *moorah* facing each other. She caught the gossip; one entertaining another; the stories are both old and new and some even stale for a child's taste; the tea cups on the small table in front were empty, negligibly left there focusing on the topic they were interested. The late afternoon tea she made for her mother and Benta-ma stood on top of small wooden table. She sat purposely with her ears tuned to their talk and learned a lot, something she had a gist of knowledge but not in detail. The talk began and ended in and around Bolchugri, about the men, about the women and about the teenagers something her mother discarded as trivial but for the other woman entertaining another, dragging her ears to it.

'Once he beat her and we ran to her house to rescue her. Her screams awoke our sleep.' Palmina—ma told her.

'We found her in the corner of their room shielding his blows.' She added.

'I got hurt shielding his blows. The scar still remains in my arm.' She ended and showed the black long scar on her right arm.

'He hit her on the stomach when she was three months pregnant. She had miscarriage and the baby died. We took her to hospital.' She said spitefully. Benta—ma listened too stunned to believe.

'Bastard.'

She gritted her teeth. Chinche never breathed even a word, about her mother; her life in a hell; the real hell with the devil of a husband she doubted not. She bore silently alone a repeated daily abuses. Her nights spent outside the house behind and at times in the merciful neighbors with her one year old son tied on her back with just plain petticoat was sad history Palmina listened and felt sorry of; she loaned her own *gana* covering her modesty out of sympathy, she said in explanation. Palmina was aghast at the plain imagination of the story she heard. She was heaped with punches and blows and drew water from the pond below their house with black swollen eyes and bruises all over in open display. It was hell, her mother confessed, to be their neighbor; they often dragged their ears towards the cries, screams and the loud wailing, unwillingly. They were helpless, she told Benta—ma with a resigned shrug. Palmina vividly saw the picture in her mind. Chinche suffered alone. She bore the pain alone. Self was her own shoulder she leant on. She felt the intensity of Chinche's pain. It endeared her to Chinche more. The story began on a sad note but with a happy ending, her mother said with sparkling eyes. Palmina saw her mother with tear brimming eyes. She died, her mother said of Chinche's mother of tuberculosis, coughing blood her husband took no care of; he drank like a fish even on her death bed when her sisters and a mother carried her off to the hospital. The neighborhood young men carried her off in a folding chair her husband knew nothing of but came late night, drunk, shouting at his wife right above their house. He shouted till he grew hoarse till he found no voice to bring a lantern. He sat where he fell and went home when tired. He went berserk at the sight of the empty house and called her names her mother shivered to speak of. Palmina heard it all; it left nothing to her imagination; she had seen it all. A last stage her mother added of her sickness, and the doctors shook their heads negatively. She died few days later there on the hospital bed. A mere skeleton, her mother described her of. Chinche was beside her on the death bed, crying profusely. A mere seven years old girl, barely old to take responsibility yet thrashed with two very young brothers to take care of. Her father came with a stale alcohol smell everyone narrowed their eyes and slanting their necks away from his evading his presence with no escape and bore it silently in respect of the dead body. He cried loudly that evoked annoyance and anger from everyone around rather than sympathy. They all knew why he cried. He lost his punching bag. He'd miss his nightly routine of shouting at her for lantern and an arm to rest half of his weight. He lost the washerwoman who washed his vomit caked clothes and urine stained pants. She had her revenge, her mother said with a spark of satisfaction with a gritted teeth, after her death; a day later she was buried, her husband sat with his friends drinking with the money her funeral brought when the bottle he held went out of his hand; it was unbelievable but true she added. He took a rod and hit blindly but the rod went out of his hand and hit him instead. She had her audiences now openly staring and replied for repeated queries directed. The broomstick swept the rooms itself and vouched herself strongly as eye witness, an intriguing little conundrum. The bliss, she ended of her death. She sighed relaxed with her death. The hell on earth and perhaps she'd be happy where she was now, she said. The topic shifted—to Tochi—ma. The talk began with heavy sarcasm. Benta—ma began out of nowhere.

'She told me your husband had a mistress in the village he works.' A young woman but her smooth skin with freckles clustered, in big black dots with working in the sun excessively. Hard life injected left her uncaring of her skin. A cup in her hand sipping tea of pure milk, unmixed with water, her long hair coiled kept wrapped inside the blue cloth, turban fashion, protected from the husk, she cleaned the day long, separated from the rice—rice for family, husk for pig, she ingratiate herself feeding tales in her favour.

'How dare she? I know my husband very well.'

Anger rose from every pore—from her eyes, nose, ears and breathed fire out, a picture of fiery dragon. Calmness and sympathetic woman of few minutes left her suddenly, aggressively. Palmina watched silently, each word sinking.

'Yes. Even their new maid servant heard if you do not believe me.'

She asserted. With her one hand feeding sweet potato to a toddler on her lap she put weight on her words, while the elder ate voraciously sat on the wooden stool as if for whole life.

'What business was it hers anyway to talk?' She raged, still fuming.

'Forget it. She was like that anyway. What did she think of her husband?'

She had sown a discord. With her intention achieved, Benta-ma tried a feign effort to lessen her hurt.

'I heard their last servant ran away because he entered her room.' She avenged.

'Yes. Now they got new one. What was her name?' she creased her forehead, trying to remember.

'Metina . . No . . No . . Mitil . . Mitilla. Let us see how long she would last.'

The thought brought relief and lessened the flaming rage. The two children had stomachs full.

'It is late I will leave. By the way can you give me two three onions.'

She asked, 'for lunch tomorrow . . ' She added a bit hesitant.

Onions in hand, three kilos of rice as labour fees, two children tagged behind, well fed, she left and the short thin man waited for her, sat in the expansive courtyard, cross legged and his face solemn. His thin moustache moved for every word uttered. He smoothened it, coiled both the tips inwards with a small *mantu bidi* in between his dark lips with Tochi-pa. Benta-ma and Benta-pa. Palmina—ma sat outside for a long time, her eyes mutinous, fuming with rage and little Palmina knew not the reason why; she muttered unintelligibly and the daughter knew not to whom it was directed, whether to her husband or to Tochi—ma but was relieved when she stood, lifted the old bucketful of waste water, rotten left over rice, and the husks mixed together and headed well towards the jackfruit tree where the young pig grunted, hungrily running around the tree in circle and entangled himself with the rope tied to him. The rope all around him tied in many rounds and he now stood immovable very close to the tree shortening the long rope. It was a hard task disentangling the entanglement and she swore and cursed the pig in her effort.

The screams, the shouts, the chorus of laughter filled the evening. A long stretchable road with neighborhood houses on either side streamed with children—both boys and girls—elder women and men. Women caught in the latest gossip. Palmina ran and joined the gang. The evening whiled with her screaming too. She ran after Milche with the ball in hand, intending to hit her and Milche stopped running. She stood, her eyes on the road, at the end stretch where she saw her mother coming with a grocery bag in full carrying the burden with her brown lady bag on her left shoulder, exhausted after a day in the office. She left the game and ran forward eagerly and took the grocery into her hand with the weight of it dragging her down but she could not careless. She tried with both hands to lift the weight and gave a girl child's full strength. She got a reward—a wrapped big square chocolate. Amul Chocolate. Jingo too ran forward and got the same wrapped chocolate. Both the brother and the sister opened the covers and licked the brown cocoa made chocolate. Their friends watched them silently, licking their lips and their mouths flooded with saliva. Palmina felt her tongue flooded with her own saliva. Jentilla shook her head wishfully and turned her eyes towards the clothes ball she made for the evening out of pieces of rags she found in the drawer.

She stood outside fresh after a bath. Her sparse hair excessively fallen after a child birth was left open. It was a late afternoon. The wet tiny hair showed not a shred of grey hair that she took it in between her tiny palm. A long *gana*, wrapped around her chest a little above her two tiny breasts, tied tightly; it skimmed her calf and covered her modestly and left her dark brown upper chest bare. Jentilla—ma. She muttered something under her breath while she squeezed the wet clothes from the bucket and let the water dropped to the ground below. '

'The bitch . . . from where she learnt to cook like that?' she muttered angrily, drying the wet clothes on the coconut rope tied from one tree in one corner to another.

'How many times I told her and showed her myself how to cook?' She complained to none.

'Still she'd never learn. Her sister cooked better.'

Jentilla came out of the kitchen and threw the dirty water. For anyone interested she looked disinterested and the words went with the air. But no; She listened but only half to her mumblings. She knew whom and where it was directed. Nokam never sink her fingers in the rice pot or in the karahi but was always awarded undeserved praise she generously allowed received. She never was given a much deserving appreciation she let it go. For several times she slapped her sparse hair from the back, drying it and squeezed it a little too. Jentilla said nothing; she hummed a popular Hindi song she heard from radio and walked past her, uncared. She had done the chore for the evening, cooked displaying the best culinary skill possible and filled the barrel with the water from the well, six hundred meters away. Her mother rejected her cooking instantly on the first taste; it neither offended her nor hurt her; she was careless, did her duty and bothered her no more. Her thoughts were somewhere else—house—house, the little houses around the giant cotton tree; the tiny little self made dolls of clothes; the tiny little crockery of tiny families.

'The house—house . . '

Reminded Palmina when they parted near their house and still rankled in her ears. When she reached the site; the small families had already settled around the giant cotton tree—Milla, Hilla, Palmina, Chinche, Jentilla took charge their own. Palmina had two young bottle gourds with four sticks each stuck below where they stood and kept them behind Milche's kitchen. Her sty set up brought instant fought between two families with that of Milche and Hilla and the verbal duel began. A thorough mock fight, imitating the elders. Jentilla played a peacemaker, a judge and gave fair judgment. The sty found a site far from two houses. By then it was darkening and the woodpecker no more pecked the giant cotton tree but the colony of birds flew and settled on top of it and made a huge commotion past caring for the little children playing below and the children too retired for the night—packing their bundles. Milche carried a little bundle with her; small miniature dolls of clothes she made herself; Palmina taught her how to make them; miniature crockery, small cut off pieces of clothes she collected from the clothes her mother made in the Singer Sewing Machine; her mother was adept at it and a very good one. It was her hobby, her pastime when left with no office on Saturdays and holidays and irked her daughter no end clamoring for attention and affection. The sewing machine stood naked and lonely in the verandah; the half sewn cloth hanged below with the border of it clipped well below and pinned—left undone for hurry, thought Milche. She paced up and down, went inside the drawing room and outside to verandah; her face dark with anger and she muttered under her breath. She saw her daughter stood aghast in open curiosity with normal motherly affection but received a goading look meant for someone instead. She dared not to ask and remained muted throughout. Jingo came out, his eyes tear streaked. He wiped his nose and then his eyes yet she still remained mute staring at them with her mouth slightly ajar soon to be closed.

'How dared he? He should return what belonged to my son?' She expostulated.

'No one can put my children down while I am still alive.'

She spat with aggression.

'He has to return what belonged to my son.'

He persisted stepping the threshold of the Verandah. Molly, their mad servant came too terrified to speak and stood beside her.

She nodded her head towards her in askance and she dumped it all in her ears. Her mother had climbed the steps already, reached the top where she usually rest but this evening she stopped not and marched purposefully towards where she headed—Palmina-ma's.

Palmina sat outside. Beside her on the *moorah* sat her mother with a small round bamboo tray; in it were slices of betel nut and green slices of betel leaves; a cup of lime stood on the low wooden table; it was freshly immersed. Jonan, Palmina's five years old brother sat on his mother's lap, stroking a little chick he had taken out from the nest; he found the nest on the tree branch two weeks back, let the eggs where they are and taken them down this evening; he brought four chicken home.

'Palmina—ma! Jonan took chicken out of Jingo's hand.'

She stood shouting from the top of the stair. There was a momentary silence with her mother unable to grasp her accuse. Then it began to dawn slowly. She was aghast, momentarily shocked and was left speechless.

'No. I did not. I found the nest, left it hatched and waited for the chicken to grow.'

Jonan protested strongly. It was him who made her aware of the happening around.

"Yes. It was Jonan who found the nest, left it hatching and waited for the chicken to grow." She replied mildly expounding.

'No. Jingo found it, waited for the hatching and waited for the chicken to grow." Milche—ma said with vehemence.

'Jonan found it. He left the chicks to grow.' Her mother reasonably answered. Words slung from one end to another and with every word the situation heated.

'What do you think? You think you can put my children down while I am still alive?' She said aggressively. The tirade continued for nearly fifteen minutes, drew the neighborhood to the spot, watching the scene with rapt attention and curiosity, murmuring, criticizing and listening to every word. Volleys of words came. They were smashed one sided only. The other side was given no chance to hit back. Palmina watched her mother took a hairless chicken out of crying Jonan's hand. The baby chick tried its utmost to flap its hairless wings in her hand in a failed attempt. Jingo returned home with a chicken not belonged to him; he smiled gleefully in triumph. Milche—ma returned satisfied and still murmuring of fight for justice and truth—a distorted truth; the justice brought upside down. Milche—ma had a phobia—fear of ostracizing of his children—Milche and Jingo. She gave them all much—love, care, affection and attention. The children had them in excess. Pampered. Spoiled. She wanted to be a mother and a father rolled into one. Her father saw it not, heard it not and felt not the pain—the humiliation. The dim light of the lantern kept on the wooden table showed Palmina two drops of tears. She remained silent companionably, her way of comforting to her mother—understanding. Milche—ma reached home, her anger subsided yet still trace of it in her face; she still muttered and murmured. Blindly. Milche stood behind. Jingo put the chicken down on the floor; he watched its wings flapped, ready for fly.

'Mum . . the chicken belonged to Jonan.'

Timidly Milche explained. Silence.

'He saw them.'

There was no response.

Palmina called Tochi-ma aunty, she neither like it nor dislike but looked at her vilely but Palmina knew she liked her; often she snubbed at her but she mostly smiled sweetly. She felt herself younger than the age she found herself in, wished it and willed it for others to know it too. She listened to her stories, much of made of, imaginary of the past she longed but never had, much to put herself up then down. Chinche, Jentilla, Milche, Hilla turned their face and walked away, scoffed, made faces from back, then turned innocent in her face. Palmina stood on the rock, listening looking at her with an intent, her eyes with curiosity much of show than the real interest; she did it out to please her and of pity. She earned a cup of tea with pure milk in her house she much like. She later learned she preferred herself calling her sister; it was a term designated for a woman younger and looked at Palmina and considered her age, then accepted grudgingly her much younger age. Palmina knew she'd preferred it otherwise given the opportunity.

'I married Tochi—pa in a very young age."

She said darting her eyes at Palmina then journeying back to the past. Palmina said nothing. She just smiled. She knew the story well and urged her on to resume.

'I was not ready for marriage then. We got married much against my wishes.' She said.

"I wore the white wedding gown, stitched beautifully."

She carried the tale proudly with gleam of pride in her eyes.

'How beautiful you must have looked?'

She asked in feigned surprise and flattery. In her boastfulness she hardly could judge the flattery and took it as compliment. She smiled with pride in condescending way.

'I passed my matriculation well, in second division.'

She ended. They said, she was dwindling like an old maid, forced herself on him. She went to his quarter where he worked in the village nearby. Her husband was the sub-divisional officer; his office was close to the village she lived working as *anganwadi madam*. She preyed on the matured officer, filled the loneliness he felt with her body in his bed. She did it purposely and had her family, uncles, aunty and brother in law, sister in law, brought and made his guilt felt charged with defiling the young blooming girl. He was left with no choice; he was cornered, and his betrothed left. They were married in a week in a hurry before further misfortune. She was ecstatic; they were ecstatic but he felt like written his own doom and he did hanged his head in shame and came late for the wedding in his old suit; his face looked gloomy like of funeral than a wedding day; she waited in her mother's white *dakmanda* and a white blouse. A borrowed lacy veil of her aunty from the year last covered her face. Later, Palmina learned, she had her result in supplementary with two back subjects, well after three years of trying, then copying from the book. She lay the book open in the latrine where she went every half an hour for piss up. She returned with a white paper pieces with blue inks; she put them beneath the answer sheet. Benta—ma brought her past life in detail. She got it from somebody she knew in her village she hailed from and relayed it to her mother. She brought her limp thin hair forward. A rat's tail, her mother remarked sarcastic once. Her hair was long, thick and very healthy, lustrous and needed bamboo railing for drying it but the motherhood spoiled it and fell excessively. She had the limp unhealthy hair from girlhood she was told later. She talked of the lavish wedding, the number of pigs killed; she began counting.

"twelve, thirteen, fourteen" rolled her eyes up then blinked,

"fifteen, sixteen, seventeen", stopped and rolled her eyes up, blinked several times and resumed,

'eighteen, nineteen, twenty, twenty one, twenty two' and ended nodding her head finished the number.

'around twenty two . . .,'

She said with pride of the pig killed on wedding day itself but the number killed before the wedding and the smaller ones, she said was left uncounted. The number of cows killed had no record, nor of the chicken, nor of the fish from their pond; his relatives she said came in a Night super Deluxe bus and satisfied with the marriage. The village had only two ponds, one of her cousin came for weaving training said, unknowingly of the story told to Palmina. One was owned by the village headman with owning large estate; the another with the village school headmaster with acres of paddy fields. The wedding, the cousin said was sudden, more like registration in the church, signing their names and witnesses with his relatives brought in public bus, jam packed; his relatives sat grumbling and angry for not hiring the bus and went back home dissatisfied. They returned with pouting mouths and with the words 'got our son cheaply.' The pigs killed was six, her cousin said; they were more from the relatives' charity; one from uncle; one from the village headman with generous hand; the another one from the upcoming politician wooing votes, one was her mother reared at home for selling and remaining other from a close distant relative with bags of rice. The meat was all cooked with powdered rice, the cousin added, not with vegetables then turned to Palmina before she left and ended.

'She perhaps gave herbal love potion to have him smitten.'

They fought a vicious fight when the herbal shrub flowered in the month of a year, she explained of those using herbal love potions for marriage. Palmina noted all these in her mind, calculated and smiled. The imaginary, ninety percent of it all, she decided but said nothing and let her lived her wish—unfulfilled yet fulfilled in her imagination. She relayed the story to Chinche, Jentilla and Hilla. Jentilla laughed. Hilla listened skeptically. There was disbelief in her face. Chinche rolled her eyes in wishful thinking and said.

"I wish I too will get that love potion to give him . . ."

She had a new admirer; the newcomer in the neighborhood she was smitten with. He had a rented small room; a serious student immune to Chinche's beauty; resisted the temptress.

The sun lost its bright red, the shiny circle around it disappeared, gone, its duty done, finished and the red round ember headed near the edge of the clouds, in the west for a short rest, then ready to return the day next in the morning. The Small narrow path in between clustered houses was a common playfield; it was strewn with the children; both boys and girls, shrieking, screaming, laughing, crying, running when the attention of the few girls got distracted and the shrieking stopped. Their running too got disrupted. They girls had their eyes pinned on the slender girl; their friend Hilla. With her hair combed shaped around her shapely face the style Palmina admired and a red pant with the bell shaped bottom she wore with a black cotton tee shirt, emblazoned with white letters she walked in heavy gait weight down by a pair of thick two inches black shoes its straps wired around her feet. Cock shoe and bell bottom pants, the fashion of the season, Milche turned to her friends and informed them proudly. Palmina sensed the pride for the knowledge; she had assessed her voice inside; it was tinged with envy or it could be of jealousy. Perhaps she found a rival, Palmina thought but muted her inner words; it was the feelings she too nurtured within. Palmina, Jentilla, Chinche and Milche gaped at her; all of them envious of her or perhaps with self pity. With their parents failing to buy; but they understood their financial constraints each wrapped in their own thoughts they whiled the evening away. Milche's mother was not. She had the money; but she hated the sight of the cock shoe. Her parents led with the tall burly man in blue jeans and blue shirt in front with a bunch of keys of his mo-bike and house dangling, the first man with the red moped motor bike around, kept one kilometers from home with the road from the pitch main PWD road of rough *kutcha*, meant for footholds not for machines that ran on wheels; the mother in yellow *churidar*, the only woman around to wear it and much frowned at for it, her thick lip stick bright red adorning the thin sweet lips, a brown lady bag below her right arm with a small boy dressed smartly in tow behind trailed, left them all still gaping till their disappearance; the children resumed the play but not with the whole heart. But the family in the elevated area left too much murmur, criticism and simple plain envy coupled with jealousy. The next day, on a Saturday, the holiday, the four friends—Palmina, Chinche, Milche, Jentilla—gathered in one place and began what they planned—to make cock shoe they saw the evening before in Hilla's feet. With their desire un-whetted the girls brought out a block of raw wood, its skin still green and with a long sharp dagger in hand, began making with their mind of only one, their desire only one on cock shoe—each pair of hand trying, desperately, unsuccessfully yet with a single desire. Palmina volunteered to cut first looked on by others with a single intent. The sharp end of the shackle landed on every part of the wood. Their desire was dishonored, their immense effort went in vain, the block came out in every shape far remotely in the cock shoe shape, in a slippery effort, the dagger cut in small steps with Palmina screaming. There was excruciating pain in her voice, the red blood spilled on the ground below. Her point finger almost severed, balanced only by the skin.

"Study well. When you become a doctor, you can have hundred pairs of cock-shoes."

Her mother refrained from scolding her but rather motivated her.

There was pain in her face. She didn't know why.

The evening brought the women-folk, stood in a circle at the narrow pathway, their faces on each other, their backs on the bamboo fencing, blaming, criticizing for the morning episode—the failed cock-shoe making. It was an issue in the evening; some listened and then injected the words in between, asserting their own opinion but they zeroed on one topic—the family in the elevated area.

'They are spoiling our children.' Tochi-ma.

'Look at the way she dress. She wears only *churidar* not *gana*.' Palmina-ma.

'Very stylish.'

Benta-ma. Not an admiration nor an appreciation but her mouth twitched with the words.

'Look at the husband. He thought great of himself, always unsmiling.' Jentilla-ma.

'Milche is nagging me for cock-shoe now, crying since morning.' Milche-ma.

'A bad influence for children.'

'Look at their daughter. She wears longpant like a boy.' Another scorned.

'They thought we are paupers and themselves as high class people.'

Another woman, neighbor. None was smiling when the dusk fell and cut off the conference bitterly.

In the early morning water was clean; it reflected their faces like a mirror; the water rose its level well up to its neck, below the craggy mouth, decorated round with the stones and the moss grow green in its wall and the long stemmed ferns sprouting from in between two stones which no one cared for removing and left them the way they pleased to grow. On the other night the men-folk came and poured a bucketful of lime water. Bolchugri girls goes to school, ran by American Christian Missionaries; the best the small town could boast of for little session fees; that was they called it, session fees, a lump-sum for a year, a small amount in comparison to the private convent schools with huge three storied buildings with preference for admission first to the children of denomination the church belonged. She had tried, Palmina remembered in the private convent school, but was rejected with her denomination unmatched with the school signify. Her father met the principal for reconsideration but met the man who shook his head negatively; a middle aged man with white skin, white hair and white beard that came not with the age but was a nature's gift to him. Original. Inborn. The colour of his race and bearing. Some cheated on the denomination but was later asked for baptism certificate they could not produce of and lost the seat. She got in the end in the Christian Missionary School, her father thought of as at par with it. He allowed grudgingly though. The bathing in the morning was their ritual. The school had a strict warning, not to come without bathing and let them known it was a disrespect shown to others, that too after kitchen work, mostly washing utensils for Palmina that she did out of compulsion than desire. The bucket was one; it was too small for four; it had the capacity of only five liters and heavy with pure but rusted steel; it was tied with a long rope to draw the water up from the bottom. There she came the new girl Tochi—ma had hired; she had a pitcher under her arm, circled at the neck; its bottom was rested well on her waist, a big steel bucket on her right arm. She stood shyly, a village girl faced the town girls and the complex fully felt; it showed in her face, body movement and her behaviour. Uncertainty. Hesitation. But compassion had its virtue seen in the girls and gave way for her.

"Here is the bucket."

Palmina handed with a rope attached to draw the water out. She took it wordlessly but with shy smile; her eyes drooped to the ground below; she was shy to unable to look up; she drew water up six or seven times, both for the pitcher now landed in between three stones; it was balanced properly from falling or moving but firmly; then she drew water to the big bucket nearby; it was big since it certainly was bigger than the one the others carry. The reason was because she was stronger than them all; she had done more hard-work than them. Then she left the well heading home. The first she went without word except for yes or no. The third, she came back and went with few words still shyly, yet opening up. The next two or three days the girls made her talk freely. In the pond, in their bathing, the friendship blossomed, a restricted friendship began; restricted for Tochi-ma hardly forgot the sudden exit of their last servant she vehemently said, poisoned and forgave not still and threatened if found someone talking to her. Mittila, she told them was her name, told them to call her "Mittil' for the full name had the mouth full. The friendship strengthened more and after a year when the man with a loosely worn shoes and a grey half sweater sauntered in to meet her father and informed of the cemented ring-well in and above the pond with the MDC scheme, the friendship was strongly sealed. But Mittila for one, hardly came out in the evening like them all but fed the pigs, darted in and out of the kitchen with the dirty water, throwing with a loose dirty *gana* on her waist, its hem below the knee, a charity from her mistress they well knew of with the blouse above, they all had seen her wearing well before and now ready to throw and darted risky glances at her town friends with forbidden wish.

CHAPTER 5

RAINY SEASON.

When June began, the rain came in its heaviest. The cleared compound green with grass, long and short, snakes and leeches crawling, attacking defensively and sucking blood red from the ankle, calf and thigh unnoticed, then fell back swollen black and tripled their size. Palmina saw a slim leech fattened with her blood, stuck hard to her ankle. She squirmed and screamed without looking at her ankle. Jentilla laughed and removed it with the stick. Later, both of them watched it disappear in the salt she brought. The long green stem year around gave a white flower; the another of its kind bloomed pink flower, the another same green but for its orange flower, the elders said of medicinal values and had magical values of its own. A charm; a love potion. The relationship sealed with it saw repercussion they claimed; once in a year when they flowered the fight began in between a couple sealed with it, something beyond their control powered by some mystic design, a belief everybody mouthed of yet remained unproved. A scream, shout came from the house with L-shaped, too close for Palmina to ignore but compelled to listen. She called Jentilla and Chinche. Three of them sat in her house and listened to their screams of fight. Jentilla laughed. Chinche put a finger to her lips and told her to listen. For them it was a drama, being heard without a picture. But they knew in the next day, Mittila would carry the tale. Hilla refused to come. Her parents disallowed her. They lived in seclusion, untouched by the illiteracy and uneducated neighbors; untouchables.

"Uneducated people live that way . . " they told their daughter. The fighting came every night since the flower bloomed with screaming, crying, wailing—the woman. The man shouted three or four times; that was all but the woman's voice rang above all. Their voices mingled with the *cling clang clang, clang, clang, clang, cling, cling, clang, clang, clang, clang, clang* sound when the pots and *karahis* flying below to the stream and hit the stones and the trees on the way and the sound stopped when they reached well in the stream. They lay there for a week or two, brought back when the screaming, crying, wailing stopped by the muttering, pouting Mittila with nothing in the kitchen but everything below on the stream went down below and brought them up. The dented pots, handle-less *karahis*, glass-less kitchen, the scattered plates were an eyesore in their kitchen later. Benta-ma came, eager to tell the news and stood with the elderly women neighborhood, forced in the story even if they were unwilling to listen and made up some of it, the beginning and the end of it dressing it up to a tale. The long stemmed grass stopped flowering; pink, white, orange went down dried, then fell wet to the ground and the fighting in a season stopped and everybody around in the neighborhood proved themselves right. It was the wonder herb with its magical values. The enchantment. The bewitchment. Benta—ma came the evening later, too eager with the tale she was bearing, something new added to her already stuffed mind ready to share forcefully. Palmina made tea for the three—herself, her mother and Benta—ma. Milche—ma joined later and her tea shifted to her even before her lips touched the tip of her cup. She took casual leave from the office she said later for the head ache Milche complained in the morning and abstained from class.

"Tochi—ma hired an *ojha* . . ."

Benta—ma twitched her mouth, unsmilingly a bitter revenge for an unspoken anger she might have stocked from the past and resumed her tale of Tochi-ma. A tale of her romance, the beginning of her love story, her lure of the man she married, something that happened long years back yet remained unraveled except now. He was unhappy with his life, her mother commented later to Milche—ma of Tochi—pa. Palmina overheard it. It was *Ojha,* the local medicine man who took a single thread out of Tochi—pa's cloth and with the thread of Tochi—ma's cloth with a charm herb. He rubbed them together and conjoined. She carried the tale lengthening it. He then put the two conjoined threads on a fresh green leave along with something nut she raked her brain to remember the name and left it in the stream on the bank pressed below the stone after chanting few *mantras*. He was paid for that, Benta—ma spoke in the end. The next day, Tochi—pa began smiling. Smiling turned to something akin to invitation. It next turned into courtship. Tochi—ma never missed the chance and lured him straight into from where she tied him down—in bed. There was no escape. She blocked the routes. He was trapped. The tale spread. It went from one neighbor to another, from Palmina to Jentilla and then to Chinche, then Milche, Hilla. Jingo spilled the lurid details to Tochi in the fight. Tochi took the words back to his mother. The mother was livid beyond sanity and vented not on the child but on the mother. She waited for Milche—ma, her simmering anger visible in her whole body. She stood on the narrow footpath, right in the middle. Milche—ma encountered vicious attack, verbal attack worst even than the physical attack. Milche—ma saw the nightmare in the broad daylight after the office hours. She had none to blame but herself. Benta—ma denied vehemently she carried the tale. Her meal came from Tochi—ma's. Mittila brought the inside story out. Palmina too eager to listen sat on the green short grass near the pond and fixed her gaze on her, transfixed. The inside story was mesmerizing and urged Mittila to carry on. She was late in coming. Tochi—ma resumed her rage and vented on her badly. Her forehead showed the twin swelling the next day in the pond. The impact of the hit received from the big spoon with the elephant's strength.

Long green drumsticks hanged down. They moved sideways when the wind blew, undamaged even by the rain and the four drumstick trees below the house gladdened her. She waited for the season for them to give flowers then to bear fruits her children so loved to eat. Now with the season in full bloom she inspected every morning and every evening when cleaning rice with her mind purely calculative—a generous neighbor till the hilt. A long bamboo pole was brought, a sickle attached on the top and she cut small branches with drumstick fruits in them, spread them on the ground below till it heap. Two handfuls each are separated—for Tochi-ma, Hilla-ma, Chinche-pa, Jentilla-ma, Benta-ma, the headman—for four meals the left over served. Palmina saw her father came, his hands full. He gave the school summer vacation, he told his wife in explanation, waited for two days for road clearance blocked by the heavy landslide he was caught and talked of the flooded rice fields, flooded bridgeless river he crossed. He had his brown trouser from sale folded upto to both his calf. The brown mud painted his exposed legs; his plastic sandals were two inches thicker with the mud he washed with half the barrel of water. He cursed. He swore at the obstinate mud and went inside the house. Her mother was happy. It was visible. She was worried for the whole week and tensed when he was away. Her face was a dead give away. The next day, he took one hundred areca nut saplings he kept in the small plastic bags he kept three years back and now sprouting with long green leaves and busied himself planting them in the empty land.

'To your future' he said to Palmina.

'It will bear fruit after few years' he said.

For Palmina and Jentilla the black leather shoes soaked the year round in the incessant rain, torn, irreparably, flapped when she walked ashamed of with her rich friends in the class made fun of, stifling giggles. The spot where her heel rested had the nail's head protruding, butted into her heel and a small store of white pus seen within burst. She grimaced in real pain and limped. For her, the pair was a more of a burden with it on and without it, the butt of teacher's ire, a tall regal woman with forever unsmiling face with her black eyes looked down at her, snorting distastefully. She was a pure snob and with her side always on rich students not the poor the girls are fully aware of but with her influence in the school and her tartar reputation nothing could hardly be done; she remembered the last time she went without a pair of shoes but a pair of slippers and afterwards sat with her knees down on the rough concrete that the blood oozed out and reeled of the blazing sun. She nearly vomited with head ache, the tartar felt no guilt of but snorted her long nose and held her arrogant head and looked down at her distastefully. The next day, Monica, their rich classmate wore fancy footwear her father brought from Delhi, proudly showing off to her friends and walked with her head held high in a nebulous mind. The tall teacher gave a glance, looked away, a spark of admiration in her eyes seen fleetingly, said nothing and began the chapel in her usual regal standing, stern and rigid but said nothing about the school—shoeless feet. It rescued Palmina's school-shoeless feet too. Jentilla too escaped unhurt for that day. She asked her mother for new school shoes; she kept mumbling something unintelligible that meant for her ears alone with a green piece of betel leaf in her left palm she rubbed with another pair and her right cheek bulging with a slice of betel nut; Jentilla heard something like the empty purse, the rice-less kitchen, the meatless curry but the green vegetables later when her voice rose. Her demand was left unattended. She was given no hope and no promise for a new school shoes. The next day, her sister was brought a new school shoes and her old worn pair fitted hers. Her father came home on the first date of the month with a pair of black uniform shoes. She was ecstatic. Her mother grumbled endlessly and complained needlessly and nagged irritatingly he said nothing of. She could not careless. Her happiness lay in his care and love. Her father smiled at her happiness, something he did rarely. His smile dimmed at his wife's unhappiness.

The street looked colorfully beautiful in the rush hour of the early morning; shades of blue, green, brown, purple and grey uniforms were the colors splashing; white was the common color none would miss of; an expensive bags rested on the backs of the well off children with colourful water bags hanging from their hands; the handloom woven cotton threads were the common bags of the commoners, something her mother skilled at weaving; the unused bottles their mothers kept at home carried the water for them. The green majestic Tura peak, stood in the backdrop and the sun rose above it from the back side, filtering to the ground below, on the streets which was both a blessing and curse to the school children. Palmina was late; she drew water from the pond whole morning, saw her with her clothes on her right arm going to the pond for bathing; she waited for her and then came ahead. Chinche said she'd give the class a miss. She attended classes on her whims and fancy and could not careless of the result. Milche went far ahead of time and waited for none. Palmina found herself alone with Hilla for a company to school few kilometers away from home. The bright and sunny morning she was greeted with suddenly changed; the sky turned grim; the dark clouds masked the bright smiling sun; the sky looked ominous; tall Sal trees stood on the left side of the pitch road swayed from side to side as the monsoon wind swept past them while the howling sound it gave chilled her body; she shivered; the dust and sand came flying, hurt her face; she closed her eyes for protection; her hair tied in a bun on top of the back of her head in a pony tail came out in disarray and gave her disheveled look; the rain was imminent and with no umbrella the panic struck her; the name of the supreme being uttered in her lips; she arranged her skirt made disarray by the wind, tied her hair tightly let loose by the wind but the wind too strong for her swept past them and lifted her skirt up and she fought hard to push it down, looked around in open embarrassment for any onlookers but found none. Everyone was too busy with themselves. Hilla took her umbrella out, a birthday present from her Doctor father, folded, sat comfortably in the bag, opened it into pink printed shade covering her; few drops of rain fell first followed by a downpour; she'd decided to retract her steps backwards; her mother would understood; the wind stopped lashing leaving only the simple rain to pour as if gripped by compassion for school children, she was grateful for; she stepped closer to Hilla protecting herself from rain but not before salvaging her bag and her right side, already drenched, dripping; she lifted it up, held it closely on her chest with both her arms; rain without sweeping wind was easy to handle; a brief glance in Hilla's direction gave an instant guilt stabbing her heart; with the other side of her body in total drenched, she looked a real waif; she neither blame rain, nor her, nor the umbrella for its size but herself; with her with the umbrella in hand the question never cropped but the guilt remained within without a word; the heavy downpour threatened the hawkers, pedestrians, taking shelters in the shops wide enough for standing but for the school children and few cars fought against it and still plying in the flooded street; her friend, a classmate with a contractor first class for a father, wealth in open display with two ambassadors and one Mahindra jeep sat in a brown of the two, in front with other girls; their neighbors sat behind and packed the jeep; two girls sat on lap of others passed by and stopped not; she gave apologetic smile she was grateful for and smiled back in open understanding; brown muddy water flooded the black pitch road and ran over their shoes and the socks inside the shoes got drenched yet they still walked; the shutters of the roadside shops are down preventing the saleable things from getting drenched; the front part of the shops used as verandahs with roofs above them but without walls are packed with pedestrians sheltering; battling with the lashing rain coupled with cold, their bodies shivering, the girls stepped into Ringrey bridge, covered with brown muddy water—flooded; a black Mahindra passed by, its four wheels sent slithering jets of water into the air and spluttered muddy water all over them, soaked them to skin, she cursed after but the jeep went off with the driver showing not a single sign of remorse; the sign of makeshift grocery shops with plastic roofs weighed down by rain, pitiable but no one showed emotions thinking of their own, selfishly; the long corridor of old school set up by the Christian missionaries in British regime warmly invited after a soaked morning, totally drenched, shivering cold at the first bell rang; the other girls already ahead run to and fro on the wooden plank of a floor. The sound was disturbing and many a times the whole class earned a period of baking in the oven hot sun but now sighed with a relief with the pure knowledge that the teacher was yet to come; a soaked umbrella Hilla left in the corridor left a little stream in its wake and with both girls headed inside the classroom they left behind two pairs of wet footsteps; both the girls crossed the threshold where Monica stood waiting with welcome smile meant not to greet her but Hilla. She was an outcast and it hurts like hell; a warm smiling good morning to Hilla, missed purposely on her with an remark tinged with sarcasm she made her wet and a vile look directed was an insult stabbed deeply and bled profusely; shame, guilt and pain trailed, inserted deep with it the tears, the unseen tears she kept hidden and let the scar remained where the wound was—in her heart; the fault was the poverty, something she never could undo but challenge and throw it back from where it came—in their face; something stilled in, etched with steely determination, a quiet determination of Saturday morning resurrected, fresh alive, strengthened; her eyes in challenging slits, narrowed but no one saw it. The evening was morose, she neither was interested in the game her friends were playing nor in the food; her mother turned dangerously aggressive when she sat in silence and ignored the task allotted—washing utensils of the day. Jentilla gave the class a miss; she hated to but left no choice. She finished her chores a little late. Her friends already left for the classes when she was still in the kitchen. She was little away from home when she saw the overcast weather; she had no umbrella and returned home only to meet heavy shower halfway; she reached home with complete soak.

In the evening Palmina sneezed badly; she went to Jentilla's house with a home work and few History notes the teacher gave. She had a bad cold the whole week round. Jentilla applied mustard oil when she reached home and escaped.

They both saw their future together till midnight.

Rain lashed incessantly, merciless for whole two weeks; the sun showed no face nor the ground remained dry; the clothes hanged inside went into a bundle foul smelling wet; the birds were no seen on the amla tree beside the house; the brown flower pots of their rich neighbor turned moss green; the small stream below their house swelled to a river to be short-lived; the leeches gate crashed to the small room she slept. She squirmed, brought salt, kept it hidden in it and found none but the water after few minutes. A curse was on everybody's lips. A hard soil loosened and streamed down below and mounted right in front of their house; with it weeds, roots, old socks and long black slimy creature crawled away for her scream; a bamboo pipe stuck out on the wall, behind their house. Flood seemed everywhere—in the plain areas and even in the hilly regions too; heavy landslide occurred; roads blocked and the buses stopped plying; loose soil took the lives and the houses; somebody got drowned in the swelling river and the boat capsized in the south somebody carried the story Palmina so eagerly listened and felt sorry for the people washed down to Bangladesh. She heard too of the mermaid girl netted in a fishing net, so beautiful to be true cried to be let off but the cruel fisherman severed her into two, ate the fish part from the waist to tail and buried the girl part from waist up to head. Jentilla heard it from some where and relayed the story; she was laughing at the story while relaying; her usual cheery way, jolly to the last, making jest of the story. Palmina listened awe-struck not finding it funny at all but felt sorry for the mermaid girl. Chinche laughed. Hilla was skeptical. She didn't believe it. He parents never allowed her to believe such false rumours nor stories. She was ingrained in it. Some horror stories too streamed in but they were no surprise for all. The rain stopped; their neighbour, fat woman with her huge swelling buttock swayed in, her small mouth looser than the old elastic. With her entry came news from all over; some mysterious water creature went past Ganol River, crossed to Dubol beel; it left the marks of a tractor's wheel on the pitch road, in between; the hot news was exciting to many and it found the listeners in everyone—men, women and children and believed; many went to see but came disappointed, abusing, cursing the tale bearers—it was an usual local news. Benta-ma with her three children in tow, her two sons in both the hands holding left the house in the middle of the night when the wind went berserk and with a struggling for survival flame of a kerosene lamp. The wind kicked the crumbling house hard and it stood no chance and reduced to mere debris. With no trace of kitchen and she camped for a week in Tochi-ma's house and returned after the house was restored back, livable, by the generosity of the neighbors—bamboo from Palmina-pa, wood for pillars from the short headman, food from Tochi-pa stocked. The young males erected the wooden posts, woven the bamboo flats, made the thatch roofs and the woven flat bamboos stood in between roof and the ground as the wall. Benta-pa watched it all with his hands on his hip, a *mantu bidi* in between his lips stuck out and declared to anyone listening shamelessly he'd built a concrete house when he got a contract of few lakhs he announced boastfully with all half ears listening but with sympathy for the children and his wife; the short man, headman, his mouth twitched, smiled sarcastically insolent and recalled the first time he was given the house with a vast expanse of betel nut trees around, much to the nagging of his wife than to his will, had no heart to turn them out for the fear of his wife than the reason the neighbors thought; he was her distant relative. A family in the locality lost house; went down with the loose soil; the elders to console and to share the family grief went; the children for fun and delight, for curiousity; Palmina along with Jentilla, Milche with big black umbrella, Hilla in yellow printed shared with Chinche shielded from slitting drizzle, with never ending love story went heading. Jentilla danced all the way, laughing and carefree; they were more interested to see it. They were aghast at the sight. Sympathy filled their hearts for the victim family of nature's fury. The site was a total wreck; a huge family of bamboo went past, pulled along the house to the stream below; the bereaved family of six, the eldest a son of ten with three sibling sisters of eight, five and two stood watching on the side with the mother, her red rimmed eyes smaller than normal spoke of the pain, sorrow, sadness of the lost and with the brush of death invoked sympathy atleast out of one with the others just staring at the site with silent inspection of the damage and their feelings too silent, wrapped; Palmina parted with an old pink frock her father brought the year last, its red stained stood prominent in front; Milche gave ash baggy pant; Jentilla donated an old beige *gana,*; Hilla with her extra flower printed bedcover the sad family are exuberantly showed gratitude and Chinche with a shirt of her brother were satisfied with their charitable deeds; the eyes lit of bereaved children, so forlorn with the devastation smiled for the first time; a tall lean man stood far aside looked at them and sent them a silent gratitude with a small smile the children understood of; The head of the family and the father of the children. The crowd thronged, on all sides; the nearest neighbor host the guests important enough to grace; a burly man, his curly hair on top of a tall body, his eyes intent on a round chubby face, showed some emotion with sympathy; an upcoming politician, someone whispered; he stayed long enough, handed something to the lean man with no emotion and made exit; duty done; just made sure the votes are cast in his favour—begging for the next election and the family are fooled, taken his action for generosity and care and felt under obligation to repay. Another man entered, a tall thin man with his cheeks shrunken; his eyes red with a grey suit over a brown v-necked sweater, revealing the pointed collars of light blue shirt inside tailed by four men; a local MLA; everyone knew, cast their votes four years back now with regret, resented. There were stories around. Everyone seemed to be carrying stories of the past two weeks of incessant rain and what it left in its wake. Some creature went past; it was foretold of by the woman with a dual life with that of the river creature in another life and of a woman in human world; she knew all ahead; the crowd started the stories, Palmina was fascinated of and believed. Chinche and Hilla stood head to head their eyes on the site but not their minds and ears certainly not on the stories circulating; the formers' mouth on the latter's ears in low tones; "My heart belongs to you", the words read, the three kittens above in the yellow, near see through tee shirt, a gift she wore for the second day and Palmina asked her mother, the night before, the meaning and got the scowling with no answer, mumbling something unintelligible harsh, then glared at her; she braved the rain for a date on Sunday with her new boyfriend and now the stories she fed to Hilla of her romance, she had no interest of whatsoever. She wondered for how long the story would last before the character changed.

They saw nothing of Hilla for few weeks.

Her parents saw Chinche as a bad influence.

Sunday came hot and sunny in the morning with the weather unpredictable; it dried the soddy ground, evaporated the water and lifted somewhere up; the sun looked strong but everyone knew her façade wore false strength and would easily wear off if the cloud came menacing, charging; with it the people ran helter skater for the weekend worship, the weekend routine of the people; the small church in the heart awaited waiting for the time to call with the bell hanging in the front. The narrow path above their house, to the well below, thronged with the people; some are going and some coming, trying utmost to finish the morning chore before the first bell chimed; each school was in its weekend holiday and the children loved it most. Palmina awoke late, leisurely; her mother was already up and her face showed of anger and hostility, unspoken anger she was well aware of. She had finished the breakfast for the children and way ahead in lunch, already kept ready on the table and had not her to help. She was ready for bath with her fresh clothes on her arms for the water ring-well few meters from their house, mulling with the neighborhood; with an empty earthen pot under her left arm, circled around its neck, on her right hand her clothes, her mother led the way; she trailed her like a puppy; the well cemented round well raised high above the ground, a raised cemented platform around the well, for washing; the well was far from deserted; the young blood neighbors sat waiting, the women neighbors elders on the platform washing, slapping clothes, few children throwing water at each other, shrieking, screaming filling the surrounding with their voices; Moren, among waiting few with his arm around Gongsin, a dark, devilish neighbor with the heart of gold, smiled with his towel from his waist to the knee, his intention clear, a merciless teaser and she was his victim.

'My princess, you came; I have been waiting for you; we can bath together.' Sudden tears blinded her eyes; not of sorrow nor of sadness or of anger but of shame'; an aluminum mug she hold covered little of her full round near teenage face. But it was the nose and upper lip that benefited much and covered.

'You look prettier with the mug,'

Her action invited more teasing; it infuriated her while her mother laughed but she wailed, howling. She cried not of sadness but of anger and embarrassment. She hated the man but the man resumed merciless in his effort. He enjoyed her discomfiture; his favourite victim.

"If I have hurt you and your heart ache, then please take chloroquine tablet to ease the pain."

He ended sheepishly. All laughed but she cried. The rumor said, he waited for her, in his uncle's house where he stayed, struggling to cross last stage of school to the college, to tie for ever till death do them apart with his uncle brought him with a promise with his lone daughter, the family heiress, he was sure to marry, not that they had much, just few hectares of land, a three roomed tin sloppy Assam type house, a separate thatch roof kitchen. His uncle had two sons and a daughter, a tall fair slender mother, her swan neck much spent stood below the jackfruit tree on a *moorah* with a permanent wooden table in front. She had betel nut and leaves permanently placed in a wide plate, a small container of lime too with a small stick stuck out, non stop grinding with an inborn red teeth, but of artificial red lips, craning assessing of the neighbors' daughters than her own. The neighbor girls' movements, behaviour, dress were much criticized of with a husband more like that of a woman than a man, his curly hair smoothened with the coconut oil. He had height shorter than his wife but his mouth and the sights wider, unsurpassed even by the wife. The wait, everyone said will take him time, with the girl still in seven class;

she was still in her mid teenage, too pretty to be his and too ambitious to tie down. She carried her aim of a white cloak and a stethoscope around her neck her as nurtured dream, unwilling with the match, still resisting and barely looking at him. She was rarely out of the room at home. She spent hours browsing over books, a whole stack of them. Her father wished to wait only for another three years and then to betroth her to his nephew. Her mother let her have her wish. Later in the day, with the church service over, the teenagers flapped in the clean blue water, in thigh deep, basked in the cool, washed away the sweat, took shelter from the heat, enjoying. All had *gana* in each, their soft budding bodies and tiny peaches underneath with their nipples hardened underneath that still stuck out. Their *ganas* covered them from chests to calf and left the other parts bare. They crawled with their fingers with their swimming skill almost naught till the water reached skimmed their mouths and noses while Mittila slapped the bucketful of water on the flat surface rock. She had the whole family's dirty clothes to wash. Chinche scrubbed her reddish clean skin with a stone and sat later on the shade beside the stream. With two handfuls of green young mangoes in hand and a small amount of salt with green chilies, burnt with white tiny black eruptions like pimples in it both wrapped in a paper, a generosity showered by Chinche, best suited for the weather, she made her friends sit on a flattened rock; mango chutney was more of fighting the heat than filling, whetting the desire of the mouth not the stomach that they decided to satisfy; Hilla peeled off the green skin of each mango, made small cuts and the white mango came out in tiny pieces into a plate brought with a purpose and mounted in the middle. She lifted the stark white seed and began the science class she had the week before with their science teacher in mind, imitating him—seed, monocotyledon, cotyledon, then feigned cough covering the mistake, they all watched amused; salt and burnt green chilies mixed with it and all swallowed their own saliva that watered the mouth; Chinche lost self control and reached out first; the others too began with a funnel shaped green leaves on their hands each as spoons;

'huh hah . . . huh hah . . . huh hah . . . huh hah . . . huh . . . hah . . . huh hah . . .'

Palmina stuck out her tongue, fanned it rapidly with her palm, saliva dripping like a tired dog. From her nose too the water dripped while her ears and cheek turned red and the others looked at her with something akin to sympathy but laughed aloud; she too laughed much later when her mouth cooled; the evening took them to Araimile, the photo studio they went opened only half the day; inside they powdered their faces white, put lip—stick, bright red, they never owned one, and showed their wrists sat on the wooden bench, all five of them—Hilla, Jentilla, Chinche, Palmina and Chinche with a vase of dusty plastic flowers in the middle. The borrowed plastic wrist watches they proudly showed had no life. An hours later, in the early evening, all four in Chinche's kitchen sat; with the inspection of her dressing table over, they were much fascinated with the green comb with its thistles wide and a long red lipstick they all tried with all their lips painted red of the same colour; the lipstick crossed the outline of each lips. They envied a bottle of 'darling perfume', a gift from her beau they called it 'essence', pronounced firstly by the shopkeeper, a tall thin man with a black moustache. He had his oily hair sleek and with sunken eyes sat in the small shop near the Rongkon bridge, perhaps he meant 'scent' but for his accent. Chinche behind the twin hearths sat on the low wooden stools, struggled, cooking a kilo of pork, her boyfriend sent; the dim lantern stood in between, its unwashed black chimney blocking the flame; the number was added to the group with Mittila joining, escaped stealthily after the dinner was made ready and livened the group with the stories in the village where she grew. With her stories over, she ended with a note,

"I want to study", sadly but recovered quick enough and hid it with a winking smile, a swollen black mole with little hairs elevated briefly and rested where it was before—below her left eyes; she called it good luck charm and smiled cheekily and said 'one day it would bring her immense luck,' something all listened with half ears, unbelieving. Kitchen work was well distributed. A big round onion she was given spilled tears out of Palmina, not of sadness, sorrow but of onion juice brought laughter from all around.

'She'd make a bad wife and a house-maker,'

Chinche said in prediction and teasingly reproved,

"You better learn how to cook or you won't get a husband."

The party extended till 8.30 later, parted with full stomach each, enjoyed and bade goodnight contented. A couple of eggs in the coop cared by the mother hen disappeared in the morning next; her mother gave morning inspection for it every day muttered angrily, cursing the big rat in the hole; it was the size of a piglet with its hole beside the kitchen.

She laid trap for it and got it too in the evening later much to her grim satisfaction and delight.

"*salah* . . I got you. Now you see . . ." with a gritted teeth she put the dead rat upside down, his slim long tail in her hand and threw it to the cat standing nearby with his green eyes feasted onto a sumptuous meal, expecting fully and was not disappointed; Palmina laughed silently alone, enjoyed escaping her wrath, guilty at the same for sending the guiltless rat into the gallows. Her mother never found the real culprit. She never revealed. Nobody knew. The photo came out, three weeks later; black and white photos with their faces all white and the clothes they wore sprinkled with black with the watches showed on their wrists as their pride, all too clear with the flower base in the middle stood that they took pride of with the plastic petals too all in pure white. All four collected five rupees each and paid twenty with three copies and a black negative, they again give it back for another three copies of printing.

The evening on the same day, one copy went into Chinche's boyfriend with a handwritten love letter and he pasted it in his album along with his; he cut it out into heart shaped, got half the body of Hilla sat near Chinche, got the half of Palmina's face and her hand without her legs. Her hand came a wide apart from her body and hanged limply near her hips. Hilla's face stood very close to Chinche's covering the left side of her. She sent another thing too, a white handkerchief with a rose embroidered, its long stem reached into one corner and two leaves on both sides; flower was in red and the leaves and the stem in green; she borrowed the threshing paper from somebody in the class and had the flower copied from it. Her interest in embroidery, filling the flower and the stems and the leaves she indented mark from the threshing paper with coloured threads had nothing to do with interest in sewing but solely to impress her boyfriend. He returned it back when she dumped him for another one.

CHAPTER 6

<u>BEGINNING OF WINTER.</u>

September came; the bamboo families clustered; in their compound; in the compound of her three friends; in the jungle nearby; on the bank of the Ringrey Stream it flowered white; the leaves too with its whole body cast green for white; the children loved the flowers. They had never seen one but for the first time they saw. They wondered and took out the onion shaped green fruit it bore. It looked delectable; delicious. Palmina had the bamboo fruits plenty in their compound near the house. Jentilla came and collected it. She put them in a round glass plate, full of it and kept the plate in the sitting room; in the corner on top of the side table. It beautified their sitting room her friends admired ad followed suit. Later, the fruits get dried and turned light brown. She brought the silver paint from Milche's and painted them all into sparkling silver and gave half of them to Milche she was seen squealing with delight to have. But the elders frowned, their foreheads creased in many lines, worried, muttering and became a topic in the whole locality, in the neighborhood with the words 'a history repeating'; a bad year ahead, they foretold, the famine, the disaster they foresaw. A bad omen. It proved true, the prediction, and few decades back when their elders were in their childhood, the bamboo flowered. The year next, the monsoon rain failed, the paddy fields remained dry in the villages, the forever wet ground cracked that widened. The people turned mere skeleton, their ribs under their skins showing but the man with the loosely worn shoes thought of nothing but of the pipeline, the PHE water, the primary school, the electricity, the need in the locality; for the umpteen time he tried, in tireless effort, failed but undauntedly persistent and blessed this time round with an opportunity—the election came round the corner, in the months coming by. A man with grim face, curly hair, tall and burly, gave him company for the time last and came back with the assurance from the local member of legislative assembly, if voted him back to power all would be theirs and they made a deal. Her father agreed, the headman too, Tochi-pa too nodded, few others male elders in the locality, each along with their families had decided to vote for him who promised but Palmina saw her mother disinterested. Her mind was occupied both in the morning and evening on the fattening two pigs tied on a mango tree, feeding them with the husk and the rotten rice, left over of both the lunch and dinner. She was fattening it with a purpose in mind—Christmas.

Palmina saw her mother busy. She had small saplings on a raised ground below their house planted from seedlings and had them taken out in the mid month, made holes, filled them soft black earth mixed with old manure her father brought and planted—tomato, pumpkin, cauliflower, spring onion, radish, cabbage and watered them everyday, weed the grasses humming under her breath. A soft soil near the stream was dug out; the water in it supplied for her garden. Palmina kept her busy every morning, watered the plants and enjoyed the work. Her friends came in the evening once and stolen ripe red tomato her mother had waited from few days back to pluck; she was angry and hummed no more for a day but grumbled both in the morning and the evening of the tomato she lost, reminded at the same time the hard work she had done on it. She got an earful. Her eardrums blasted. On Saturday, when the sun shone beaming with pride the school gave half a day. Jentilla, Chinche, Hilla and Palmina went down to the Ringrey stream and jumped from one rock to another close by, going further down searching for a shade to sit and enjoy watching the stream flowing. Flap .. flap .. flap .. flap .. flap .. flap ... flap ... flap .. flap .. flap .. flapp .. flap .. flap .. flap .. flap ... sound filled the downstream. Jentilla shrieked excitedly. Milche stayed back. Her mother caught their plan and imprisoned her at home; too protective; too possessive; Milche watched at them through the window tearfully. The women slapped the family's clothes brought and slapped them hard on the rocks sapping their strength; their children shrieked and scream and jumped from the rock splashing water. They flapped their legs and hit the water.

From either side, the stream was bordered by thick shrubs and trees, creeping vines up the trees. They saw a big banyan tree, its branches all bending and its thick leaves shading below on the big flat rock and their eyes gleamed. They sat there with no words uttered. Palmina looked around. She took stock of all. The stream water bouncing over the rocks gleefully with the butterflies black and white printed, pure yellow, pure black, cream colored ones fly in the air mating. On the tree above, birds flew to and fro from one tree to another chirping sweetly like an excited little child, then flew down to the river sighting perhaps swimming fishes, sat on the small rock bending its green head and swooped down and flew off with a wriggling fish in its beak.

"Look . . look . . . look"

Jentilla shouted excitedly and smiled happily; all stopped to look and enjoyed the sight. Gentle breeze seemed caring for she chose that time to caress the little princesses softly that Palmina chose to close her eyes with her arms in open embracing savouring its gentleness, loving each moment they were gifted with. They wished to fish, fulfilled their desire but got nothing but the tadpoles swimming in the stream.

Screams, shouts, the splashing of the water came from two hundred meters from where they sat, relaxing. They saw half naked and full naked bodies made head diving from the big rock. The deep green water where they dived into stretched into hundred meters. Two boys somersaulted and went inside. Six black heads emerged out of the water, bobbing. Their bodies immersed well from the neck down. One pulled a big dead log from the bank. It floated in the deep water. Aimlessly. It went nowhere. Six right hands held the log under their arms and floated with it. Their left hands rowed the log to the water end. Then one counted till three. Then they dived again and left the bobbing log alone. They emerged well in the middle and began flapping their legs, swimming towards the other ends. Their hands supported them. Palmina looked at Jentilla wishfully; her desire written well in her smile and eyes. The water was deep. The colour of it was well evitable. Palmina knew how to crawl. She was a novice. Jentilla was well versed in swimming. Her friends had a name for her. A fish. Palmina loved shallow water. Jentilla loved deep water. Deep water terrified Hilla; she retreated far behind and sat below the tree towering over the big rock. She had broad expanse of flat rock before her. She had a stealth escape from home, much tempted by the water risking her parents' wrath. Chinche loved it for fishing but she had no rod. Jentilla stood and jumped from the big flat rock they sat. Thud, she landed on the smaller triangular rock below. She stopped not there but climbed the higher rock. With her one leg and a hand she clambered. From there, there was no stopping and she stood above on the rock towering over the deep blue water. She looked at them and smiled. Her friends well knew her intention and slowly followed suit. Two boys left the water and stood on the rock on the other side. Their water sleek bodies shivering. Water dripping endlessly from the unfit short pants both wore. Their teeth clattering. They spent too much time in it. The two others reached below where they stood. The another two still flapped in the water and called out others. The other night it rained heavily and the rock was slippery. Palmina slipped her feet and had nothing to hold with her flailing hands. She wished desperately to hold something. None. Her heart sank. Panic gripped her.

"Ahhhhhhhahhhhhhhhhhhhhhhhhhhhhhhhhhhhh" She shouted for few seconds. Loud splash of water tailed. She struggled vainly to put her feet on something below while her hands beat the water. There was nothing below and nothing above. Just the plain liquid she could not hold into. The water was merciless. She went down with her ears, eyes and mouth well inside. Breathing was impossible. Water went into her stomach. Her mind stopped working. The water went inside through her mouth and nose. The current was swift, pulling her below and then into a whirlwind. Death was inevitable and the water seemed cruelly laughing. She thought nothing of it. Suddenly she felt pain in her head and her hair being pulled. Her face above the water and she breathed long and hard. She saw nothing but felt her body being dragged towards the bank. She blackened out. Her eyes peeled opened few minutes later to the worried and shivering four pairs of eyes peering down at her. Jentilla rescued her from the jaws of death.

They breathed not a single word of her brush with death. All remained muted, tightly sealed their mouth. They all are well aware of the result. At night, her near swallowed into a watery grave shuddered her still. She vomited the water out again. Her dinner was wasted. On the bed, the exhaustion overtook her. Her eyes were closing half. She tried to keep awake. The story her mother said was thoroughly regaling. It was a fairy tale, a story of a princess abducted by the certain giant and the announcement of the king, the father that whoever could rescue the princess would his son in law—an usual story. A man took the challenge, slay the giant, then rescued the princess and they lived happily ever after. Her imagination soared high and she saw herself as the princess and felt blissfully romantic.

'When a name is called in heavennn . . . I will be thereeee . . .' a familiar voice slurred drunkenly singing a hymn loudly in the night. The song ended only when Palmina heard the loose pebbles slipping with the heavy weight with a loud thud. Next, she heard the man swore an unmentionable word; Obscene word; Objectionable word. But none bothered. Her mother smiled, knowingly, not caring in either way. Palmina felt the apprehension of the inevitable, worried about Chinche and prayed silently.

'Mujhe du . . niya . . walo sarabhi . . na . . samjo . . '

He began the song he sang consistently for a long time. His drunken slur filtered into the neighboring houses when he closed on towards his house. Then she heard the father calling out to the daughter, loudly, commandingly and demandingly.

'Bring the lamp. I . . cannot see.' He shouted.

There was silence later. But Palmina still hold her heart still with fear. She was not disappointed.

"Bring the lamp . . . ."only few seconds later.

"What is taking you so long?"

"Bring fast . . ."

There was abuse.

He swore.

There were loose pebbles slipping and the slipping of the sandals.

'Cling, clang, clang . . . clang . . . clang . . . clang . . . clang . . .' The sound of the utensils falling reverberated few minutes later.

"Aaghh . . . . . . aaghhh . . . aaghhh . . ."

The cry of a girl was tinged with pain and was more of a scream than a cry.

"Why did you cook this for me?" a drunken voice followed in a rage and more clanging followed. The plates, bowls, saucepans seemed going everywhere.

'Take this, and this and this . . ' a savage snarl.

'Aaaghhh . . . aaaghhh . . ." More of girl's wailing. Pitiful cry.

She cringed.

The footsteps echoed, running, escaping; it sounded towards their house, closer, and closer, and she escaped and the knock sounded on their door a minute later; her mother opened the door and took stock of the tear streaked, battered and bruised Chinche and let her in; she later bundled beside her, in the bed, still sobbing late at night and then hiccups disturbing Palmina. Her two brothers slept in the house seasoned with his verbal torture; they never received his torture physically but his verbal abuse they well were used to could not careless. They were timid children Chinche tried to shelter, from every pain. The next morning, her grandparents came, a short fat man with his thinning hair sparse on the forehead with white scalp shown with full view with a short woman in tow, another fatso, both looking dangerously serious and grim; her cousin too came heavy with six months of second pregnancy beside her husband, a tall dark man, a caring husband for the world around, looked at his wife every now and then, asked her comfort but the sinuous eyes and the meaning within only Chinche knew; a three months stay in their place after one of the episodes of the night before in their four roomed house, spacious in the heart of the town said all she wished not to know; insinuations in the suggestive words, his actions, his gifts, lingering eyes on her untouched two ripe peaches without a knowledge of his wife, all done with a motive she knew well ahead and spurned off; his sinister design raveled but she had none to share with none to believe. She left for home after a month, back to her drunken father, relieved, safer and secured; they crossed from the town outside; her cousin sister with her brother in law sat outside the house with the sitting room too small for the fifteen people—her parents, the elderly neighbors, couples, the village headman for fit in—the chairs were brought from the neighbors and sat in rows; the tea with tapioca boiling was given for everyone. Jentilla and Palmina moved around with trays and Chinche and Milche struggled with the smoke, the wet firewood and they swore and cursed the lifeless wet firewood with two pairs of eyes with tears streaming, batting the lids to wash the burn away. Chinche's hand stuck in the middle of long handle of spoon with its head round big, stirring. Hilla was missing, not that the friends care; her parents are strict, they all know; her presence at home was seen by her doting parents. He cried, her father in front of all presence with his penance realized and said it was alcohol doing and not his doing, relishing the guilt with the burden shifted, his fear too real of losing his children, swore to quit but all remained silent; they all knew it was a crocodiles' tears and was certainly not the first time he cried but the hundredth time with the promise he'd never do it again, stayed silent for a week only to be repeated the week later much to Chinche's consternation and chagrin; but his in laws took two boys away, looked in askance at Chinche. She shook her head in open refusal, believing the man sired her, perhaps loving him in—spite of everything. A responsibility of daughter to a lone father realized. The next day, Palmina saw Hilla outside the house and waving frantically; she neither called out her name loudly nor shout; her parents saw it to well and disciplined never to call out loudly; it was not refined way, she was told, undone by the educated people. Mittila had a day off and stood with her; her mistress went marketing with a big bag, wads of notes in it; Palmina was hesitated, looked at Mittila uncertainly; She understood it and shook her head negatively and motioned her; she was servant she knew well, not of their league to set her foot there, the fact both realized even Hilla she was uncomfortable with. She knew her parents well, their attitude towards servants and even her friends—not of their class. She went running up, much glad to be invited she had reservation about going and sat inside the sitting room. A stack of piled comics in the small corner table instantly drawn her eyes and she reached out for three top—Bahadur, Phantom and Tarzan, she was fascinated with and began flipping. The plump cushion below, a comfort added gave her instant concentration and she began to immerse in it, waiting at the same for bathing Hilla with her parents went out with her brother in tow. The footsteps echoed, heavy with the lighter one faint, almost drowned in the heavy steps; she tensed and wished desperately for friends; alone she felt naked, bare, uneasy—rattled. There he entered in blue tee shirt, blue jeans, a pair of sport shoes, expensive even for her eyes looked at her but threw no smile at and went straight inside their bedroom on the left. His wife followed, threw her charming best smile that came not from heart but from the face, in a pink churidar, dazzlingly beautiful, asked her politely of her daughter, more of courtesy than an interest. She shifted from side to side, uncomfortably.

"They are like a bunch of monkeys. They are not of our league"

A male voice said conversationally in the room next but carried to where she sat with a soft chuckling of his wife, discussing of the fought between neighbors—Tochi-ma and Milche-ma—in some way pierced her painfully and shamefully, a deep embarrassment felt. Discomfort and uneasy reigned supreme in her mind and she felt the sudden need to flee, feeling like a total vermin, an outcast but waited for her friend. A curtain of class was drawn for the first time, between the rich and poor—and she jolted in. The stark reality staring. Something unavoidable and where she was born. She came silently back home without a word to her friend and thought of it for a week, shamefully. Saturday morning was a free day for school children; a play-day to be precise. Brunch with watery *dhal* where tiny pieces of onions swam, eaten with young leaves of sweet potato, fried and tasted good to the children, left hungry without proper breakfast. The shrieks, shouts, laughter reverberated the morning, cheering the surrounding. It lighted Palmina and Salmina, her sister's eyes and hurried, helter—skelter bridging small gap in between in no time, merged with their friends playing house and house on the shades below an oasis of tall Sal trees; Hilla and Chinche were a couple in acting; the husband Hilla went to office; the wife Chinche screamed at him like a fishwife for failing to bring chilly home. She pointed at their daughter, a self made doll, a white *markin* cloth with cotton stuffed tightly, her two slanting black eyes on a round neck-less head above twin holes black nose and red lips below, its hands fingerless and the legs toeless sat near, unmoved and wordlessly; Jentilla, a shopkeeper, sat on a sack spread on the ground with leg wrapped up. A tiny baby jackfruit in two slices, young tiny bamboo shoot, young tapioca leaves were her sell laid in front of her, lined up and named the price for anyone interested but no takers; Milche fed her piggery, fattening two green young gourds with four sticks on each below, told to no one but herself to sell them for Christmas. It would bring good money she said alone. She wore two black wires tied with a rope in the middle with the both ends on her ears, wore a white long coat of her nurse aunty and checked Chinche's pulse; she with no company seized Samina's hand, acted as couple besotted, eager to marry with no pastor and got one in her; Palmina agreed not because she fancied the idea but she saw three slices of cakes ready for the wedding feast; the ceremony began with a wedding hymn, the bride with a white lacy nightdress of her spinster aunty and the groom with a black baggy pant and a white shirt; all came and graced it; far from them behind their kitchen below a mango tree, a figure straightened, her hands sprayed with wet grinded husk, left hand holding an old aluminum pot, dented, dirty, feeding the swine and eyed them longingly; they waved, she shook her head sadly; the shout in the background asking her what took her long was an answer for them; they shrieked. A loud wail nearby where the younger boys played with a ball disrupted the ceremony; two boys, one that of Chinche's brother, another Tochi, both in similar age fought; Chinche's brother fled home with a punch to Tochi; he wailed loudly like that of a child; a short man rushed out with a long stick in left hand, his face in furious rage and asked no reason and the culprit but gave a three beating to Jonan and took his son home; a boy tried to pacify the fight; the boy cried an innocent cry; it stabbed Palmina fiercely, cruelly; tears streamed out with an inexpressible emotion and pain; Jonan, with no fault was her brother but she knew, he was guilty of one thing—Poverty, a curse. The night was a torment; sleep eluded her; she told nothing to her mother; but the wound was so deep; the scar won't go no matter what; the haunt began from that evening; the decision began, strong and solid; a challenge to insult, to swallow the poverty with wealth, the power; a quiet determination to it all. An idea conceived in advance was sealed. A flag stood put high on the Summit. In her mind. A flag of white with green and red printed afar off. It looked small but it waved at her, moving for the wind. It was beckoning.

Few years crossed with nothing changed but everything remained same; a routine. Palmina goes to school regularly; Jentilla too. They both passed each year not topping the class but in the first top ten ranking, never below it not above. Chinche failed once; if through then without ranking. She seemed losing interest in studies but more seemed love-struck that became more of temporary than permanent. Hilla was serious too. She attended classes without a taint of soot in her fingers in the morning nor with a single flex of her muscle. Yet something had changed; everybody was agog with it, talking about it, dreaming about it, asking dreams from everyone around, then calculating with their fingers and then the number came. Palmina had the information in the school. Dream was necessity, Milche said one morning on the way to school. In the morning, dreams took center stage but the numbers replaced in the evening. All seemed interested in the dreams they had at night, interpreted it, calculated and came out with a number—ten, thirteen, thirty three fifteen, fourteen, sixty, eighty, ninety, forty, fifty, zero five, zero two, seventy six, thirty six, double zero, single one, ninety nine, twelve, ninety eight, eighty nine, fifty one, fifty two, sixty one, twenty two, sixty five, forty eight, forty six, forty seven, eleven, fourteen, twenty four, forty three, thirty one, seventy one, seventy nine—any number from one to hundred. Everyone seemed eager to hit the jackpot. They tried desperately to buy the number blindly and waited for the evening. Some are lucky and earned but others lost. It was just a pure gamble. Palmina took big strides for her morning chapel. The round wall clock told her it was eight forty, late by ten minutes than her routine. She crossed Benta—pa on the way.

'What is your dream last night?'. He stopped her for few seconds with his question.

'I dreamt of an elephant with his trunk around me'. She lied in a split second and rushed forward. He missed her stifling her giggle and believed it. He passed the dream to Tochi—pa the same morning, elated with the dream.

'Eighty four.' he said calculatively and bought eighty four and forty eight in reverse and waited for the result in the evening, expectedly. She knew of it from Tochi—ma later. They bought a new sofa set and told the story; they got teer of one hundred and then hit the jackpot. Benta—ma carried the story around; it spread but Hilla—pa was skeptical, believed it not and wrinkled his large nose. A culvert given to the given to the village in his block never appeared, he mumbled with few texts missing. The next day, early morning, Benta—pa came excited asked the dream; her father told him and smiled at his back Palmina saw and smiled at her mother. In the evening he came when the number was out.

'I missed,' he said 'just by a single number' and shook his head.

'The dream was precise, a woman with an earthen vessel below her armpits; her one arm around the neck.'

'forty six, four for a woman and six for an earthen vessel." he interpreted not looking at anyone but staring blankly and smoking his *mantu* bidi.

But the number he bought came next to the one they selected for the day.

'I bought 45 (forty five).'

Benta-pa spoke, a sheepish smile and a brown *mantu bidi* in between his dark lips, sat on the moorah with her father, a table before them and asked what dream he had. He dreamt, he replied of none but him, replied her father. Benta—pa missed the mischievous smile in his eyes.

'You stood naked on the road.' He said hiding his smile.

His face was dead pan, in all seriousness. Both seemed to consider it seriously for a moment, thoughtful, silence in gap;

'perhaps some sadness,' predicted Benta-pa for himself, morose.

"00 zero" (double zero) perhaps." Palmina—pa spoke slowly, thoughtfully, solemnly with dead-pan face. A chorus of laughter reverberated.

He laughed joined by his wife, one irritated, red-faced, the another heartily, enjoyed other's discomfiture. A plate of betel nut, leaves, lime, two cups of tea, white with the pure milk bought from Nepali boy, Kancha, they called him, with dozen cattle reared they called it *battan*, outside in the remote jungle and rice cake Tochi-ma made in the morning with the grounded rice powder and jaggery, Benta-ma grounded with her whole strength in it the whole morning, stretched into the day for a kilo of rice but went home with a tiffin full of rice cakes, a bonus for the hard work; he eyed it wolfishly. It tasted well in his mouth as well in the stomach; he ate full.

'I had been to Taj Mahal. Now I would like to see Gate Way Of India". Tochi-pa said conversationally.

'Oh . . Gate Way Of India. It is in Delhi.' He lifted his nose up and let the white smoke ascend with all knowing attitude.

'No. It is in Bombay.'

'Oh Yes. I forgot. I visit Delhi long years back' He feigned memory loss, unashamedly lied when he never reached as far as Guwahati.

He spent his evening smoking bidi, waiting for result, a piece of paper in his hand and asked for anyone coming from the bazaar what number they shot but with no luck and regretted his own dream interpretation.

One night it was decided—a meeting was called; the male elders sat in a circle; a short man, the village headman spoke first, his mouth twitched and stressed the need to cut down the giant tree and gave reasons; very old, he said, risky with nothing but hollow trunk.

'It looks strong but just surviving on the skin.'

He darted his glance on left, right and centre, shrewdly watching others and their reaction. Silence. All seemed thinking, considering.

'It would come crashing on our houses in the next cyclone.'

Another triggered their minds. Then the meeting turned into a market place, arguing, talking, agreeing, then rejecting, each in their own but not for the children.

A breeding ground for snakes.

Bloody owl never let me sleep.

The tree gave not much cotton.

Headless, legless white cloak figure roam out of it at night.

The week later, a giant elephant rope was brought; a man scaled to the top, tied near the tip with one in the middle and the axes were brought;

six men were hired and the cutting began. One day, two day, three day, the men were exhausted; the four day and it began to shake and the fifth day and the whole village pulled and like a big mountain it crashed to the ground with earth shaking thunder, they never had heard before. The children watched helplessly and sadly. The wide planks were made, the branches dried burned in the kitchens, cooked their food for the whole of rainy season—the floor of the village headman became fully wooden.

The owl never hooted again.

The woodpecker seemed permanently disappeared.

They never made commotion again.

But the children lost much. They played no more house—house.

The year drew to an end and the dreaded news it carried, not by newspaper, not by television, that two neighbors of Palmina had bought but by a man, a policeman in the neighborhood that the male elders waited with their radio on for the details in the evening late; indeed it carried, the news.

This is All India Radio, Shillong. The headlines are being read by newsreader along with her name. The headlines—Chief Minister visited the flood affected areas at Pulbari and Rajabala. In Williamnagar, dreaded dacoit Tilok Singh made a jail break. Police fired rounds but he managed to escape.

The dreaded dacoit Tilok Singh made a jail break, scaled ten feet concrete wall and the newsreader, the lady with a voice somber went in detail later, a series of cases of his involvement—looting, robbing, dacoity,—spine chilling to the listeners, the major crimes very few committed, then added he was shot but managed to flee with an injury, more of a headline than the brief story but still a comfort, later defused it with the news by the lone policeman, he jumped into the nearby forest, unhurt and the pistol shot never hit him. The evening was silent, the children left the playfields early and slept at home, jumpy for every sound, for each footstep and for each dog barking, scurrying towards their parents, leaping. The nights too were like a funeral time, silent, a fear psychosis created, every heart beating loudly, their thought only with 'what if he comes here?'; but Palmina looked at the gun, looked at her father smoking hookah, past caring and found solace on his lap when he erased the fear with the beautiful woman sailing in the open empty sky sat in the midst of a large lily, protected by its petals and came to meet a love stricken prince, waiting for her to be disappeared the early next morning and finished, "you must study well and be someone in life" and added "I passed my matric in first division" his trademark words, sheepishly.

CHAPTER 7

CHRISTMAS

The year's last month, December, spoke of Christmas; it meant new clothes, dancing to the tune of drumbeats, partying and eating. The young and old, parents and children waited for long eagerly for it. The students with smiles laden and with incessant chatter, excitedly received it warmly. Once the first week stepped into, the moods of children, teenagers, adults and old changed—the children for new clothes vied; the teenagers waited with excitement for late night parties, the relatives for meeting one another and adults for community gathering and the old men and women to visit their grandchildren. For everyone around it was the month of festive activity, full of joy, anxiety and happiness. The church leaders began their yearly collection, counting heads from each household for the community feast in the week last with their mind on nothing but of pork, beef, chicken, left out mutton and fish. A whole two year old round pig was chosen; its twin white tusks stick out, its flesh below its eyes near—hidden the eyes, the fat below cascading to the ground below with its short little tail almost hidden behind. A whole cow bought from Garobada on Tuesday on a market day was kept in the Church Secretary's house, its neck tied with a rope to the tree attached to the house. He had his servant fed him with the thick branches of the jackfruit tree, fattening well before eating. The church heard the devotees nothing but the festival; the devotees thronged more in the year end than the beginning and the middle and brightened the church. Festive mood gripped the bazaar too; the markets became the hub of festive activity—silver and gold jingle bells in the shops, red and white Santa Clause with his big round belly stuck out stood in the shop corners, the multi colored balloons baldly hanged inside and the front side of the shops, a big evergreen plastic Christmas tree stood in the corner, the folded plastic stars of color variety and multi colored small decorated light bulbs in packets flooded the sleepy Tura bazaar. Slim crackers, rocket cracker and big square crackers too sat in front of the shops, waited to be picked. Jingle bell, silent night, feliz navidad, the children hardly caught the lyrics, nor understood the meaning blared out from the musical shops. Chinche, Palmina, Jentilla, Milchc and Hilla went to bazaar on Saturday, more to enjoy and watched the shoppers than shopping. Mittila decided to go along; she heard of the village trip her mistress made for the day but cancelled in the last minute that deterred her from going. Chinche bought a lovely closed black pump shoe with one inch heel and earned the envy of her friends. Her grandparents came the day before and gave her money for shopping, she told them delightedly. Hilla returned with a pair of shoes and a maroon pull over. Milche bought new Levis blue jeans. Palmina and Jentilla returned home not sharing the excitement their friends are floating in. Back home, Palmina and her friends sang "Feliz Never Dance as POLICE NEVER DANCE, earning the wrath of their policeman neighbor. 'Heark the herald angels sing,' sang out the houses with tape recorders and livened the small town. The pounding sounds filled the days in the week last with every house the sticky rice grinded, readied for the rice cakes. The youths took out drums from the first date of December and began dancing in a small playground outside the church, in a small circle. They had the song leader and the drummer in the middle with others circling, jostling with the girls in two or three groups in a line singing and circling the drummer and the leader. Tension, anxiety and joy filled the students; their final exam was over and they awaited their results with apprehension with their Christmas presents depended on it.

December came finally, the last month of the year. It brought along the final exam of the students, older, younger and the youngest—the matric exam, the high school exams, the middle board exam, the middle classes exam, primary, lower primary exam all began in the week first and ended with the result in the third; Hilla passed with distinction; Jentilla pulled through; Palmina lost her weekly test book and lost marks and her ranking went down; she was sad not because she lost marks but her father showed indifference; she remembered the year last when she stood second and her father made it to every house the same evening and made it a point to talk about it with a pride and a smile. Chinche failed and

her father knew not about it, not he asked nor cared about it. He knew
it not whether it was a Christmas; progress card was shown to them; She
got much in English; her Mathematics was within the red circle and also
her science along with two others that sealed her fate; the teachers in the
school disliked her; she neither misbehaved nor acted manner-less, nor
indiscipline in conduct but they saw her weekly test book with a love
letter in it written with blood. She was branded as a demirep, a girl with a
loose moral and eyed with difference. Head Mistress treated her badly and
scolded her badly in the chapel for a trivial thing. Tears glistened her eyes
and cried profusely later behind the students' toilet. Palmina and Jentilla
sat with her there and said something to comfort that failed miserably.
The gap of five years between her and Palmina made the elder wiser. The
friends laughed later, much to ease her sadness and recalled in a jest of the
handwork exam she did two years back; she sew running stitch in place
of hemming stitch and could not differentiate between cross stitch and
running stitch; her baby woolen socks half yearly home work was done
by Jentilla and was paid for it from the pocket of her father. They laughed
out aloud later, heartily. The exam over and the drum beats began, the
collecting of rice and money for the Christmas feast; a bagful of sticky
rice and another bagful of scented rice arrived and dropped mercifully
in her kitchen, a generosity shown by her grandparents in a village with
countless acres of paddy field with a verbal message delivered—a herd
of wild elephants had destroyed the much paddy and much damage had
been done by the flood but her mother could not careless, scowled rather
than smile, muttering something unintelligible to anyone, Palmina knew
whom it was directed, on her grandmother, a short small woman, doted
on her son but resented her, brought the year round—rice of every season,
bananas, brinjal, chili, bottle gourde, pumpkin, cucumber and fish from
family pond and marked it purposely with the words "for my son". She
was an itch her mother could not scratch but bore silently, feared her
father and gave to her children everything she brought; perhaps Palmina
guessed wildly, an affection, she thought, an exclusive domain of her being
gate-crashed; but Palmina waived it, her mind of the Christmas, the rice
cakes and all eateries with delight. The headman came tagged along with
few elders and sat in front of her house, saw the pig tied on the mango
tree, fattened with its stomach drooping and they saw nothing but the
slices of thick white fat in their mind and their tongues started dripping.
The deal was done and her mother close her right palm with few notes

that had her smiling, went to the market and brought—new frock for both her daughters, a pair of shoes each for her two sons, a piece of cloth for her husband for new pant, a tiny piglet for the year's rearing for the year next and nothing for herself. The result over on the week third, a sated Palmina jumped, danced with the group collecting rice and money in the nights, and began; the church elders collected money per head from each household for Christmas feast, her father had seen to—for her, her mother, her sister Salmina, himself and her two brothers. The third week heard of pounding sound in each household. Drama connecting Christmas was prepared, Moren was in charge of it and began searching for both willing and unwilling actors and actresses and found Milche, Palmina, Jentilla, Hilla for lambs with their heads covered but with little cavorting and fluttering her long eyelashes Chinche got the role of a shepherd sated not but agreed in the end, still fighting till the last for the role of Mary, she was refused with. Her father erected two banana trees at the entrance to the house, cut down from the garden, beside the house, its leaves wiry, stuck out, connected with another, leaves removed, that had 'WELCOME' above in black letters in white paper and "MERRY CHRISTMAS", below in a colour variety—green, yellow, red, blue for letter each—on an golden shiny and slippery paper with the bottom cut into many pointed arrows downwards, she had disapproved of but silent with a scowl from him—imitation of his village Christmas she remark scathingly, out of his earshot.

On the Christmas eve, drama displayed of Christmas scene and Jentilla, Milche, Palmina Hilla stooped and crawled like the sheep on top of six wooden benches joined together and covered with an old rug below the makeshift roof of Sal leaves and branches drying after three days of sheltering; their heads were covered and the light of the gas lamp hanging from the roof shone on their heads as they crawled with a man nearby coming everytime it began dimming and pushing in the pump and brought back the brightness for all to watch. Chinche was a shepherd boy she was much disgruntled with unable to get the role of Mary, she wished much to act as. A yearly news was reported; the fought between Jentilla—ma and Tochi—ma was read out first; the reason, news reader reported over the pig; One kept herself busy with the toddler on her lap she was lucky to carry, adjusting the cap of the well slept child that was uncalled for and the other dusted off the imaginary dirt out of the betel leaf, a habit or an embarrassment proof no one could put their finger on.

Somebody's fear of ghost also was reported and also of the pigs roaming freely; the voting, newsreader said was done on the biggest stomach and Palmina's father won the vote. Chortle of laughter was for every news; all seemed to catch their stomachs with no hard feelings but just for fun for all.

All seemed eager for the Christmas service, the church well decorated with colourful papers and balloons of all colours and a green Christmas tree stood in the corner, its small branches lifting weightless miniature red father of the day, gift wrapped shiny plastic boxes and white cotton pieces like snow capped tree. The friends went to the church not that they wished to worship but they all wore new clothes they were proud to show off; Palmina wore a cream frock, rose printed of the same coloured missed miserably if not with an in-depth stare, a Christmas present from her father but she earned it with a good result in her annual exam she prided on; Jentilla and her sister Nokam wore same frock of yellow printed, hand sewn by their mother a month back, both flaring from the waist and a little tie behind with the black school shoes and white socks served for the purpose of two. Chinche wore in the end, a grey pant and a shirt, fought with a tailor two times for failing to deliver it on time, a bespectacled man with thick big square frames, made one leg shorter in anger, infuriating already angry Chinche and wore it with a new stitch she herself had done. Mittila came not for the service; her work doubled; but the real reason, her friends guessed was something else; she missed home and her parents in a house and her two young brothers. She told them all about it, their little house on the roadside and their imagination came alive vivid; the only bus to Baghmara, a small town in the another corner ran past the border road, she prided; the road was kutcha with big boulders sprouting in the middle; it toppled from side to side and the jam packed bus with passengers even at the open top hanged into the narrow railing and saved themselves. She saw it, Mittila said, the men went under the wheels and crushed beneath, flooding the road with blood. They squirmed and cringed at the imaginative scene. She told of them, the Bangladeshi people across the border; they were hard working and watered the dry cracking paddy fields with water brought in earthen pitcher from a stream afar off with their husbands behind the cows, sweating walking behind with the plough in their shoulders. She told them of the horror stories too; the cattle lifting by the men across the border, their long indigenous gleaming swords, slitting the throats and the sleepless nights the villagers spent at night guarding the village. Mittila had nothing new for Christmas. Chinche came with an idea everyone agreed.

Milche parted with her once worn frock from the suitcase.

Chinche with the pair of old fashioned shoes she lost interest.

Palmina asked her mother for a *gana,* woven from the left over thread of two and half meter.

Jentilla with nothing but a new handkerchief sewn and Hilla with a sweater she hated. Together they all made her Christmas.

Little Santa Clauses.

She was ecstatic. Overjoyed. Happy. She cried and they all cried.

They all smiled. Happy.

In an expansive lawn, in front of a small local church, a community feast was held. Each family sat on the edges, family wise. In the middle, many wooden posts lifted the small roof made of tree branches. It had its wall bare, left opened and on the chairs inside, the elder male members sat with one in the middle with the register in his hand. In the corner stood four big empty *karahis* with the local cuisine of various taste in green plantain leaves, in thousands rows of mouth watering dishes they well imagined of. The necks of the plantain leaves are tied with the bamboo strings leaving the round bottoms where the meat cooked well stored. The food got cook from the early morning by the men folk, and the women too kept themselves busy cooking rice. Palmina sat on the mat, woven of bamboo strips. Her mother sat beside on the *moorah,* looking with intent at the elderly women wrapping the cooked food in plantain leaves, kept in lines ready to eat, listening ceaselessly of complaint made by the neighbor family sat next of starvation, cursing at the same; Her stomach at the same, groaning loudly with the nearby seaters looking at her and smiling understandably. Rice wrapped in plantain leaves were kept in open mouthed plastic bag where beside sat a small old woman wrapped in white shawl of cashmere, Jentilla was absent, noticeably. Her mother waited patiently beside an empty *moorah,* kept for her father in the make shift kitchen of the day busy with other elderly males smiling at their jokes. Hilla and her family too were absent conspicuously. Their absence brought few raised eyebrows. Palmina saw people whispering in the ears of the one sitting nearest. She heard then from the grapevine circulation that they left for the family gathering in the main town. The First Class

People, someone remarked scathingly and all around smiled with sarcasm. Her stomach groaned, this time loudly, with everyone around looking, smiling compassionately.

'Hungry?' It was her mother, compassionately.

'Obviously. They surely are taking time." Replied, the neighbor, sat on the *moorah,* cross legged, her eyes haggard, worn-out face, indulgently on her side.

At that moment stood, the short stocky man with a register opened in his hand, began calling the names of the head, the male members of the family much to the welcome relief and smiles of everyone around.

'Three beef, five pork, four chicken.' He announced while his mouth twitched.

'Six pork, two beef, five chicken.' For a family of five.

'Four pork, four beef, three chicken.' For a family of six.

'Ten pork, five beef, three chicken.' For a family of eight. They got much number with the fat sum they gave much before Christmas. The number was on rise per head in the family and the amount they gave. It almost took forever for the man to call out her father, with his name in the list's end and when his name was called, she finished half of the rice of wrapped rice without curry for the taste. When the night came, Chinche, Jentilla, Milche, Hilla came, with Hilla still in her grandparents, all dressed in the best dress they all could afford took a bite of rice-cake her mother had a master of making with a jaggery, then began towards Jentilla's house with Palmina too joining the group for the *jakkep,* only her mother had a gift to make, had their stomachs filled, then into Milche's where only her mother had a flair for making *sakkin* and lastly into Chinche where she had nothing she made of her own but few sweets and ready made cake from bakery, they all enjoyed and had their fill.

A round banana cake on the dining table, coconut laddoo, *pitas, sakkin, jakkep* all came from her grandmother, her uncles and aunties from the town, sent by a maid servant the evening last with a message for her to come with her brothers for Christmas week and for New Year celebration. At times, Chinche had a pride of having rich relatives, she hardly speak of, partly perhaps she was totally disinterested in their existence but the reason she and her brothers got respect in Bolchugri was their existence and relation they maintained, who came, remembered them on occasions, she never knew about or hardly thought of it but her life around in and out.

Her father, she knew was not a bad man at all as neighborhood pictured him but just plain violent when drunk, lost his sanity along with it, she was accustomed with and lived with and became a habit nothing else. Her brothers went to the town to her rich aunties for Christmas but she stayed just the same not because she could not live without her father but she had for the Christmas a plan, a night together with her boyfriend she professed she loved him much, invited for food, the extent of it her friends doubted and tired of. One night before Christmas, on twenty-third night, Palmina, Jentilla, Milche came not of their own but she called them so, to eat coconut laddoo all of them loved and their mothers never made. Hilla missed it, not she was uninvited but she went to her grandmother's place with her parents for Christmas and Mittila had a late night working still pounding, grinding the rice to powder for *pitta,* her mistress behind breathing raggedly on her willing her for a machine than human. Sollen too came, her boyfriend, young and boyish, in black jeans and a sweater inside, the bottom end of his jeans tugged inside the cow boy boot he wore, chained till mid calf and a black over coat over, its bottom touching his mid-calf, borrowed he said from his brother in police, came for Christmas and was generous enough to loan it to him. The short hair above hidden by a woolen cap, obviously knitted by Chinche, her handiwork seen in it and was obvious love token he wore to please her complimenting her sentiments. They chatted excitedly, sat around the fire, their pairs of palms opened towards it, warming, heating, eating, Chinche well behind her boyfriend, her hands on his shoulders, balancing her body on his, a perfect show of intimacy and kept the stories burning a word here, a sentence there where it needed most, unaware of the knock on the door perhaps the sound of their voices, laughter, deafened their ears. Sollen heard it first.

'I heard a knock on the door.' He turned, facing his Chinche and informed her rather gently.

'Who would come now?' She doubted and patted him lightly, playfully.

'Your father?'

'ohh . . He went to his friends and by now must be somewhere still.' She waived off.

The second knock was louder and all heard.

Chinche rushed out, opened the door with a bang.

Then screamed, terrifying, heart wrenchingly and rushed towards them.

She jumped over the kitchen threshold.

They all stood, looked at her aghast, not knowing about it.

She stood before them, her breath ragged, swift, her head up and down with the rhythm of her breath with stark terror in her eyes.

Her fingers pointed at backwards. Fear robbed her speech unable to speak when they all looked at her for a word for the reason of her terror stricken face.

'Ghost . . . ghost . . . ghost . . ' She managed in a voice so small, rasping for breath.

The girls screamed, all of them, circling around Sollen, the only male around for protection.

'Ghost?' he sounded skeptical yet showing he was not scared. There was no more knocks, just simply sound of like a growl, loud and clear. The girls screamed more, tightening around Sollen like a ball.

'Let us go and see. I doubt it is a ghost.' He inserted courage. The girls came behind, on his side, both left and right, clutching tightly.

On the long chair, a man stretched his body long, fast asleep; his legs set apart, one above the chair arm, another on the ground below. Around his neck a new round wreath with flowers fresh sat; the room reeked of his breath of exhaled whisky smell.

Her father.

Perhaps he went to somebody's grave and came out from graveyard. The girls let out a shaky laugh.

'Take it off.' He ordered gently no one listened too but shrinked further away from him.

He knew it had to be him. He gently removed the round wreath off his neck and took it outside and threw far away in the dark. Chinche removed his shoes and socks covering his nose and mouth at the same. All let him have his beauty sleep and went to the kitchen again. At deep midnight when everybody still remained awake, Palmina felt drowsy and yawned with her mouth uncovered. The last night's late night demanded her to give time to sleep. Jentilla saw her and laughed loudly.

'I am feeling sleepy.' She told her friend.

'Even I am.' She agreed and rose to leave.

Both started home. Everywhere around the sound of drum beats filled. The night was far from silent and the roads far from deserted. The dark night was lighted with crackers shooting in the air and breaking into thousand tiny stars. Jentilla reached home and stood for a while outside the gate looking at the crackers. They saw two sleeping bundles just near the gate. Palmina torched the light she carried and saw the familiar faces. Jingo and Tochi. Their alcohol reeked mouth emanated the stench smell both ran to evade.

A week later, Bolchugri had brimming tales to tell; Benta—ma sat with Tochi—ma. Palmina—ma too joined in the evening; they had nothing to talk but everything to talk. The talk circled on Chinche; the Christmas night in her house, of her boyfriend, the night he spent there. Pstssttpsssttpsstttpsssttpsssttpssttpsssttpssttpssttpssttpssttpsssttpsssssttt psstttpsssttpssstttbzzzbzzzbzzzbzzzbzzzbzzzzbzzzbzzzbzzzbzzzb bzzzzzbbzzzzbbzzzzbzzzzbzzzzbzzzbzzzbzzz. The words spread far and fast. Palmina was well thrashed. She was told later to evade her. Milche—ma blamed Chinche for teaching bad things to Milche. Jentilla had a good advice from her father and an earful from a mother. Hilla was well escaped; her mother heard nothing about the grape vine; aloof and alienated that was what Milche—ma called her she heard nothing of and could not careless even heard of. She had a reason to head ache the same evening. Palmina opened her mouth. Tochi—ma heard it and beaten Tochi black and blue. Tochi showed his two palms opened at his mother and lifted his right leg up to his knee and stood a monkey pose. Something he saw in the Chinese kungfu movie in the town's lone cinema hall. His action infuriated his mother more and he ran when she went to get the bamboo stick. Milche—ma adopted another tactic and tenderly asked her son. He denied vehemently and heaped mouthful of abuses at Palmina. His mother believed him not but stroked his head and blamed Palmina. Palmina received the slandering blame and said nothing. She got an earful from her mother too.

CHAPTER 8

BEGINNING OF LATE EIGHTIES.

With December gone, vanished Christmas and all the hub of festive activity taking along with it—drumbeats, carols, music and merry making not that she missed it all but the rice-cakes that brought saliva to her mouth even now. When January stepped in dullness and silence enveloped reminding everyone of the funeral right after the child birth. Cold wrapped the small growing town both at night and in the morning coupled with white mist deposited tiny round dew drops on the green leaves and the grasses that rolled away when moved while the deadness of the night was marked by not hearing of even the sound of the dog barking. The festival had seen the people spending their whole month's earning leaving them dry the whole of the first month of the year that even the flies steadfastly refused to enter peoples houses; the used plantain leaves, below the church compound began rotting, emanating smell with left over food of community feast in the festival. The tall Sal trees began casting their leaves heaped on the ground below with only the near naked body exhibiting pathetic sight. Few drunkards vowed on the first day in the church service, their eyes still red tinged, their unkempt hair sleekly combed, oil-soaked, a common practice, not to drink but to lead a chaste and pure life, kept it for the first week and resumed their old habits, for the worst till the year end. The small church, on the hillock full for the first week, began slowly thinning in the second and emptied on the fourth and by the end of February, the church survived with just few devotees. For the students the month was the best part of the year with the winter vacation in it and with no books to fix their eyes into but more to play. Come March, they would need to sweat it out in the morning, afternoon, evening and at night with the monsoon rain flooding the whole town, rivers and streams. Each household chose January to stock firewood to last for the whole rainy season and the stocking began with even Palmina's mother worried of the summer rain but for Palmina and her friends more of fun, adventure and spending time with nature than anything else.

It was cold morning of the first month. But the Winter coldness deterred not the children from love for the nature. They grew with it. They loved it. It was their fascination; their environment; their enchantment; their best friend. The thought of spending with it brought sparkle into their eyes. They all were eager to spend the day with it. At seven thirty in the morning, it was too early both for the breakfast and so also for the lunch. But her mother awoke at the touch of dawn, her routine. Cooking for children's lunch early before their school made her so. Palmina had a tea in the early morning. Her mother finished her cooking. Palmina had a plan for the whole day. She kept her mother uninformed about it. She feared a block to her exit. She brunched in haste, chewing rice only twice, literally swallowing the rice and swiftly letting it go down into her stomach and gulping down a half of aluminum mug when it blocked her throat and saving her life. The fried sweet potato leaves and yellow watery dhal that went to her stomach tasted good to her mouth or it must be the hunger that forced her so. The low wooden stool moved to and fro every time she leant out to scoop out the rice from the steel plate in front of her on the ground below.

'Where are you going?' demanded a voice. Even without looking up the familiarity of the voice told her the owner who had the knack of knowing her habits and who would not if the person had delivered her, nursed her, tended her, cooked for her for more than the past twelve years. Hasty eating that too early in the morning meant going out and she knew where. It was the season. Silence was her answer while the attack on the food persisted without a dot for the answer from her meant earful and she hated that early in the morning.

"To collect wood from the jungle." Was the crisp reply. She knew she already had the answer while in her silence. Perhaps she had seen her friends on the road waiting for her.

'You needed not go, as if the whole year we are using the wood you had collected." Scorned her mother. "Besides I heard that the herd is roaming in the jungle."

She added in the same scorning tone.

'There was no "Yes" nor "No" while she kept on eating without a look-up nor minding what she was saying but with a single minded determination to do her heart's desire. The sound of the brooks, the songs of the birds, tall whispering trees and swaying bamboos, thousands of cascading tiny drops of water on the green moss-covered rocks and baby fishes swimming in the clear ankle deep stream and sandy beaches beckoned her in her mind's eye which was simply too irresistible to control. Inside she thought her twelve years gave her permission to go where she desired. The brunch was over. She washed her plate in a hurry, deaf to the barrage of words her mother was stuffing in her ears, wiped her mouth with water from the steel basin and rushed out of the kitchen into the main house opposite to it. On top rung of ulna, she found an old grey '*gana*' bordered with white given to her by her spinster aunty two years back, wrapped it around her waist, on top of the old pink frock brought by her father from Shillong when he went for training that had a partition in it with an elastic just above the waist giving it a flare below the hem of which reached just below her knee covering her modesty. Very furtively she looked around the house and the compound outside for her mother not for fear of not allowing her but for fear of embarrassing her in front of her friends waiting for her which she had a knack to do. She was relieved by her absence but was still dreading when she slipped out of the house unseen and on her toes and ascended the narrow rocky one at the two and reached to a junction of the road where all her friends had gathered waiting for her impatiently.

"What took you so long? We were about to leave without you." Chided Jentilla shaking her straight deep brown haired-head in obvious anger with a long blue towel slung from her right shoulder and with an indigenous wood cutter whose long wooden handle had under her grip. In height she was two inches shorter but in age, three years older which deterred them not from being friends though both differed in personality and it was the humble background to which both belonged that bound them together. Jentilla loved music, food, cooking, flowers and gardening; in total contrast to it she loved nature, clothes, solitude to be in deep thought, fishing and in games while the former loved 'bo' and seven stones and it was the art of fighting that captured her fascination. Both loved to share laughter together, always for everything even for tragedy. With woven bamboo basket rested on her back, balanced by the strip made of a bark of a tree whose both ends are tied on the narrow bottom of the basket with the other round end resting on her head, Mittila with Jentilla, Palmina, Hilla, Milche and Chinche descended the narrow track on the small hillock which ran between two houses with bamboo fencing on both sides of the track that ran down to the Ringrey stream, gave a slice of raw betel nut each, thin slice of green leaf along, a digestive while the thin black dog with a short tail, its heavy breasts drooping, thick nipples on each sides pointed charged towards them barking squeezing in between two parallel bamboo poles of the gate of the house nearby the stream, fiercely protective of the two puppies still trying to cling on its heavy nipples with the owner shouting at her behind to stop. The girls shrieked, screamed and ran down, terrified. They stopped on reaching a huge family of bamboo with its members leaning to all sides, one bending and blocking their path they evaded and went in semi circle to the rocky steps leading down to the Ringrey stream.

"Must be *beera*..."Chinche dropped the spooky name, all too suddenly, her eyes with fear; she too evaded the bending bamboo with a shudder running through her body she once was a victim of this mischievous imp. Chinche had outgrown her early teenage and with late teen and adulthood on either side she stood ready to step. She'd be seventeen in the coming May and at her prime sweet sixteen. With no mother to speak of, Chinche, the second among the four siblings, the youngest was the brother she doted, had the gift of fair flawless complexion, tall in height, slender, sharp pointed nose, something of instant attraction in her face, small slanting eyes in a heart shaped face but the long curly hair she was gifted did no justice to her prettiness; still she had to fend off boy's attention even in that young age unsuccessfully; now her fighting doubled. She had a weakness for them and enjoyed the attention showered to her, shamelessly, unblinkingly, changing them on routine; the butt of ire of other neighborhood mothers, of envy by other girls and competition by young men for her attention, love and affection; gifted in sewing, she made a most of it; she sewed a white pillow cover, she boasted proudly. It was frilled in edges, with "Sweet dreams", embroidered in it, with the green and red, her favorite colors. She gifted it for her boyfriend, who she claimed slept on top of it and dreamed of her at night. She had the latest admirer, a young engineering student, smitten with her and been tailing her for months. She had melted down and been talking of dumping the present. An engineer husband, the status, the money had been in her mind for sometime now. He was the toasts of the mothers—Tochi—ma invited him over for dinner. She had him in mind for a brother in law. He went but rejected the girl. He had seen Chinche, well after *beera* left her. The *beera* had a cunning way of stalking unsuspected walkers by placing long bamboo poles across the road and pulling them up, in between their mid sections, a popular primitive belief proved true. Few months back, Chinche lay in bed, suffered terribly; she told them later, a man lay on her bed in the middle of the night; his body all hairy and she screamed later; from the very next day she fell seriously ill; she screamed, terrified and pointed at nothing and said the man was entering her room to the consternation of everyone who saw nothing. Then the *ojha*, a local medicine man was called. He gave her herbal medicine to take, a green paste and a list of menu to be avoided—ginger, pumpkin, gourd, tapioca, yum, bitter gourd, turmeric powder, red meat—left almost nothing to eat that she hated to do but was compelled and survived on rice and salt and boiled white dhal. He said it was male *beera*, tamed by some *ojha* long time back, freed after the death of his owner and was smitten with her. Still she wore a brass metal tied by a thin thread around her waist, she called '*tabees*' to ward off the evil eye and with it strict rule to follow—avoid hospital, deliveries, funerals and the list goes on; the remedy worked on her; She never suffered again.

The sight of Ringrey stream with huge boulders and rocks was elation to Palmina and for others too that she calculated it by the ecstasy on their faces and the eager way they rushed towards it. Rather than jumping from one rock to another to cross the stream like others are doing, the urge to feel the clear flowing water was simply irresistible and she let her legs down into the water and shrink as the cold water sent shiver to all over her body that she chose the small flattened rocks with footholds in them to cross the stream and landed on the dry ground on the other side of the stream.

'Julie . . . . . . ah . . . . . . I love you . . .'Mittila sang with a voice that sounded more like a goat bleating jumping from one rock to another with bamboo woven basket resting on her back with an axe inside that swung from one corner to the other with each jump. A kitchen help hailed from a remote place, somewhere in the Bangladesh border, Mittila, a sincere and hard working girl had no education to speak of but was brought with a promise with monthly payment for her services by their loud speaker neighbor who forgot her promise once her services were given or the alternative of school education she was promised in place of money,

Mittila ardently wished. In few years of her service, she got money half yearly, not monthly. She was promised monthly, a promise left vacuum. She dared not uttered a word. Her mistress said nothing. Her poor parents needed it. There was no telephone at home. Her parents fed them with daily labour. A trip to the town costs them their half a week's earning, her father could not afford of. Her brothers and her mother needed to eat. The poor girl had not receive any for the past four months, got the same answer 'next month' for every query about her dues not for herself but for the two mouths at home in the village but when the next month came the answer stretched forth, unending. Just the other day Tochi-ma who also had an elastic mouth on her rare visit to their house loudly criticized the poor girl of being insincere and poor cooking giving them half-cooked rice and slow in work with her doing most of the work and she got paid in huge sum which was all fabricated saving her own reputation. Palmina was saddened seeing her sat above their house below a tree at night surrounded by the darkness on her return from Jentilla's place and asked her what she was doing on recognizing her after few moments of heart beat thinking her form for a ghost for which her answer was her wood cutter father was sick and she needed money but she had none. It was pure pathetic. But the character she had left no one but to admire which even with earful of tongue she could go on singing spree throughout the whole day. The other night her mistress took her along to an industrial exhibition held at Government College Field not because she wished her to see it but to carry her two year old son and stayed back to watch a free cinema show. The great effect the film had on her stayed on her through out the whole day with her mind filled with film and the songs that her joyful mood and the happiness in some way was a source of entertainment to the entire group. She had not seen the film but heard the song and seen its picturisation in "Chitrahaar" broadcasted in D-D-1 in the house she served, newly bought, after waiting for the whole evening just for it, where she sat on the floor with other children just to watch it, gulping a lungful of contaminated air, a secret farting revealed with no culprit found. Once landed on the dry ground on the other side of the stream, they all looked up and sighted shrubs, young budding trees and the birds chirping singing in glory with their God given freedom which exhilarated the young minds. Nature had always been her first love and would always be; deep inside her heart sang out of pure joy not because of the film-story Mittila was regaling the group to which she was half-muted while Jentilla and others were listening with rapt attention, uninterrupted. Except for the tall grasses with blades that with one cut could reach to the human bones crossing the flesh on the other side of the narrow path and shrubs, no big trees are to be sighted which was the result of the cruelty of human inflicted on the nature, the place being too close for the human habitation and got paid for it.

"They were not allowed to marry by Julie's mother".

She finished on a sad note as if the whole story had been hers.

'Then what?' someone prompted eagerly.

'In the end, she allowed and they got married."

She ended with a smile that creased her whole dry black face as they reached an old desolate abandoned village, with people living in it less privilege and civilize than the other part of the town but a blessed place for the children—village flowing with tamarind, jackfruits, mangoes, bell fruits, a place of milk and honey, Canaan of the children. Relief and happiness brought smile on everyone's face; one for the story ending in happy note and another, their destination came closer.

None wore watch. All of their wrists are empty. Their parents haven't got one for any of them. But Hilla had one at home; an expensive gold colour slim wrist watch her father brought from Guwahati. They had spent nearly half of the day inside the forest and enjoyed its silent beauty. It was time for them to return. They looked at the sky for the time. The sun had crossed the middle of the sky. The winter heat was cooler in the past afternoon. 'Around two thirty' Mittila calculated roughly in the absence of the watch. Everyone agreed. Palmina felt the tinge of chillness in her arms and suggested it was time they return. She turned and looked at the crushed dead leaves of bed she slept and mouthed a silent good bye. They knew it must have been either mid-day or past it when they reached their destination. The weak sun was weaker even than the first morning sunlight of the Summer. They had crossed the same stream seven times going zigzag towards the west to merge with Ganol River, left on the way a big banyan tree with long thick roots hanging out of it where she had gone swinging like tarzan, crossed pure white sandy beaches, sunk their small feet and thousand pebbles from where Mittila had taken few to scratch dirt from her body, stopped at a place where they shouted, the rock walls facing shouted back, passed it to another, shouting, listening to their own voices echoing, crossed a big green moss-covered stretchable rock wall where thousand drops of water are cascading to the stream below. Green ferns sprouted from every corner. On every encounter with the birds on the trees Mittila, silenced everyone with a finger, took a stone from the ground and threw it towards it for a kill and it nearly hit on one occasion and was angry with her for making a sound that triggered its flying away to her delight. She only thought of eating them. Jentilla let out a shout of delight. Palmina laughed loudly. Happily. Chinche and Hilla gaped at them, looking both at them then to Mittila. Mittila was openly angry. They missed out the reason. Milche expounded. Their destination, the locally given an apt name to it was full of trees in mixture with bamboos and dry twigs which they saw even from the sand they stood and made a queue through a small opening between the different families of bamboos used by the wood cutters. They saw a man, barefooted, short and stocky with his short towel covering his bottom reaching just above his thigh revealing half of his muscled thigh and muscled calf and old sweat dampened blue shirt with a big log on his right shoulder coming out of the jungle, with his forehead glistening due to excessive sweat and the drops of it falling to the ground but not wetting it. They made way for him as there was no way he would stop for them and the foul smell emanated from him as he crossed them that she nauseated. Even if he was panting for breath still he took a moment to stop near them and paused for a breath.

'Big one is there. Don't go deep inside.'

With that warning he shifted his log to the left and resumed his walking as if he said nothing leaving a whiff of bad body odour in its wake. The children needed no warning on that; few thick green droppings that lay on the way belonged not to the cattle and no cattle was seen grazing nearby and were dead proof of their presence. They were fresh. They saw the old droppings too—the yellowish bamboo strands. A warning for them all. They knew something. An elephants often traced their old droppings. The sun headed too far to the west when they started for the east with all their burdens; Mittila with her bamboo woven basket full of dead woods and bamboos, shortened into same sizes attached to her back with the support of the strip of the bark of the tree from her head that was keeping the basket on the place while the others with the dead logs, Hilla returned empty handed with her bare long hands swinging with her fair sun scorched face red. She was much worried for wrath from her parents, dotted and pampered her like a real living princess with not even a speck of dust in her fingertip allowed. Jentilla returned with the slim but the

99

long body of the tree with its leaves and small branches removed to make it comfortable for carrying and which she found on the ground cut down and left by someone before her, dissatisfied with it. To speak the truth she felled not a single tree, spent nearly half the afternoon lying on the bed of dry dead leaves on the shade below the tree that stood beside the cool stream listening to the music of its flow that ran down from the hill top and met in the Ringrey stream, below and the cool breeze fanning away her sweat that made her to lie in laze, dreaming, a pair of eyes lazily yet enchanted on the blue birds, wild, their white back towards her, perched precariously on the thin branch, flew after a while to another tree with the other one to tailing. They were a couple, she thought and she had desired of sighting of mating of the wild birds she had never seen any; brown ants lined up in thousands, busy in their walking, some going up while the others are coming down with their community house, an ants' nest swayed softly on top of the little branch. The nest skillfully made was out of leaves, circular in shape while the birds chirp around and flew to and fro. A small slim log on her shoulder, picked up from the sand by the side of the Ringrey Stream that was left by somebody when it was time to go home, light in the start but more weight added with each step, which brought sweat out and slowed her steps, pulling her backwards rather than pushing her forward. The old "*gana*" which she carried was folded into several and made it into a small but thick square to reduce the pain on her shoulder on which her burden was placed and dried after used it in the stream as a fishing net by Hilla and Chinche in the morning, caught nothing but the black slimy big round head with long slim tail. The tadpole. Squeamish little thing. Palmina refrained her fingers. Except for occasional "let us stop here" and 'let us drink water' and "I'm so tired"; let us rest for a while" there was total silence among them and with an obvious reason. Returning was not same as going. Though no single complain came from anybody yet everybody was counting seconds and minutes wondering when they would reach, that to fast and eagerly. All wore tired face, eyes, and even in the peak winter sweat glistened on their foreheads, dampened their clothes and made their hairs disarray. Near every spring they stopped after each three or four hundred steps to quench their thirst that in some way made up for the hunger making their stomachs groan to which seemed like a mirage, unreachable. Just a fraction before the sun disappeared beyond the horizon at the fag end of their energy and strength which they never knew from where they had mustered they reached home, sagging and drooping to the ground—Palmina to a worried mother, Hilla to an empty house with her parents in her granny's much to her delight, Jentilla to ever nagging and grumbling mother and Mittila to disgruntled unsatisfied mistress, and but all with relief.

CHAPTER 9

THE ELECTION, WILL AND HUNTER.

The sleepy place saw a sudden buzz of activity—the motor cars, mostly open jeeps, jam packed drove in the narrow pitch roads. The pitch roads are uneven with pot holes in them. The front with the flags stood on the long sticks to the jeeps attached, waving; frantically waving, all desperate for attention. The flags of colours variety with the pictures variety needed attention. The man with turbans, their ears covered from top to bottom with silver earrings, their bodies warmed with the second hand coats worn with wide legged short khaki half pants sat proudly holding their heads high. The plastic shoes they wore below with thick socks were oversize and clucked every time they walked. The typical village headmen, their followers, the party workers enjoying the election ride; their once in a five years' ride from their member's house to their village. They came, they ate, they slept and were promised heaven and they returned satisfied; the innocent trust of the simple villager in the town people. In their display of genuine concern for their problem; the need for a bridge, the pitch road, the primary school, the hospital, the electricity, the drinking water. They promised something they never meant and willed something they never knew. The nights heard of two three words, 'vote for"; the posters stuck in rows on the bamboo fencing of their compound, big black letters unevenly adorned the freshly painted white culverts, on either sides of the main street, messing rather than displaying, unattractively repelling; a big banner put up, in the party offices, outside had the party symbol. Other than that the picture of the candidate, the symbol, his name and title no one, small and big, old and young, rich and poor, illiterate and literate easily could forget also stood staring smiling and begging for vote straight out of the picture. They saw in the town other symbols too—chair, table, sickle, rose, drum, leaf with the pictures of another person, another name and title. They centered on one and only one. Election. Hot debates followed; the crowd favourite, the likely winner, the party, the family members, the wives of the contestants, each child and their behaviors were scanned; the place saw no other topic but the election. The women assembled, the men too separately stood in the evening when their dinner was over.

'He had an extra marital affair, an illegitimate daughter.'

The first was judged.

'His wife is a snob, spoke not to the people.' the second contestant dismissed.

'He is stingy. Food is not given for the visitors.'

The third too was waived.

'His children are all over-smart, disrespect the people.'

The fourth too was dismissed.

'He treated people like dirty creatures and washed his hands after shaking hands with the people.'

The fifth was also condemned.

'He washed his hands with soap before meal.'

Another added with conviction.

'Ishhh . . . what kind of member he'd be if considered his people dirty.

"Do you know his children are so arrogant?"

The question was an answer itself.

'Last time I went to their house, the daughter walked halfway and said her father was not at home and never let me in.'

'Believe me. I came back without a cup of tea." He tried to convince others.

Each background was judged, rejected, with none perfect but each with a flaw; The contestants were in their mercy. God, the one accepted seemed angel; the whole family too; nothing imperfect found for the voting, unbelievably true. Benta—pa seemed took most of it. From door to door he peeped with the neighbors as his target. He sat, he smoke, he drank tea and spoke of the election as if he was the master player. He had someone in mind; someone he was campaigning for, someone from whom he got and needed something to return, someone in whom his two or three months' food came from. He spoke of the man with the chair as his symbol, sang praises of him, of his inner and outer qualities, of his family, with no mention of his sons. His sons, the notorious duo who fought in the vicinity, left somebody near death, jailed twice. His was a campaign not for what the locality would get but what he could get out of him, ended always with "you should vote for him", a *mantu bidi* in between his dark lips, touching the thin moustache with the tips of his fingers, twirling and twitching it; the wife, his wife relayed to the womenfolk was soft spoken with good manners, respect all and sundry, rich and poor, small or big with smile permanently plastered in her lips but the sarcastic smile said they threw at her back said they all needed to know—she shouted at the people. If they ate in their house, she ridiculed them as slum people, disrespecting the poor but smiled only to the rich. A pure snob nobody missed and rejected outright. They came, the contestants and sat in the separate meeting. The village headman was the host of each, not only was it his duty but he got they said money from each, for the tea party on the polling day as his excuse half of which was used on the polling day; the male elders attended, listened and demanded from each—the electricity, PHE pipeline, the pitch road, the local primary school. They nodded, accepted, promised if voted him to power, they too agreed readily to whet their demand. Whether they kept the promise remained to be seen, well after the election; Palmina saw her house swarming. From the village where her father works, the villagers came to meet their candidate, a strong contender from a strong party, met him and stayed in their house rather than his. Palmina cooked. Her mother cooked. Palmina stayed late working and cursed. Jentilla had no guests. She burnt midnight oil and fared well in the semester exam. Palmina faired badly in her semester exam and was saddened. Her uncle came, next in number to her father, a leader of the village council and said they'd choose new candidate. The sitting one never cared, he hotly criticized. The demand for primary school still remain unmet, he criticized. He was vehement. Aggressive. The makeshift bamboo bridge across the river washed away in the last heavy rainfall. The bridge was a necessity, he spoke informing to Palmina and her mother. It was the students from the other side of the river facing the wrath of the monsoon rain and the heavy flood. Two students met their watery grave in the year last in the heavy river swell and washed away only to be recovered their dead bodies later when the water receded, he sighed with the tragedy and resigned with the fate. Palmina and her sister sat silently, quietly. Her mother spoke words of sympathy and was hugely visibly relieved when he left early next morning. Polling day came. Men, women thronged the road, made their way early in the morning to the nearest L.P. School, their polling booth—Palmina-ma, Tochi-ma went early. Their intention clear, evasion of standing in a long queue, the bad body odour and the heat of the day; the polling agents sat outside and gave piece of paper with each voter's name hoping against hope they'd vote for their candidate. First five to cast their vote her mother evaded standing in the queue and went back with nothing but a black mark on the back of her point finger and crossed the headman's house on the way. White smoke went up, a huge pot put up in front of the house above the three big stones below where firewood stacked and was burning heating the pot. Three women stood nearby, one was stirring it while other two just stood watching but they came, their piece of paper slipped into the ballot box, came back with the black mark on their fingers. Different groups of supporters—for sickle, kettle, chair, rose, book, lamp, drum; Tochi-pa, Palmina-pa, and Benta-pa, a man with loosely worn shoes for the same symbol they ticked in the paper. For a chair they cast, with the back of their nails blackened in little dot; Hilla-pa and short headman cast for another. They both waited for the result, arguing intensely, siding for the symbol they cast. They both have something in their mind nobody knew about. Something of their own, differed from others. They all got nothing but for Benta—pa. A bundle of new CIC sheets behind the house he rented shined out in the sun yet Benta-pa slapped his palms three times, took the tobacco, mixed well with the lime, put it in his mouth, a new habit acquired with the election campaign he busied himself with before the poll; the counting day was awaited much with enthusiasm, anxiety, fear, trepidation all mixed; it began in the morning early. Palmina saw her mother biting her nail in tension. Her father sat with his neighbor friends. When the leading margin was announced, the male, female elders, the young and adults and children sat near the Philips radio and tuned it in. It was the best her father said when he bought it, its two antennas straight up, one shorter and the another longer and when the result was announced after a tired wait; the victory was theirs. Her father hid his eyes well in a full heartfelt smile Palmina knew was his rarest. Tochi—pa was exuberant. Benta—pa stood with 'it was my work' stance and mixed tobacco well with the lime in his palm and chew betel nut. The man with loosely worn shoes showed his rarest show of exhilaration. They all saw PHE water, electricity, Primary school and the pitch wide road. A tall burly man turned grim, his anger obvious, disappointed, ready to depart from where they all stood in a group with a radio on but gave a parting shot.

"Your candidate won with the votes of Bangladeshi refugees . . ." a scathing contempt of pure scorn but none to challenge but to accept the reality; Bangladeshi refugees on the other side of the stream, separated, stuck hard in the government land, tried hard by the department for eviction but for the political support. They were a vote bank, they knew well but kept mum with the winning more important than the voters; Benta-ma took her children; twelve year Benta, two brothers in tag, her mother and the father smoothened his moustache, lit the slim white wills filter in between his dark lips and proudly announced the victor wished him there for the party. A kitchen closed.

Three years elapsed since the election last; two years to the election next. The Member of Legislative Assembly was elected. Their persistent effort and consistency paid. It was a great achievement; he went, the man with loosely worn shoes clucking behind him and met the minister, lay the demand he fought for fifteen years, undauntedly alone. The man won with absolute majority. Bolchugri voted ninety five percent. He could no escape. It was announced in the counting he hardly could ignore. He promised, grudgingly for fear of losing in the election, he needed badly to win. He had a house that remained incomplete. One year before the election next, giant pipelines arrived. Each sat comfortably on twelve shoulders, slowly, with no motorable road, queues from the giant main tank, two kilometers down, joined together later. A man with the loosely worn shoes smiled for the first, fully, his face widened, his mouth opened, white teeth shown fully but marred by the wrinkled lines brought not by the age but by the fatigue, thanked each for the effort but downplayed his own, humbly in the assembly at the courtyard of the headman circled by the elder males. His smile was genuine. His happiness all too real. The burly grim man sat in the wooden arm chair, smiling, relaxed, the short headman with his mouth twitched spoke gratitude to the man who made it, his tireless efforts appreciated; Palmina's father too was proud and contented, his eyes smaller while smiling while Tochi-pa and the other male elders in the locality too spoke of happiness; a short thin man, smoothened his moustache, seemed thought hard for sometime and spoke in the end; he said he asked the member in the election last for the water; he showed his importance, the pseudo weight of his words that the member paid attention to. Two or three months later, the water spilled out of the small pipelines in the public tapes; the one behind the house of Tochi-ma supplied for the six houses with a long queue in the morning also in the evening on a square cemented platform strewn with clothes of various sizes—bed-sheets, long-pants, children's shirts, petticoats, blouses of one house but it was the babies nappies that Benta-ma brought had everyone frowning and turning away their eyes and for some even revolting violently. With the well water left unused, it turned red uncared, iron-filled—a field day for Benta-ma; Private connection few could afford. Only Tochi-pa, headman, a burly grim man were the lucky few for the privilege . . Her uncle came again and again. His demands are still unmet. With the election left another two years, he thought of getting the demand. From a borrowed legislator. The master liar, had acres of land bought near the town and had an old house demolished and erected massive building frowned upon by many that sealed his fate in the election next he cared not. He had stored for a lifetime.

Three years and half had gone since the election last. Palmina crossed her teenage stage and at her fourteen years. Her father still hunt, not sincerely for meat but for pleasure and for a sport with his friends in the village where he worked for the weekdays, almost every night but here too at home with Benta-ma and at times with Tochi-pa in weekends and rewarded almost every weekend night with small sports he was contented with, gleaming his face priding on his good target and bragging about it and gave tips here and there to his friends. The meat in the kitchen always was of smoked venison and other animals of the same family with their short and small horns filling the small store room behind the kitchen and some even given to the neighbors or whoever had the fancy for them nearing teenage Palmina had neither approved nor disapproved of. Her mother was livid, nagged him to stop hunting; they all knew why. He came back one night; his fear was unfounded. He hid it behind the smile but tremor in his voice betrayed him. It was a long chase he told them, well covered the foothills of two, of the deer; the deer stopped for breath below the huge family of bamboo, a well fifty meters from where they stood; then they saw her father said, the large twin ears, the sound they emitted while fanning. It was a huge, too huge for a deer. They ran for their dear lives. A narrow escape. Her mother worried sick for his safety refrained him from hunting and said in no uncertain terms they'd live without the meat he brought and Palmina loved the evening she spent with him. He rested from his hunting for months; the three months of vacation he gave for winter; she neither told him to go or not to go. She was relieved and enjoyed the evenings with him; her mother was relaxed, tension free. Weeks later his overdue promotion came. He ruled the school now with iron hand; a comedy head master; in the school he was both feared and loved. He showed his funny sides too, people talked about laughingly. He chaired the condolence of a student absent in class, alive and kicking. His life history was read out—a good student, disciplined, well mannered, a good boy while in reality he was mischievous, naughty boy who often sat with his knee down in the sun for the ruckus he caused; but everyone though vividly remembered his every deed stood benumbed; the teachers shed tears; the students cried; his good friends stood each and spoke of him well; it was a great loss to the school, his class teacher who often was at the butt of his pranks said solemnly, tearfully. They prayed for the departed soul and the aggrieved family. Two days later, he came in health and hearty and sent all students scurrying, running helter skelter in fear. The girls scream and shrieked in terror.

'Ghost . . . . . . ghost . . . . . . ghost . . . . . . ghost . . . . . ghost . . . . . .ghost . . . . . ghost . . . . . . ghost . . .'He was bewildered and totally confused.

He came out, stood aghast and stared at him open mouthed. The other teachers too came out, saw the dead man walking and they too stood aghast. The confusion was cleared. He was misinformed. He had the identity of the dead mixed up. It turned out as a good joke later. All laughed, a good hearty laugh. The incident neither embarrassed him nor shamed him. Rather he laughed at his own mistake and carried the story home and made her mother and children laughed at him. Palmina and her mother saw something in his few months of sabbatical retreat he took from hunting. He was restless at night. In the weekends when at home, he took out his air-gun, took them out parts by parts and cleaned them well with rifle oil and dried the pellets in the sun. He had the barrel cleaned well and shining and let Palmina had a glimpse of it too. The barrel shone like a mirror inside. His desire to hunt was never missed either by the daughter or the mother. And he took the rifle to the village where he worked for his safety he reasoned to his wife with elephants visiting at night. But she knew and Palmina too knew. After a month when he came home brought a wild boar home, smoked well in the kitchen in the village where he worked in a bag full of its long slices and dropped on one surprise evening. Her father still hunt well and could hardly part with it, her mother explained to Palmina one evening when she complained to her. Two months later he sat in the courtyard, smoked hookah with the pipe well in his mouth, silently with a deep thought as if seriously thinking of something. Her mother came, placed tea on the small table infront, boiled maize for a company when he spoke.

"I have thought of stopping my hunting"

It was a total surprise coming from a man unable to spend the nights without being seen with his rifle, his constant companion and a bosom friend. Why? What happened of her mother's interest brought the whole story out. He said he had a dream of a man with a face unfamiliar yet creating unease within telling him he had a boar tied on the tree somewhere in the jungle waited for his hunt and that easily could fill his stomach, then disappeared like a genie leaving him bewildered; the dream had an effect on him he said, gave him sleepless nights they all noticed, even Palmina silently noticed in the brooding silence he smoked but thought nothing further. He further added, a headman and the hunter with not a single shot missing from the village where he work died two years back in the jungle after he too had the same dream, went for hunting after telling his family the dream, even joked about it perhaps indeed with a fattened boar waiting the village would see a community feast they all longed for simply to have his body brought back home, lifeless with the whole village in a community feast in his compound with wailing and howling a sight; he saw a deer, they said who accompanied him, shot it on the leg that managed to run away with him behind chasing for second, third and fourth shot for kill but the deer tirelessly ran far, extraordinarily far for one with a shot taken on the leg and stared at him above a cliff, waiting for him when he aimed again, the deer ran and he too took few steps but fell into the deep gorge, hundred meters below and lay flattened bloody red on the flat rocky surface. The dream, he said thoughtfully was not a mere dream but a warning, though he never knew from where and whom.

But he heeded for the better. The year seemed blessed. The school he headed had a government favour, became full fledged and his salary became regular, monthly with the increments that had him smiling all time so did her mother.

Mitilla, began Tochi-ma, roam each night, the night last she caught her red handed she told to anyone interested in listening and found many pairs of ears listening. They all stood on the narrow footpath in between rows of houses. She came very late, she began her exaggeration of her kitchen help, must be after twelve, meeting her boyfriend she presumed and gave her a thrashing deserved with a warning but Palmina believed it not; they came together, an early night all of them had with many witness against her. Chinche turned her face towards her and raised her eyebrow in disbelief. Milche and Palmina saw her action and the latter laughed. Milche stifled a giggle. The evening later, Mitilla, her arm around a steel pot, both eyes swollen red, one black, long slitting bruises all over, showed from the naked left arm, uncovered, red blood still clotted in tiny dots in a long queue, drew water from the ring-well with Palmina on the platform slapping a bucketful of clothes, her uniform and her brothers clothes and she bared her heart out with none around. Her much restrained tears unable to contain spilled in few drops that she hid with a swift smile and then winked at her and then they are gone with the wipe with back of her hand; she was charged she told Palmina after their night in Chinche's for tryst with a ghost boyfriend and slammed a hard bamboo stick on her body and broke it on top, left few bruises in the shape of the stick on her back she showed her. Palmina flinched and she burst out again with her uncontrollable tears broke the dam and surged like a gushing water that she wiped them and ended with a note, she'd leave for her village where her poor parents never even touch a strand of her hair. But she stayed anyway; her parents needed to eat. The next morning, Palmina had her mother's *gana* hid her naked body. Her tiny peaches well hidden. Her shoulder blades well exposed and her creamy white neck in complete contrast to her dark face. Her ankle well hidden with the bottom of the *gana*. Her exposed shoulder blades with small soapy bubbles, scrubbing hard with dried spongy gourd. Jentilla was there too, ready to bath. Mittila came, in her usual way, entertained them with the last afternoon's story. Benta-ma came, Mitilla told Palmina and talked of her mother with her two sons in tow; they sat in courtyard, with her mistress all ears and fed what she wished to hear; Mittila said she took a tray of tea and overheard their conversation; Palmina's mother, disrespected her husband, cook poorly, ate only dhal with no meat, unhygienic. Then she relayed the words she claimed spoken by Palmina's mother of Tochi—ma.

'She said your husband entered servant's room at night', then looked at her for conviction, her eyes shrewdly calculative; Tochi-ma fumed, eyes in angry slits, smoke out of every pores—nose, ears, mouth and eyes but she with a tact calmed her with the words.

"You are richer, why care?" and her confidence and favour won she ended with a note, "'By the way, can you lend me two kilos of rice? I will return it next week."

She left with two kilos of rice, her two sons well—fed with two slices of bread each but with a sure that the two kilos of rice won't return. The cold war began. Innuendoes and suggestive remarks filled the gap in between. Palmina saw her mother tense with no clue yet the tinged of her meaning with no prove. She restrained her feet from their neighbor; their neighbor looked not their way for a month. The month next, she came smiling, hiding the embarrassment, her guilt well hidden and sat outside their house; Her mother said nothing, no reminder, everything forgotten, forgiven; she sat with her outside the house. Palmina went inside the kitchen and brought two cups of tea; she placed them on the table and watched them both sipped. She brought the story, about Benta—ma—The daughter, the mother and the stepfather; their relation, the inside story, the elopement. Her mother was shocked. She opened her mouth—shocked for a moment.

The sun seemed mesmerized by the horizon hurrying forward, yet with a remote distance it seemed running faster when Jentilla crossed the threshold of the main gate, the pink bougainvilleas, its thorns stuck out wired around it; Jimmy bounced, wagged its tail, nuzzled its head and snorted its nose asking in his tongue of her where about, licked her palm when she patted his head. It was an affectionate gesture and left her with a feeling of love, wanted, missed and headed straight towards the door. She was starving and she took her strides big, so eager to reach and to fill her empty stomach. Her wary feet stepped into the small drawing room. On the left side with its back to the bamboo wall stood a long three seater wooden settee of jackfruit wood planked on each side by the small rectangle tables with one seater each on the side opposite with flattening cushions of what were once plump cushions. The one long rectangle wooden table stood in the middle dominated the room covered by green, embroidered in red of three roses with its leaves of green, circled all the three roses with the white. Bunch of fresh roses, the queen of flowers were her favorite—pink, deep red, white, orange in a flower vase stood, hand picked in the morning from the garden, withering with the heat. The glass vase stood in the middle of embroidered red, the pride of place and honored to beautify. The flattening cushion on the settee, bogged with her weight she neither cared nor bothered threw her bag beside. She slipped out her only four months old white socks lay crumpled on her feet, its elastic top loosened with the black leather belted pair of shoes below, lent by Hilla out of twin pair she owned. She appreciated her generosity much but the repeated soaking in the rain, gave it tear open with a black patch over invited snorting remark from their class teacher, a pure snob and insensitive bitch. She needed a new pair again she knew and owed her father a word but tightly sealed it. She knew their financial crunch with her mother's incessant complain of it. Her stomach groaned. It was a heart wrenching sound with a stark hunger pulling her where it would be filled. Up, she rose and headed toward the kitchen, lifted the lid of the steel bowl in the middle of the round table high, peered into it. Round *puris* within brought out saliva.

'Leave three *puris* for Nokam. She'd come late today." A lion's share. A short—stature grey haired woman stood outside the door.

'Hmmm . . ."one *puri* dropped into the bowl below.

'Fetch water from the public tape after your tea and fill the barrel.' Her evening routine.

'Hmmmm . . .' she needed not be told.

Two *puris* half filled her but the three exuded belching she much enjoyed letting out with none within a hearing distance and she went beyond warning of her mother she could not careless and delightedly went where she was asked to be, to fetch water from the public tape. It was a long queue. All waited for the water with their silver aluminum bucket in each hand. The empty pots dangled carelessly with their hand clutch at the lips of the mouth. It was the only public tape in the vicinity connected to the main big silver pipeline with less water in it with the water half filling the big pipeline and not reaching the private connectors at the other end. Jentilla's family was the worst sufferer of it. With the lone public tape as their lone saviour, they bee-lined around it. Jentilla and Palmina too stood at the fifth and sixth row. The waiting robbed half an hour of her time and she yawned and got the much waited water. With her arm circled around the neck, the water—filled pot rested on her hip heavy to carry yet comfortably balanced that almost weighed her down, she stood rested on the concrete foot path fighting with the exhaustion that sapped her strength. With her strength regained she shifted pot to the left side but it slipped. It was a vain effort something she was unused to do. She much felt the comfort carrying filled pots on her right side of her hip. The slippery pot reverted back to the right where it sat well balanced. It rested well there. With great care she crossed the threshold of the outer gate, in the middle of an expansive courtyard and headed towards the kitchen. The black barrel outside the kitchen had the water up to the neck. Jentilla saw to it and filled half of it in the morning and another half in the evening. It was black with the bitumen her mother had PWD labourers as donors. She repaired the whole barrel and stopped the leakage. The water well could last the morning next and spared her of energy waste, she consoled herself, relieved of the burden the next morning.

"Why didn't you leave three *puris* for Nokam?" It was a thundering accusation spelling danger. Jentilla startled; her delight in her work short-lived at the sight of her mother.

One hand on her hip, bamboo pole in another, she stood ramrod straight. Her eyes were in furious slits, fumes emitted out of her wide nostrils, her heart with a heavy rhythmic breathing and advanced menacingly. Behind, Nokam stood, tear streaked, her mouth openly and stubbornly pouted.

"Crack . . . crack . . . crack . . . crack . . ."

The bamboo pole made contact on her back, hips, thighs and calf, she screamed, cried out in pain, the loud crashing sound and the pot landed near her trembling feet, missing her toes by few inches; the water spilled out, wetting the dry ground, and washed her feet but the tears flowed freely, rolling non stop like a summer rain.

'Salah . . . Now you know.'

Her teeth clenched, gritted and her eyes widened in pure stark anger.

'Now you get out of the house.'

A parting shot stung her to the bones.

The breeze whispered, the leaves whistled, the dark daunting, the frogs croaking in the nearby stream and the silence reigned but she neither moved nor rose but sat on the foot on the thick root of ancient jackfruit tree, behind the house, planted by her grandfather. She cried, cried her heart out but no one heard just the deep quietue of darkness surrounding her. She sobbed, big sobs and small sobs till they reduced to hiccups. When the tears stopped but the questions in chain invaded.

She laid her heart bare to none but the jackfruit tree and asked herself. Why was her sister favoured? Why not her? She worked hard, unlike her. But all best things in life came first for her—clothes, shoes, books, bags, food, love and care. She was the apple of her eyes, the undivided recipient and the family custodian. She wished for death but for her dear father, the overworked father, his love and care were her only surviving instinct. It was late, near midnight when he returned home, exhausted, with none to give food for him. With the food on the table went cold, not warmed and he knew whom he missed; he asked Nokam first, who replied nothing, then his wife who gave the twisted version of the story shortly and he searched the whole compound and found her asleep with her slender teenage body bundled into a small round ball, at the foot of the tree. She slept with hiccups still invading, patted lightly, tenderly on her back and then shook her gently when she awoke. She was no longer a child but she still was his child, his daughter whom he loved, protected and cared. He brought her home, lay her on the single bed and ate the cold food alone and spoke few harsh words that frozen her mouth for two days only to open her mouth two days later with wad of notes he was paid for the private tuition he gave. Two weeks later, his wife waited, eagerly for his return. She had something she wished to talk. It was in her mind for sometime now. Something she thought of seriously. Something she knew she'd had to fight a hell lot with him. But she knew him, knew him too well. Her husband of long years. She knew too, one thing—his weakness and her strength. Her weapon and his defenseless body and she chose the place—the bed. The pillow talk. She chose the topic very carefully. They talked, a middle aged couple, the husband atleast twenty years older, deciding about the future of the property they owned, not that they had much but a small plot of land where they housed in, few hectares of betel nut plantation, a daughter who would look after them in their old age, tend them when they are sick in dotage when the man removed the loose shoes he wore, then a pair of socks, a grey half sweater, then his shirt and lastly his grey pant put on a thin white towel with white banyan covering his upper part when the wife spoke sharp already decided from eons, waiting only for the right moment to talk and suggested her choice he was reluctant with. He decided for the eldest; she loved him most, looked after him well, fed him, he said casually. The younger maintained house, sweep the rooms, took proper care of everything inside, she argued, advocating. He was not persuasive but she was affectionately forceful. She'd be given the land for house—building but not the house, she cajoled, persistently; she was relentless and his energy sapped and he loved her most, many years younger to him, someone who stole his heart while teaching in the class she was in. It was long years back but he looked back; her long black hair, her thick lashes she fluttered at him, shyly and the slow melting of his heart day by day still warmed him; his insecurity for the age gap, her looks, a bone of contention once before marriage with the man smitten with and lost to him being a jobless student. His secured job sealed his fate. The fate that smiled at him and he had no heart to lose the smile. He was adamant with his decision intact, tactfully but gave in after much persuasion and cajoling and using of feminine wiles she was adept at. The youngest daughter was chosen, the family heiress with everything in her name. The eldest remained for future—a homeless. Somebody eavesdropped. Her ears stung. Her pain was excruciating, too real. Dam burst and water gushed out uncontrollably the night long. The water flooded where it fell. Soft light pillow soaked. She was let down.

CHAPTER 10

TURA, THE BLAME, NARROW ESCAPE AND HAUNTED.

A green majestic Tura peak stood on the east, dignified, towering over the small town, in the midst of the summer evening, unchanging even in the mid eighties. The shouting of the hullocks in group, the diminishing sound with the diminishing numbers, faint sound unlike before when their shouting echoed all over the small town. It was balming, soothing and entertaining for Palmina but noisy and irritating to Jentilla that sent her scowling. Both Palmina and Jentilla walked back home in companionable silence, each wrapped in their own thoughts. Hilla had already gone with Monica and co., something she formed as a habit after the class. She made them to feel discriminated by her action. The blazing summer sun left a weak trailing heat while facing the west, before disappearing beyond the horizon, blissful for a short snooze. On the day was a sweating hard, the heat still strong enough to give a blow to the famished school children on their way home after a tiring day in the class. In sailing, it shone on the scattered tall leafy trees, towering over the pitch PWD road, on either sides in rows, that gave shady spots below, a blessing to the sun-scorched pedestrians and to the weary school children too. The children some with and some without their umbrellas, took rest, relieved of heat, their eyes fatigued, their dark sun burnt faces glistened with sweat in tiny droplets. Their energy boosted with the short rest, they lifted their legs, dragged their protesting feet forward, towards home, the another half an hour walking distance, after an hour's passed. The street was empty. The two wheelers, mo-bikes and Bajaj scooters the rich owned were the only the passing vehicles in the town with the town boasting of a very few rich people and their cars. The ambassadors were their pride, a pure display of wealth and also of the town even in the mid eighties. The pavements and footpaths bordering on the side of the blackened pitch road with the left side of it strewn with famished, wearied school goers, their waist line to the knee below decorated—navy blue, violet, black, brown and green—the sweat dampened common white shirts above the waistline bathing them. Black naughty boy shoes they wore streaked brown while the soles caked with brown mud adding extra inch to half an inch heels they wore below. Their white nylon socks turned brown covering their feet with the empty water bags hanged from their hands, swinging to and fro with their multi colored school bags on the backs, some hanging from their shoulders below the hips slapping their thighs for every pace they made, they chatted, laughed, giggled, portraying the picture of gay abandon, they headed home, unheeding of the pain. Palmina with a handloom woven green bag slung across her shoulder with her wrapped thoughts, rehashing the scene vivid from the period last in the class, smiled alone. Her lips twitched, her face creased, unaware of the ripples created in the surrounding, staring at her, some even murmuring something in other's ears with their eyes solely fixed in her. The scene was too vivid to remiss. Merina, her seatmate, on the bench last, folded the pink umbrella, flower printed with her mind riveted, diverted from the cleanliness Teacher Sodini lectured, dreaded by all for her unsparing strict attitude for the matters trivial. Hollering and howling were her hobby if caught inattentive in the class. With her powerful spectacles her insignia, a symbol of strictness she scowled down at her. With her eyes above the top of her spectacle's rims she seemed seeing her better without her lens than with them on she thundered and rattled poor Merina. With her hands stilled on the umbrella Merina stuttered and stammered with no single word for immediate answer and was a butt of teacher's ire with her eyes widening in fear, stunned. Teacher Sodini was unforgiving and dissatisfied with her fear closed on her. A second later she stood on top of the desk, her opened umbrella above with no rain or sun but protecting from the ceiling, a punishment for impatience. It roared the whole class with laughter, enjoying her discomfiture, while the old woman satisfied with her anger quelled, rubbed the both corners of her mouth with the light blue handkerchief and the tiny red particles of the betel nut grinding in between her red—stained teeth landed on Palmina's face. The poor seatmate, fair face red with embarrassment took it neither light nor funny, compressed her lips tight, blocking the moisture in her eyes welling with both the mixture of pity and smile flooding her in the rehash, broken rudely by the sudden sound from the Tura peak, the cry of hullock seemed to be in a group and had she not know better she would think so but somebody said of it, had he been a singer even a lone hillock needed no need of loud speaker in a jest. She jolted at the nudge she got below her arm and stared blindly at visibly amused Jentilla, laughing at her. She looked around and saw the curious eyes of other school goers on her and felt like the total idiot. She sped towards home taking long steps her long legs afford. She came late from school today, later than other days and found a high drama she found repelling.

She had a hectic day. Three sections of mounted files on her table took a toll of her energy. She sat sprawled on the long chair, breathing in rhythm counting her every breath. Palmina sat with Milche inside the kitchen peeling potato watching at the same Mittila chopping chicken. Milche brought a hot cup of strong tea like the way she liked. She smiled in warm welcome.

'Who is making dinner?' Her voice tinged with fatigue.

'Mittila.' She answered. She sipped her tea slowly and said nothing.

'What is she cooking?'

'Chicken.'

She thought of chicken leg and smiled.

From where she lay, her eyes straight faced the twenty five steps leading down to their house. The wide window showed the dusk outside when a single clean chimney of a kerosene lamp lighted the room. Suddenly she sighted a figure of a woman loomed on top of the step. She could vaguely recognize the identity and confirmed when heard her voice. Tochi—ma. Her shouting and yelling shook her and she jumped suddenly. It was not calling nor invitation nor a courtesy calling but an angry accusation. She was taken aback. It was sudden, uninformed and without warning verbal war. Her reaction was slow. She came out and stood in the verandah with its wooden floor raised few inches from the ground with the verandah, too half-walled with the wired nets above. The lone door in between flung open where Milche-ma stood, her mouth gaped open unable to understand the cause and directed at whom but the fiery eyes were pointed straight at her and it began to dawn slowly. Mittila. She came two days back, her body bruised blue, beaten badly brought by Benta-ma on hearing of searching for a maid, their own left home with the news of her ailing father without whom the household chore like a milestone on her neck. She was chased out, she sobbed, the pitiful words supported by her guide, not out of concern but she needed a cup of sugar for morning and she let her stay with the thought it was God-sent and gladly parted with the cupful of sugar. But the charge now was totally twisted or perhaps the truth; she was branded—a thief, a robber—the names were called; her mother sent her to her house maid and thus her responsibility. She tried to explain but there was no gap, the woman had the gift of gab that was not given to her by her maker, shouted at the other woman rudely the confidence her mother had in her in sending and in a fit of rage Milche-ma shouted at the poor girl to leave to her former mistress venting her anger on Jentilla rather than Tochi—ma. Palmina had her sympathy flooded. The poor girl got an earful, perhaps even blasted her eardrum. She left unwillingly, tearfully much sure of earful even a beating she got much than feared and spent the night in self pity and buckets of tears soaking the small pillow where her head rested. She woke with swollen red eyes and the protesting body the morning next and lowered her eyes when in the kitchen and later lowered her eyes at the still glowering eyes of her mistress she hated that bore on her. Palmina, Jentilla and Milche met her in the pond two days later and she showed the black stripes.

It was a hot Summer Sunday. The whole locality of men, women and children went to the church that stood majestic on top of a hillock in the heart of this small locality, almost hidden from the eyes outside by the young green leaves of the Sal trees that surrounded it. Outside the church, small young groups of elderly men and women gathered in the shade given by the Sal trees, laughing and talking about what God only knew while another group of young men and women stood in a circle with a decision to explore the abandoned village for mouth-watering sweet ripened tamarind which in reality was to while away their holiday. Palmina, Jentilla, Hilla, Milche and Chinche were also seen among others. Poor Mittila wished fervently to go but the fear of her mistress without whose permission it would be death knell for her decided to stay back, grudgingly with half her heart with them. She watched them disappearing, her eyes too longing but with no choice of her own and they could no help except feeling sorry. It was a long caravan with young boys also adding to the long line, playing all the way with each other. She looked at the two girls and three boys, much elder than them, far left behind the protection of their parents. They had freedom to move anywhere of their hearts' desire, anytime, unhinged. The teenage stage they still stuck they far left behind, the envy for which gnawed at her tinged with jealousy. For every small thing to do or to go anywhere, 'No' and "Yes" are two essential words, the latter she was hardly blessed with and there was only lone answer. She sneaked out with them, uncaring for the consequences awaited for her in the evening from her over protective mother. The lengthy three hundred and ten concrete steps led down to the stream below was partly shaded by the roadside trees while the halfway down the sun had not spared it from its scorching heat but the children were too excited and braved the heat and crossed to the other side of the stream away from the civilization, they fell instantly in love. The summer heat beat on the young teenagers as they followed adults in line and with no proper road to their destination except for the narrow beaten track just broad enough to put a feet with tall grasses on each side of the track, home of any creepy crawlies she could think of and seen. Twice, a green and brown snake crossed their way while the children shrieked in fright, jumping and running forward each time. It was soon forgotten when they caught sight of beautiful blue bird much larger in size than other birds its long red beak stuck out sat on the branch of a tree searching, looking left and right past caring for the passers-by but for food. The life far different from their ordinary life was enchanting and mesmerized the young minds, exhilarating. An hour passed by in simple walking in the sun amidst occasional breezes that fanned their sweat away till they reached long four roomed Assam type house, nearly vandalized with no occupants and left empty by whoever built it for what purpose but it served just the same for another purpose and for some people—For romance seekers, for lovers and for closeting. The doors and windows left bare empty, white washed walls turned brown and black with the scribbling, graphiti, rough drawn pictures of nude men and women by charcoal and red stones or perhaps with charcoal and red stones or perhaps with chalk, the lovers decided to express their feelings with "I love you" and to declare "Rabin love Silma" on it with snippets and gossips found in it while the long open verandah welcomed the droppings of cows and goats, the stench of their urination, purely repugnant and undesirable place for teenagers to step into but was a destination of the adults. The adults' footsteps stopped, stepped inside it, with teenagers little knowledge of their business in a god-forsaken place nor was it their business to know but to resume their steps forward, non stop. Jentilla made a face. Both her eyes rolled towards one corner and Palmina laughed. They reached where they headed. It was an old and abandoned village far outside the town they stepped their feet into, a very old hamlet with the thatch roof houses scattered here and there, just after crossing the narrow stream by a leapt to the other side welcomed them with open arms. The tall trees like mango, tamarind, jackfruit, bell tree threw shade on the track below they stood for a while to catch their breath back, sweat rolling down from both sides of the cheeks panting for breath but with delight. The sun was merciless but a long walk bore fruitful; showed small opening among the tall grasses and shrubs, went straight to the fruit bearing old ancient jackfruit tree of its branches like ladders from near the ground, a gift for the unskillful climbers. The children stopped, looked up, feast their eyes into armies of green spiky fruits, hanging, smiled at her that said all she needed to know, urging, time for her knack; with no second urging needed but with a passion she pulled up her body to the lowest branch, she stopped, access to the others and then to the group of green fruits, patting. The third patting invoked smile with its sound, too different from others, not only in her but the others below too smiled that said all; she let it down with difficulty and care with her bottom firmly on a branch where she sat with her two feet hanging to below and resumed till two, attempted to lower herself but her eyes moved to something a little distance from where the others stood below. It was human, she could see clearly from up.

"Run . . . It is . . . him . . . the madman . . "

She shouted in warning, slipped swiftly down in fear.

'Run . . ." Someone shouted; the kids ran, their lives in peril with the devil himself chasing them. He was a half madman and spared none. If he had something in his hand meant he came for a kill. He meant it.

"You thieves . . . stealing jackfruit from my garden. I will kill you."

The male angry voice broke in the silence of the forest; a glimpsed of a big angry man with a big khaki half pant swishing and running towards them, a long indigenous wood cutter in his hand looked menacing; its sharp edges glistened in the penetrating sun reflecting on her eyes scurried her behind her friends; two of them still with jackfruits in their breasts, in the open track out of reach and with heavy breaths, they had a lucky escape; she had a close inspection of her body later, delighted with the few bruises on her belly near the navel with the blood clotted, red but considered herself lucky with it; she shuddered later with the thought of almost caught by the half mad man who they heard had no mercy for anyone but vented his anger on anyone dared to challenge his anger. They sat, had it stored well in their bodies that nearly cost their lives, caught baby fishes from the cool stream below much with rocks than with water, much for the pleasure than to whet their culinary taste and headed back when the sun retreated towards the horizon, fun fulfilled, its heat weak that seemed to be gritting its teeth failing to harm them. The sun already disappeared and they climbed up, the top of the long step a heaven where they stopped, they caught their breath sighting few thatch roof houses of Bolchugri; the cool gentle breeze like an angel, fanned and dried their sweats more like caressing, a much pleasure for the children only to be disrupted by the shouts, angrily and aggressively from the left below the footpath thronged by the people watching the scene, pulling their eyes towards it; they too joined slowly without a rush out of curiosity not for pleasure. The scene was a common sight. The neighbour audiences, in a large group they stood on the concrete path, eyes on the scene below, rooted, some with critical talk, some laughing enjoying, few others siding either of the two; a short stature woman, aging than her age, her graying hair thinning with the excessive hair fall, coiled on the nape of her neck, her forehead creased in few lines above her fiery eyes was shouting on her top voice with her small lips moving with every shrill shout. Her fingers busy with the betel leaf cleaning she stood on the edge of an expansive courtyard and looked down at the couple much below where she stood. With a man in grey hair behind, sleek with oil, shiny, sweeping the dead leaves from the expansive family courtyard, barefoot, a short sleeve white banyan and a green towel around his waist as his only briefs he attempted restraining his uncontrollable wife with no control at all. She seemed to cast her spell on him for his soft words turned futile, drowned in the shrillness of her voice. Perhaps not the spell but dominating wife. If she was a shrew, the other younger woman far down below the mango tree, a short middle age man in behind, a yellow towel around his bottom, shouting back, her finger in threatening point depending the family honour was no lesser; Tochi-ma had her pig tied on the mango tree, had no sty, crossed the boundary, the older woman's vegetable garden destroyed; silly and embarrassing. Jentilla gave her mother a dirty look, not seen by the latter but she dared not throw it right on her face risking an earful and embarrassment but not missed by her friends.

"Those fought for the land got a curse."

An elderly audience remarked spitefully.

"Only for trivial matter . . ."

Another put in disgustedly; none gave fair judgment, only lopsided.

'Tochi—pa seemed unable to control his wife.' Somebody remarked.

'How could he? He is under—petticoat.'

Another informed with heavy sarcasm.

The two women parted. The audience too dispersed all with scathing remarks, not siding with any in the dusk and the children and teenagers too retired for the night, excitedly chatting and amused at the scene. Palmina mingled in the dispersing crowd on her short way home and heard much than her friends. The short man had the bottom of the silver pot in their marital scuffle with their family crockery dented or shapeless in each spouse fight which she always won. Two elderly women walking ahead were talking, a story Palmina opened her ears wider interestedly and fed herself for the evening delightedly.

Benta-ma, Mittila relayed, allied with Tochi-ma, the week after the boundary fight; she camped there permanently, went home only for the night; she listened, sided not with other party but with her; she injected words if needed any poisoning her mind and watched Tochi-ma called her neighbor every names, belittled; Tochi—ma talked negatively in detail with their family's dirty linen washed out, blackly; it was not even grey; she prided on their wealth, challenging alone to compare with their wealth; she earned every evening for aligning—a cup of sugar, a wrapped packet of dry fish, a cup of mustard oil, a handful of onion, a kilo of rice and the short thin man sat at home, cross legged, smoking mantu bidi, smoothed his thin moustache, smiling but the week later, a slim white wills filter stuck out of his mouth and the wife stopped coming much to the consternation of Tochi-ma needing ally; she loudly announced on the street clustered, the teeth hurt of much pork grinding; rumour was that he won *teer*, his ten rupees earned back with good investment, one hundred for one rupee. But nobody saw the bearded man, a betel nut trader from Dhubri came to his house at night and paid him for bagfuls of betel nut. He later told the owner, the storm had done much damage; squirrel and bats had meals of whatever was left off by the storm and sent him very few bags of left over, much to his discontentment. The owner said nothing, not that he wanted to but scared of his wife. Benta—ma talked much about others; she muted her mouth when needed to. A week later her inner fears were founded. Her speculation mounted. In the kitchen, Benta stood towered over twin *chulha* hearths; she took a sip of gravy, checking the taste of the salt; she reached out for the small plastic container, scooped out a half in a small spoon.

Her loose tee shirt covered her top; the round low necked opened a gaping mouth and showed the richly juiced young melons she was blessed with. Somebody licked; his eyes greedy; his tongue licking; his mind sinuous. He stood outside the kitchen. Perhaps another time, he seemed to have thought. He left still licking his tongue.

There he sat right in the middle, on the *moorah*, rounded by Palmina and her friends, their eyes transfixed, fear, excited and thrilling saved Mittila who sat fearless and his two male friends putting and inserting every now and then in between with the words her and the words there as Moren regaled them the stories. Palmina had her eyes explored every contour of his face and body and fed her mind and adoringly unrelentingly gazed at him.

The crush of a teenager on the matured adult and hated the girl he was betrothed. She eyes him amorously he not took notice of or even if he had he never showed or perhaps he was pointedly avoiding or plain careless. The stories were all horror stories collected at the moment yet true or that was what he said, occurred in his village, somewhere in Assam—Meghalaya border; they could well imagine the scene flashed in their minds eye; a sudden death of a man after a night's return from a neighborhood village who crossed the graveyard a night before; his grave dug in six months time, found the body intact with nothing rotten; that was done to unravel the mystery, he said; some monster came out of the very grave then entered the houses he thought was his latest victim and the loss of lives. Every night someone or the other died and always with the same symptom that was too ridiculous to be true, igniting fear, panic and even fleeing of some from the village. Fear psychosis gripped the village and the night turned out to be real graveyard with none daring to come out. Yet the monster killer was unstoppable and preyed on its whims and fancy he found interested in. Some time later, some bravadoes came in pursuit, found it going in the grave, a ghost in the human form, formed into a beetle and sneaked inside with a hole little bigger than its small body; a small hole was found beside the cross, fresh grave, with the wreaths still hanging around with withered leaves and flowers. Palmina could well imagine the scene. It was chilling and goose bumps appeared on her arms and she shivered, moved closer to the lantern lighted dimly orange and stood in between where her friends closed in, looking with intensity at the teller who seemed to keep it suspense; the other girls were no better, their eyes too widened in fear, closed around the three older male adults and hold their hands; they laughed aloud; the footsteps echoed clucking outside the house, the loose and familiar footsteps; the girls sat straight, their body stiff with deep breaths, tensed and with their widened eyes listened aptly; their imagination of the horror character of the stories they just heard seemed too real now; Jentilla relaxed first, and she announced with a smile her father had come; indeed he came in; a tall lean figure, in grey half sweater above long sleeve light blue shirt tucked inside grey trouser above a loose black leather shoe he wore with a pair of ash colored socks; his thin face gave a weak smile, his sunken eyes with complete haggard, the top of his grey hair stood with walking; without a word he went inside to the bedroom, left clucking sound by his oversized shoes; the teenage in her came matured and the humanity in her felt compassion; a teacher in a government school, he struggled to feed his nine children with Jentilla among her sibling was the fifth, with a meager salary he earned monthly; the extra tuition he gave to some children nearby made no difference; the wife with no meat for a single meal throw tantrums not the children; the vegetables green was their favorites; Jentilla made a quick exit towards the kitchen; her routine to feed and serve her father she loved most and she his; she put two spoonfuls of rice on the plate and brought a bowl of fish curry nearby and poured a glass of water from the jug; she watched him smile at her and took a mouthful from his hand; she made no way home, stayed with Jentilla, squeezed herself on a single bed without a movement to be disrupted by the angry voice with her name called out later in the near mid night; a woman stood outside, lantern in one hand, her eyes angry, face complete grim, hair in total disarray and gave her earful on the way back home. Discipline.

At eight thirty in the morning, she finished her brunch, washed utensils from the other night and filled half of the barrel with water; the chapel in the missionary school where she goes start an hour later; the late arrival for the chapel meant the late bench in the left wing with the question and punishment later, she very much was dreaded of; fifty minutes to bridge the gap in between; the navy blue skirt she wore faded with a dull look due to much washing; her pride for the whole last year but a cause of embarrassment this year; they all wore new skirts in the class and she too longed for one but settled uncomfortably with the crunched; the maturity in her understood her parents, their difficulties, their struggles, their need to fend her brothers and sister and their exorbitant tuition fees too and determined in her heart that a day would come to ease their burden unloading on her shoulder something she desperately looked forward and to relief them; a white shirt she wore with it from second hand stall with armies of black dots survived three seasons, a tell tale sign of well worn she wished to discard badly but with no choice given bravely still wore it; a Naughty Boy shoe from below the bed, a big black patch on the left pair prominent had the skirt for the age; a pair of white socks in her hands, she inspected with disdain had loosened elastics on the top; the time waited for none; the voice shrill enough and familiar called her name from the road above; the time for school; Jentilla had impatience as her virtue; no compromise with it, she knew; Just one answer, affirmative from the top voice, hurriedly shoved her socks clad feet into the shoes, grabbed her handloom woven bulky green bag and rushed out; she mounted the graveled steps two at the time, paused on the top and grimaced; Jentilla already moving, impatient, angry.

'Ohhhhhh' He sat on the culvert, cross-legged, a cigarette dangled in between his fingers, out with the smoke and gave mock pitiful look, shaking his head from side to side.

"Why take the pain of going to school? It's no use." He took a long puff and gave white fumes out into the air.

"Why not?" the girls chorused, irritated, their eyes challenging.

'In the end, you will ended only in washing your husbands' dirty under—wears.'

Moren sat laughing at their anger, enjoying. The completely irrepressible man, thought Palmina and threw a vile look meant to silence him with no success and took bigger stride than was before. But she felt her heart elated and smiled alone the whole day in the class her friends caught her smiling alone and whispered in each other's ears. Thick bulky books of the week whole in a handloom woven bag, green with cover, white lines in it remarkably noticed weighed down heavily from her shoulder. It was sewn for school bag of the piece not wide for *gana*, thus into one it was sewn by her mother; she wore with her white shirt, a wide gaping hole on the right shoulder where the weight of her books rested hidden it well. Her class teacher looked at her scornfully the other day with her snobbish chin lifted, her small eyes narrowed almost sleepily, insultingly. Humiliating; it was humiliating. She lowered her eyes unable to meet her eyes and asked her mother for new pair, not for the costly terri cotton but from the sale in Ringrey, the cheapest in sale; but she asked from a carved statue, not flesh and blood human and certainly not from a mother; the week later her sister asked the same; she was brought, the stark white shirt and the old worn shirt fitted her. Hilla had two spares; one faded well worn with half the year she wished to donate for charity. Jentilla enjoyed it. Palmina still wore the old shirt from sale dotted with black. Monica saw it and stared at it hard and long; she lowered her eyes with shame and embarrassment and saw nothing of the twitched mouth insultingly.

Few minutes later, a gang of five came and their mouths twitched; their derisive insinuation said everything she feared. They knew. It hurts. It pains. The wound bled. Palmina felt sorry.

Bolchugri had a tale humming; it reached all ears—women and men, old and young, children and adult. It was early morning still but everyone left home, eager to see what was being said; all are excited; children tagged to their mothers are scared yet eager to watch and they went half believing the story and with half disbelieve. Chinche came early morning and told her so; she passed on the story to Jentilla, then to Mittila, then to Hilla. Milche heard it and they all went to the site, right below Chinche's house. What they saw was unbelievable yet true; the scene seemed the real horror movie; Stones came from all sides; hit the old bamboo woven walls turned white with the age, the sloppy thatch roof above, both of whom stood on the bamboo woven floor rested comfortably on twelve big stones below; nothing in the old house escaped the curse; that was what the huge gathering thought; the stones came with no one in act and from where in sight; it just came from all direction; mysterious, eerie and spooky; the children squirmed, clutched their mothers hand but still curious and waited like others with bathed breath to unravel the mystery, the source; Palmina sat squatted, eyes intent, curious, waiting, small thin lips apart, showing stark four front teeth; Jentilla and Mittila stood near, talking, Mittila mastered over the subject, regaled some experiences of its kind of the village, in and around, proud; Hilla and Chinche more interested in the topic of their own, the latter with the cream colored handkerchief, the embroidery in it with the red and green with the words, "forget me not", the three lettered words in the finishing touch, her hands kept busy, a love token for her new boyfriend; the sun shone, full bright with the summer heat in force, beating in the early morning; the *ojha* came; his worn ash colored pant from sale folded at the bottom, revealed his thick dry cracked foot visible; his fair face in hundred lines not with age but of dryness; his white tee shirt unmatched but he could not careless; the crowd waited for the miracle, to unravel the mystery with the *ojha* as their only hope; he talked to the man stood outside the house with his lean wife beside, her long neck skinny with all blood vessels showing with no flesh on; their two tiny children in tow, holding both their mothers hands; the man seemed expounding; the wife joined, excited, eager, expounding, more in her face than the words; the *ojha* nodded, seemed considering something, his face serious but not that of fear; he began, sat on the corner of the house, began chanting, his mantra; he stood, a small brass pot in hand, sprinkled water in four corners of the house and began chanting; minutes later, the stones stopped but he continued with the things better known to him; there was a stir in the crowd, the smiles, amazed by the sight, the trick of his magic; he stopped not, took a stick and let it led him where and why; the stick pointed towards the thick family of bamboo near the house and led him slowly towards it; he followed; it stopped near to it and stopped; he dug the ground below it and took out the round hairy roots from underneath and held for open display; the mystery solved; the crowd dispersed, satisfied; a few office goers missed their offices and children, their school, walked away with excited talk but shivering.

CHAPTER 11

THE EASTER, VICTORY AND BITTERNESS.

Came early March, too early for the summer rain to come with a shower in the late March that would bring forceful sweeping wind uprooting trees, kicking roofs with little rain damaging this small town and taking toll of people's lives and with it, the changed of season, the lives of both animals and man. In tall Sal trees this small locality was known for, the fresh green leaves emerged out of on the branches, blooming the hearts of anyone seeing them and refreshing their minds. A new fruit bearing mango tree behind their toilet had given much flowers than leaves that covered the whole tree where the bees hovered, sucking and humming filling the silence of the house. White petals of flowers clustered in the long straight young and tender branches of an old drumstick tree, the giant black bees rain-bowed their whole bodies, both mouths and bottoms touching the nectar, flying away with the flowers with rat tailed drumsticks ignored, their juice dried, seemed safe from the suckers. The hailstorm would come heavy; her mother said by the sight, creasing her forehead in worry and went on burning the dead banana leaves outside the kitchen without further a word, intent. Black ants lined up in thousands, white food bigger than themselves in their mouths, unending and heading towards the hole near the main post of the toilet; the sight that made her mother to say heavy rain would follow suit. The shrieks, screams, shouts and laughter echoing in the Saturday evening, coming from a long broad road, a playfield for children that ran between the rows of houses on both sides, below, filled the small part of this town. Every player of the game was scattered on all sides, some on the North, some South, some on the

East and some on the West while on the middle stood a tall thin man with a black face with an ugly scar on his forehead which ran down to near his left eye and a curly hair with cloths-made ball under his grip beaming with a triumphant smile that gave him a satanic look, his stark white teeth prominent guarding the seven round flat stones fallen on the ground from being piled up. Hilla crept up from behind; he suddenly turned, aimed the ball at her, pelted, missed the target and it went rolling down far below; with a glee, they piled up and the game was over and they won. The winning team again piled up the stones, after hitting the pile; this time around 'kalia', meaning black, the devilish looking man, the popular name given to him for his black complexion was smarter, looked here and there, threw the ball passing it round to his team mates and the game turned to their party's way, much to his delight and others enjoyment. The ball hit the piled up stones for the third time, both the teams eager to win and battled to wrest the game from each others' hand that muted Palmina's ears to the calling coming from few meters away from where she stood; Hilla pointed her eyes behind her with a worried frown and the moment she chose to look behind and saw her mother coming like a raging bull with a long bamboo stick in her hand, her intention clear. The other end of the long bamboo stick just brushed her left arm while she trying to evade it from landing on top of her back while she fled from her wrath, escaped, unhurt, straight to face the music in her ears, in the kitchen during dinner in her lone ears.

Much awaited Easter holidays began, a festive weekend for all; the elders for the church service had the special orange juice party organized; the Sunday school children for the drama they prepared and to walk inside the church shouting "hosanna" with green palm branches in their hands, more of ritual than remembrance, the teenagers for the seasonal picnic day on Monday. On Palm Sunday Church grandly celebrated it. They no longer were children but felt on that day like ones. Palmina, Hilla, Jentilla, Chinche, Milche went to church, their hands with green boughs, but Palmina with a betel nut bough impressed others. She walked with pride, felt tall even shortest in height in her cream new butterfly frock, and Milche with a flower printed maxi, flowing right down to her ankle, a brown cock shoe her mother gifted, she was proud of. Good Friday followed suit but meant nothing to the teenagers but waited with fervor for the Monday, a popular picnic day, their spirits high, elated. Chinche with a new boyfriend in the list, a man among girls saw the bonus, a decade older than Chinche's sexy eighteen, two sizes larger, two inches taller, his face double of hers, the shape of twenty paisa, that Palmina thought as wide enough for helipad, though she had seen none, the hair in small curls like a steel wool critical of her choice both within and outside, within her ears and without her hearing it but not hurting her. Her distaste of the grey pant he wore so low below on his hips with a red cotton underwear for pure show had Palmina wondering the choice and taste Chinche had degraded herself into and openly showed it. Her former boyfriend Chinche had dumped for him had the looks, charm and anything a girls cook look for. She thought her friend made a mistake or perhaps it was her making drastic judgment she never had inkling. Palmina knew what to speak to Chinche and also what she loved to hear. Chinche loved to hear her being complimented and could not put her finger whether her words were compliments or flattery. While she denigrate him and Chinche lowering she flattered her and said she deserved someone thousand better than him with her beauty that lifted high of her spirits and sent her smiling. He was in his last, in the engineering college he went, a man Chinche love loyally for three years in row more for loving his status, security and money he stood for than loving him for who he was.

The money was collected, twenty each, Palmina gave out of the piggy bank, saved from the year last, in a earthen piggy bank, whatever coin she got out of her daily allowance that she collected more than hundred, Jentilla with her father's mercy and the rest with no worry seen the day. Milche had the doted mother for a donor and Chinche with her boyfriend's charity. Hilla spent the day in a family picnic. They gave much importance to family gathering than to mix with their neighbors. But On Sunday, all went for shopping. The market streamed with easter shoppers. Palmina and her group had their eyes and lips full of smiles while marketing, opened only on the day in a year's Sunday. They carried each tomato, potato, pumpkin, onion, green chilies, garlic, ginger, *garam masala,* meat *masala* and two kilos of fish and a chicken. Three kilos of pork with hairs removed and cleaned, their skin burnt removed and cut into pieces, then boiled waited for the Monday in Chinche's kitchen. The utensils are carried on the day; two karahis, each with Palmina and Jentilla holding, two aluminum pots, four steel spoons, one plate each, steel glasses too and pair of clothes for changing after swim. They headed for the river side, a popular picnic spot, beside the green-blue river with big rocks sprouting their black heads, inviting but for the chasm in between. In the past noon after half the days journey of trudging and hiking the jungle pathway to the spot, the plump leech stuck on Chinche out of the dwarf way—side wet grasses since it rained the night before swollen fat with her blood; she screamed kicking when the blood red spotted on her feet and saved by her beau smiling indulgently. He lifted her feet tenderly and removed it with a stick. He then squeezed the green juice out of the roadside herb and dabbed it. The herb worked magic and her bleeding stopped. But she walked all the remaining way clinging like a limpet onto his arm and screaming for even a small earthworm crossing sides. The river bank saw parties of picnickers on either side. The smoke ascending from all corners and bushes with triangular *chulha,* was common to all; they chose the shade below the ancient giant banyan tree, its sturdy giant roots crawled over the massive rock like tentacles sloping towards the deep blue river filled with shrieking and shouting with the children hanging onto old motor tyres. They were floating black in the deep, a life saver. The sound of the swimmers splashing mostly drunken men was a sight to watch.

'Where is my panty? Where is my panty? Where is my panty?' a man wade from the shallow shore towards the deeper middle, beating the water angrily in searching. He was drunk with his eyes red, near naked saved for his brown underwear he was unaware of wearing. His penis stood erected with the cool water; his underwear was not protecting its ward, then fell into the water, splashing over the swimmers; Palmina watched it smiling. She embarrassed at the same time; Jentilla too. She was worried too as the man waded further into the deep; the water closed into his chest. He looked as if not in condition to swim. It was the timely help of his friend who came and pulled him back into the shallow water that saved him. Everybody knew how the water was; very wild few dared to mess up with. It had taken many lives and kept taking every year. Every time Palmina waded into the knee length water her heart skipped beating thinking perhaps she was the next. She avoided water like the plague. The sun was hot, beating, its impact on the glittering white sand, their feet on it burned. Chinche cooked; tomato and pork were her specialty, Milche tried her culinary skill with chicken and potato; Jentilla with fish and potato; the rest gathered firewood from the nearby jungle where it stocked the year round and Palmina with a salad enjoyed the day; she sunk her feet on the hot sand, scorching, her feet burning. With the red flower as her aim she slowly walked towards it and heard the voices. It was the couple sat on the shade, right in the beach with the tall grasses blessing and protecting them from the scorching summer sun and she peered, unseen by them; with her thigh rested against his, her slender soft hands well within his rough hands, her slender fingers were under inspection, lovingly by the pair of male gaze while he nuzzled his stubble chin on her swan neck caressing, froze her. She rooted on the spot, stealth behind the grasses and sat facing the sun, eager at the same to know how the couple talk and unashamedly eavesdropped.

"You are so pretty." He muffled.

"Hmmm . . ." she giggled and teased him.

'I took from my mother.'

"She must be beautiful." It was a genuine praise.

'She was. She died when I was ten.' Sadness tinged.

"Do you miss her?" a concern.

"Yes, when my brothers became a burden."

"your father never care?"

Silence but it was the answer.

'I need somebody to lean on to. The burden was heavy.'

A small muffled voice.

Then Silence reigned.

The food was good, tasty; the dry fish chutney Jentilla made hot with much green chilli and shot her nose upward at the praise that was her pride and Palmina's envy; none said anything and she knew why; her sentiment matters and the friends cared. They made home in the early evening. The forest on the other side was already moving and breaking of bamboos already heard around. With the big dropping they saw both old and new the late afternoon was threatening and made for safety zone but saw instead the dilapidated house quite nearby, trampled with its big logs divided by the herd. Palmina stuck in her tongue, found the two girls sat on the rock with the two others wading. Their steps were slow with the blue-green water soaking till their thighs, sickle in one hand for their own protection with the river known well for its wildness. Palmina watched, helpless while the others frantically waved and called her but she shook her head in negative with her imagination ran wild with the electric eel electrocuting.

"Careful. Don't go to the water." Her mother's repeated warning still rang in her ears and pulled her. They had other effects too—scared her.

It was the first time she was allowed out for a picnic with friends and she dared not jeopardized her future outings. Perhaps her mother thought she was old enough for picnicking with friends she always forbade. But when they returned home late in the evening in the dusk she had something waiting. Her mother had changed from loving and caring person to an angry raging bull ready to attack. In the evening later she escaped physical hurt but had her ears blasted. Tochi—ma came in the morning and dropped everything she desired to drop, not a mince of single word. Bitterly. Angrily. An avenging angel. She willed the man Chinche chose to be her brother in law, to the youngest sister sitting in one class two yearly and in her eight class, beauty without brains whom she brought solely for one thing in mind. Marriage. It escaped out of her hand. She called Chinche all names and pushed venom into her mother too. Now her mother tarred her with the same brush Chinche was tarred and blackened her day. She got a warning. Chinche was a bad influence.

The electricity, the grey haired man, his loosely worn shoes rested without clucking informed others coolly their locality was being blessed with the next, the local Member of Legislative assembly acceded finally, he said. The male elders in the locality met in the headman's house; Palmina's father, headman, Tochi-pa amongst others listened attentively. The talk of it began long time back, said a short thin man smoothened his moustache, twirling, showing off with none noticing but everyone ignoring him pointedly. A primary school, he said of the next locality would be gifted. Everybody talked, their voices loudly above others; nobody listened. Excited. The talk rose to excitement, tea was served, white and pure milk brought by kancha, owning dozen cattle; the pain, tension and shame forgotten, someone remarked excitedly and his painstaking effort paid, he added much with exuberance looking at the grey haired man with loosely worn shoes. The next month, big posts were brought, erected, a short gap in between, the lines connecting each. A triumph. With one man's effort, the whole lot gained but the effort went thankless, the man went out quietly, silently in his style, humbly; the elders basked. Everyone talked about it. The old and young, teenagers and children, lauded the grey haired man with loosely worn shoes. Benta—pa tried in vain effort to pull the credit to himself. Everybody ignored. It was Jentilla's pride but Hilla's jealousy. With the years passing life style in Bolchugri began to change; a black and white portable television made entry in Hilla's sitting room, an Onida, she was proud of and much boasted of in the class as well amidst the neighborhood friends who waited on the Wednesday evening for 8.30 show, an hour before, her plush sitting room packed, on the carpeted floor, on the *moorahs,* the chairs for the family left, empty no matter and for none spared. The Knight Rider shown in Bangladesh television channel was much hyped of and not wasted. The channel was gifted. It gave much programme than DD—1. The reason was simple. The place was close to Bangladesh. They showed much English channel than Bangladeshi films they were delighted with. The night was too hot and with the sweat slicking the girls sat with a lone man amidst near Chinche, too close for anybody's comfort but not close enough for the couple's want. The black car talk. It drove by itself and it was a wonder car and much loved with by its owner as well by the viewers. When it was over, Chitrahaar began in the Indian channel the girls went gaga over. With the free air in flow fanning, outside the door, the magic box in direct view, kept on top of the four storied show cased, eyes glued smiling on the girls singing, hands flailing, the men chasing them around the trees, pulling them gently from the tip of their *sarees* while the heroine came closer, shyly unable to meet his eyes, turning away.

The evening next when the sun set, the women clustered, blocked the narrow pathway, stood in a circle, their backs to their houses, their dinner over.

'You know, I heard he embraced her last night in Hilla's courtyard.' One injected.

'Shameless. How could he in full view?'

'But I heard he tried to kiss her but she averted.'

'I heard he fondled her.'

'Itching always. She asked for it.' One spat.

'Slut.' It ended.

Dogs barked every night, mercilessly. Balluk ran up down the steep below the house, charging, then retreating frightened by something or someone. Her mother stayed awake for few nights alerted with their dog. Their barking disturbed their sleep, frightening the children and angering the elders. A furore arose. Everyone was agog and made enquiries. Few nights later, the neighborhood announced a hen—thief. Two fat roosters with mother hen reported stolen by Tochi-ma. She announced it the early morning later loudly and angrily. The mother hen left twelve newly hatched chickens motherless she angrily declared pointing at none but Bangladeshi refugees on the other side of the stream. The next night utensils in Benta-ma's kitchen are lifted and the furore began—a new pot, karahi, two vessels are lost; a meeting was called; short stocky man headed, decided, all in unison, a need to guard the locality, the area surrounding and for the young male blood the responsibility shifted; three tall burly men with long daggers sheathed, coiled around their waists with their daggers gleaming even in the dark crossed the locality the night before, someone announced blindly; all ears perked, tensed and the truth not proved but believed blindly but the twelve young male selected said not to worry,

'uhh . . . they will be like this,' his little finger stood before the male elders, while his mouth compressed, a real challenge and a show of his bravado; 'my fists are itching . . .'

Gongsin oiled his tight fisted hand, smoothing, his teeth clenched; impressed, the male elders ended the meeting; they were satisfied; their duties are done and their worry over; they now had the young brood to care of; they were being volunteered. The guarding began on the full moon night, all armed—daggers, knives, iron rods and one or two with guns, one that of the village headman and other that of her father, Palmina approved not with no voice to reprove but rather infused with courage. With their duties alternatively done the guarding stretched for three four nights when the families slept soundly, beyond caring. When the dog began to bark, Palmina took comfort from the locality guards and turned to sleep with no iota of worry. The moonlight night left the short stint, vacated their area; the nights began with simmering dark, and the new month entered; with it, the male young blood and the stories began at the daybreak; Moren with her father's double barrel *cartouse,* he got after much persuasion. He pleaded from his father reluctant for it. He was warned it kicked hard and he had no knowledge of but two cigar size red bullets with hundred pellets inside with Gongsin in company. They both chose Tochi-pa's kitchen, sat waited below mango tree behind for the unseen enemy. They both faced opposites with a big distance in between, their backs towards each other and with the night growing into middle, both moved slowly, their steps backwards but still facing where they faced, opposites. When the wolves began howling in the nearby jungle, their backs touched, bumping into each other. They both turned swiftly, one with a gun loaded with his fingers in the double trigger and the other with the gleaming well—sharpened dagger out of the sheath, ready. It was the shout and the instant recognition that averted the disaster. Both hearts started beating, pounding faster than the super express train they lost control of. The night saw the guards their duty half done. The guarding stopped.

She cried, a strong woman who faced much hardship in life. Her tears cascaded in droplets down her cheek and tasted in her mouth. It had been long, a very long time since she last cried. She lost her child, her first child, much before Benta was conceived. Time was different then. Life was beautiful. She had a husband, supporting and comforting her with his arms. Today, she had none. Life had taught her what she was made of. Insult of this evening was too painful to bear.

"Don't bring all that crap to me. If you want sugar, take, but don't tell me all that." The words rang again and again, in her ears and filled her mind and nearly drove her crazy—shame, embarrassment and pain. The memories flooded, revived of old unforgotten fifteen years. The house of wooden floor, L-shaped, wide verandah, the wooden chairs in a sitting room, pork dried hanging above the *chulha* hearths, beef too and the freshwater fish for almost every dinner; he was a fisher man, a hard worker, a teacher in the primary school but kept her like a princess; a good husband, a good father, lulled their infant daughter to sleep with the feeding bottle; she slept fitfully and awoke the morning next to the sucking infant; he overslept and said nothing; she saw him no more and heard no more but guessed he must have re-married and felt instant jealousy for the faceless woman he must have devoted with no right to do so. It pained to blame herself. She shifted the blame—he was away constantly, in the place he worked; she blamed the business he ran too, trading of areca-nut from their village to the traders of Assam. She was contented; he was not; she thought of present; he thought of future. She missed him often. He understood not. Even the lonely nights she spent. He came as his friend, gave his hours. Hours stretched into days. Later on nights too. He filled the gap his absence caused. He brought her here, in the middle of the night, stole from the man who loved her, his promises unending she had dreamed on and hoped. She had him by her side—hours, days and nights, that meant nothing now. In the heat of embarrassment and shame.

'I will keep you like a princess.' She smiled sarcastically with pure disgust, looked up the ceiling, the tiny holes in it with sunlight filtering and the inundated rooms in the rainy season, not owned but charity by the village headman, a short stocky man with extra properties he no longer could manage, the one where they housed in had a vast betel nut trees surrounding, the fruits stolen every season with no caretaker, a kind hearted husband of a distant cousin of her; the foodless nights she spent, alone, her stomach churning, groaning empty but above all the shame. Palmina-ma, this evening shouted at her angrily, she was ashamed of but thought of the breakfast and worried.

In the deadness of the night when nothing but barking of the dogs are heard, the full round moon disappeared behind the clouds feared by the forceful sweeping wind kicking the roof of their house; the poor tin lost the nut keeping it intact giving a loud flapping sound awaking the huddled sleeping families, sat them straight on the beds, their eyes wide awake; the second wave of wind struck forcefully; the tiny flame of lantern fanned wildly, threatened black-out but she shielded it, her own body blocking it, no matter how terrified of the wind and the impending storm. On the big double bed three boys slept, huddled, one still in a mother's breast, his eyes wide awake, uncared, intrepid but his food as his sole interest; the third wave came more forceful than the second and hit the wooden window and gave a crashing sound with their bodies trembling and terrified but for the mother, their pillar and a strength; a tall betel nut tree near the house moved sideways seen through the ventilation below the roof, swaying from side to side; more and more wave came and the whole world seemed enveloped by the thundering force. The sound was eerie and their house gave a creaking sound with the drum beats in her heart only sound with the thought what was next; it was followed by the light rain, blown inside through the little ventilation and wet their heads and the bed sheet; a shack in the corner covered the ventilation and with it the wetting stopped and with it the relief; the way it came it made an abrupt exit to where and how but would come the next day or the other; it was her season and they were at her mercy and its victims—the poor not the rich with solid buildings; the family lay asleep, dreamless, relaxed and fearlessly much later in the night only to awake to the streaming sun, the birds chirping and rubbed her eyes painful though for lack of sleep but rushed out with her slippers on to see the night's damage. The front house with leaves strewn, short polythene bags, two dirty shacks and a big branch invoked grimace out of her; the world looked like a garbage dump and she a cleaning girl the whole morning and left it spotlessly clean and missed the class much to her chagrin.

CHAPTER 12

THE PAIN, THE LOST AND DETERMINATION.

The full moon chose, every month in the month last to bloom. It has no jealousy, fear, but unrivalled, gave its finest bloom; the lovers, the couples and the children benefited much. They enjoy basking in its bloom and chose merry making half the night long. The flowers smiled, the trees too, the river water silvery danced, gleefully over the rocks under its bloom; the world too drawn, the magnet too strong enjoy with it; he was the patron of it all; the children too, came out, from all surrounding neighborhood, gathered in her place; National Panasonic, the family's pride, two in one, single speaker brought from Baghmara, an international border town with Bangladesh, sat on top of a wooden table, played "I am a Disco Dancer" followed by "Jimmy . . . Jimmy . . . Jimmy . . . Aaja . . . aaja . . . aaja . . ."; the children shook their legs, wrenched their bodies, imitated Mithun, her parents their good audience, their faces in moonlight with smiles, their eyes in the dark beset with pride; the moon still bloomed late, at night when the other children, their faces glistened with sweat, took out their clothes, some fanning themselves with the old hard cover of the exercise book, desired to leave; she dropped Jentilla home, Milche, Hilla, along with. Chinche had outgrown dancing with them. She chose dancing in her own way. With the man she chose. Something different. Erotic. Seductive—the art she had mastered and they all are innocently ignorant. Halfway on the roadside stood a tree, below on the raised big roots sat a human form, silent; the moonlight showed the face; they went near; Mittila, sat, alone, her face with full of tears streaming, sobbing pitifully; they asked her why; she replied not but averted her face to one side; with her hands clutched around her, head rested on her knees; they sat, sympathetic, but mostly to unravel the truth, to help; it took long but it came out, in the open, the truth; a dirty truth. The painful truth. She would go home, tomorrow, to the village where she belonged, Tochi-ma told her so; the children understood not why it was a bad idea; she talked not more but the children probed more, then out, she blurted, the truth in the open, shocking them; she was accused, she just said, nothing more; it was enough; she whimpered, her hands around her folded legs, chin rested on the knees, wound too raw, open, like a wounded kitten The morning next she was gone, disappeared. Jentilla heard it first and spread it later. They looked at each other; a knowing look; an understanding look; look of pain and sadness not for themselves. Tochi—ma later took the tale around; the neighborhood was fed with her version. She let her go and paid her bus fare. She was lazy, irresponsible, slow in work and a bad character. Neighborhood listened only with half ears. Palmina remained silent. Her year's saving took her home. Bolchugri heard of her no more.

They thronged the road on Thursday—men, women and children, laughing, talking excitedly, eagerly sped towards the top of a long step; it took no time to learn where and why; an *ojha* was coming; some mysterious happening in the neighborhood; in a headman's house. A *beera* creating havoc, stealing women's knickers, hanged outside at night for drying, to be found in the cattle-shed of a couple of massive Jersey cows of their neighborhood; she saw him the other evening before, the owner, his tall head down in shame with his wife, a short fat woman in tow. When heard of it first, Palmina covered her mouth and giggled shyly. Her mother stared at the informer open mouthed. It took few seconds for her to grasp and then she relayed the story to her husband. Her husband took it in a light hearted banter and erupted with a chortle of laughter. It was nothing new. But it was a laughter at somebody's expense and took a gig at the man for his self fun the man took it as no banter.

'I heard you are collecting women's under-wears and bras in the cowshed' her ever ready to tease father spoke casually, partly teasing, partly conversing, an effort to pump out the truth of the gossips, his eyes with smile; his face went red, purely embarrassed, muttered something incomprehensible under his breath, only his eyes slitting said about his anger; the wife too muttered something, obviously conveying to him the message both took it hard, shame faced and with pure outrage; must be shame or embarrassment Palmina thought and annoyed at her father for his insensitiveness. The subject seemed touchy for the couple and understandably so while for the people it was pure fun, an entertainment they all needed; curiosity and excitement made her the tail of the throng; she called her friends along. Jentilla was excited. Milche grinned half believing yet went along. Hilla was plainly curious. Chinche joined them later, half interested and other half of her mind purely somewhere else if her eyes darting here and there and her disinterest in their excited chatter was anything to go by. An *ojha* was there already ahead of them stood with his back on the people watching the scene, at the open cowshed with just plain thatch roof above sheltering the two brown jersey cows inside. He seemed engrossed with his near bald head on a tall stature shining with excessive oil, his sparse hair combed back showed his scalp, his eyes red, his thirty two teeth black-red, stained with much betel nut eating; tiny red particles oozed out from both corners of his mouth, repulsing, dirty; but he stopped not put another into even before it finish; Saturday, Tuesday and Thursday were the only days the magic works he told the gathering and began his work. He mixed the soil at the foot of the Neem tree with water, smoothened it, spread plantain leaves beside, bananas and a chicken with a throat slit placed on top of it. He fingered out a vermillion of the tin container, with it red dot on top of the smoothened soil and began chanting *mantras*; in the midst a male Jersey cow mowed loudly, almost like a shriek but he gave not in but resumed till it gave a last very loud heart-rending mow that could have twisted anything; he seemed relax; the cow looked calm and tired, not agitated like he was before; that was it; he had chased *beera* away. The cow he began chewed a male *beera* herb; a bachelor, frustrated and fascinated only by women and thus their inner-wears.

The evening darkened into the night with total darkness all around; the electricity a luxury few families are blessed with, not their locality but rather cursed with the black pitch nights with few nights of blessing of the moon towards the end of the month; the lantern the only light lighting in the dark and gas lamp the people used for occasions are cast aside but Bolchugri still cried for street lighting without which the darkness itself was terribly horrifying; the road ahead wrapped fully in the dark cautioned her to tread carefully; her whole body was engrossed in it, her legs, hands and mind; a soft foothold below her feet sank, the ground beneath sandy, ready to give away, to sink, to drag her below; the gorge below was an open-mouthed monster to swallow; she with great caution stepped her sandal feet into each foothold, reached the other side safely and heaved a huge sigh of relief; with the worst one crossed, the graveled *kutcha* road posed better, wider, safer; she walked down, blindly, slipped and fell but rose and resumed her pace, ignored the pain accompanied by her fall. Deep within she felt a slight tremor, a lone walker on the deserted road, in the darkness; not for another human but for untouched and unseen force something she often heard but have not seen; her imagination ran amok—a headless, legless form in stark white dress brought goose bumps all over; her imagination came true; in the darkness an outline of a tall figure headed towards her, his big strides ready to dwarf her any moment dangerously menacing; she shivered with fright; her heartbeat quickened, beating erratically and she felt she heard her own heartbeats drumming loudly; her mind was filled with five letters—GHOST; she blinked several times, did a cross sign with the hope to vanish it, vainly; the moment of sanity made her remember the best ghost busters, an action, an advice given by her friends in the class; the dark shadow kept moving more towards her, unheeded, closer each second with no way to escape; the road was narrow and straight; on the right a solid wall blocked her desperate wish to escape; on the left was a sharp steep where if she fell she'd break her bones; she thought she would faint, closed her eyes with no solution in mind, waited for it to cross and to walk away; but no; the ghost spoke and voice was very near. It was a familiar male voice tinged with concern and called out her name suddenly; she opened her eyes, relief with instant recognition and warm; she looked up; the tall and hefty man towering over, silhouetted against the back drop of faint light coming from the Indian Oil Petrol Pump in a far distance, his dark and handsome face hidden by the blackness of the night with only his white teeth shown, she spoke, delighted with bright hope inside and her drumming with fear turned into different sound; he asked curiously the reason of her outing at night; from her friend's birthday party, an instant reply came on her lips, an outright lie yet safer; he asked why in the dark and doubted her bravado that faltered her words and gave her earful for walking alone at night; It was true in the real sense but no admittance in her mouth of her fear; with the last order of the big brother not that he was but acted like one, he moved where she knew not and without further ado, hurried home, groping in the darkness relieved at the same thanking heavens for him;

the road towards home seemed endless, more risky than safe with the area below the locality's lone church eerier, more scary and for her dangerous with the old belief it was haunted; Just the tall Sal trees, outlined in the pitch dark like hundred nemesis above the road, below the imposing still church stood majestic on the top hillock, chilled the inside of her deeply; she shivered, scared beyond belief, her heart beat drumming loudly in her ears but braved the dark till her last ounce of bravado and ran with super rapidity and crossed the danger zone; the road basked in the bright illuminated from the green painted concrete RCC house, half constructed with provisioned for three but only with two rooms done and relieved, to be short lived; from somewhere in the compound corner the dog rushed out, barking; his attention riveted purely on her though she posed no danger to its owner; the door banged opened suddenly; the bulky woman came out; her intention obvious, to check the focus of their dog; saw her, strained her eyes to get the correct view; a corner of her mouth twitched; she shouted at the dog to stop barking and went inside; the dog with the stern command went into immediate obedience and she shook her head and cursed herself; she a night hawker would be the victim of the woman's stretchable mouth, the venue would be the school where she taught the high school students; the base from where it would grace the four town corners; the bitter smile with a remembrance the number of times she, the target of her bad tongue and the tarnished image; the church felt real empty without her on Sundays; she knew and never missed, a 'holier than thou' attitude she wore to everyone around and she painted as a worst sinner; the tomorrow's headlines would make her; she in the continued walking with imaginary figure in mind, the dread of meeting it and the long stretchable dark graveled road with sharp curve before their house had high numbers with horror stories, exaggerated or real but nonetheless she shivered with her whole body trembling; the glimpse of pitch darkness waiting seemed ready to swallow her but braved herself, went into it and ran for her dear life till the gate that marked their compound came to view; she paused, took a deep breath and sat on the top of the step leading down to the house, relaxed, unwind. Nobody knew why she went out. She needed to get away, to relax her mind, to think, to dream, to plan for the future, a strategy to achieve her goal. The house stuffed her mind.

Palmina sat on top of the step below the paved footpath; sweat made her grey cotton shirt wet; her thick cotton pant gave her unbearable heat;

she pulled the bottom of her pant up to her knee, let her legs got the much needed air. It was a hot summer night but the soft breeze came from nowhere, fanned her body and dried her sweats away; silence stretched all around; the world seemed in sound sleep; the cry of the child of a neighbor and the dog barking are the only sound comforting; it must be near midnight but her wrist without watch was no help; it was time for her to go home and sleep; the I style tinned roof half constructed house looked uninviting and unwelcome; she dragged her body down unwilling with less enthusiasm but with no option; the house with provision for three rooms in reality had only two; the third room bare and wall less, an eyesore; the house loan taken over without completion but left to pay it; its completion a luxury the family hardly could afford. The faint light came from St. Mary's school shone on the tin roof reflecting on her eyes and outshone the dim light coming from the room inside; unwillingly she descended the rocky steps just wide enough to put her feet, reached the last two steps; balluk came wagging his tail at the bottom step, licked her legs, nuzzled his face and made snorting sound; it spoke of two things, one that of question of her where about and the other he missed her; she stroked his head, a gesture of love and affection and headed towards the door with no latch; it stood ajar, expecting her; She pushed it very slowly with caution; the whole family in deep sleep, she knew; her mother a very light sleeper; she was apprehensive of entering but with no alternative; a harsh voice demanded of the identity; she responded, a reply that was barely audible, for fear of reprimanding; the tone in the next question showed no softening; she replied in the same level of tone; the next question of where about was harsher than ever accused her of some criminal act she never did; it was a birth day of her class mate, the lie was easy; it muted her mouth, stopping the barrage of words; On top of the high round table in the corner, a lantern stood, its chimney blackened with the shoots and reduced the light; the flame gave dim light to the whole room; a sight of her mother sleeping huddled with her three brothers on the double bed disgusted her; the living condition was a sorry sight; the remembrance of the refugee camps sickened her; nothing could be done; the other room a big godown was half done; the building materials all lay strewn, stocked; nails of all sizes, hammers, saws, wooden planks and blade; a strips of bamboo mat stood in a roll in the corner; she took it out, spread it on the floor, took a thin printed bed sheet from the foot of the bed and spread it on top; a bulky jacket from sale hanging on the ulna, folded, made her pillow; it took no time; she lay her body, flat on her back, her hand on her head and went into dreamless sleep; shouting and screaming came from far distance; it was in the background with no direction but the eyes refused to open with it mind too; it came nearer and nearer till it came close on her ears; she awoke startled; the scream and cry of the terrified mother hen in her coop; her mother shouting at the top of her voice; balluk ran up and down from back of the house to the coop, barking, charging, then retreating; her mother charged out with plastic sandal on, hairs disarray, her loosened *gana* adjusted though none on sight; she too followed suit; stood in the backyard with the coop in front she stood like a mother hen, ready to protect, to defend, her little chicks; she took one big stone and rolled it down towards the stream, balluk still barking; balluk emboldened ran down the slope towards the stream halfway, retreated, daunted by something or someone down; the reason of uproar no one knew but the dog with no voice; fox or hen thief; the people on the other side with more criminal records than the other part, their suspect; balluk frustrated unable to catch still ran up and down; it took minutes but the furore died; balluk too quieted down and made a grunting sound with it silence—the midnight silence; both the mother and the daughter went inside and resumed their sleep but sleep did elude her for a long time; the first phase of the cock crowed; she closed her eyes and knew nothing minutes later, wakened only by the heat of the morning sun and the rude crashing sound; the morning beautiful and bright, serene and relaxed and she with joyous abandon opened her eyes; the next rude crashing sound spoiled and crushed her smile; the lazy bones, and their mother a servant, shameless, she muttered loudly; the words so biting, it dragged her on her feet; the first face she saw spoiled her morning, angry, dirty look she gave to her; it was accusing; she felt instant guilt yet not knew her fault; the heap of utensils of the dinner answered her; she took her place. The loud voices from the road above their house created attention to both the mother and the daughter; the elder was the first to go; she too followed suit; both stood at the bottom step and looked up; three men and a woman, their neighbors stood facing, talking, their voices excited; a shop was ransacked the other night; their village headman lose his goods from the grocery shop his wife ran; who, how, and when, were the questioned unanswered and debated; headman was livid and had given the matter to the police with police still finding for the clue. She too listened, calculated, then

146

something dawned and she knew; nobody suspected him; and she stuck her tongue in, steadfast. Her love for him waned.

A white packet of gold flake with the top cover open lay on the table in front. Slim white cigars loosely kept stuck out of it inviting anyone looking at it. A new silver lighter lay beside. With one cigar stuck out from between two dark lips below the thin moustache, the tips on the both ends straight up, Benta-pa relaxed on the arm chair, his back rested behind with her father sat on the moorah.

"Drut . . . drut . . . drut . . . drut . . ." His hookah stood in front something he never cast even with the time when the world around him no longer smoke hookah. He too was relaxed, just reached home for the weekend, complained of heat and demanded for two cups of good tea. Palmina knew what good tea meant—strong tea with overdose milk, topping with the cream; for him a light tea was a total distaste, he called it 'saheb tea' and she knew what it meant, "English tea." She wondered the source of gold flake with a *mantu beedi* cast aside, soon to be answered;

'Benta—ma dreamt of a man with a snake in his hand upside down." He said began slowly not looking at her.

'I calculated it and came up with 76 (seventy six). I have only ten rupees in my hand.' He finished mischievously; perhaps he saw her narrowed inquisitive eyes when placing tea cups on the table and felt obliged to tell.

'In the evening when I went to the shop, the slate has got the number boldly written in chalk. Deep inside she felt the need to, believed what she heard only to hear the truth next morning. Half of the betel nuts, its fruits fully ripe ready, disappeared two nights before from the garden he guarded. Somebody came with the news with him as the culprit who sent off at night fifteen sacks-full. Somebody claimed him seen with the trader of Mankachar at daytime. Benta-pa left early, much to her pleasure; her father had a lot to answer for and she had a lot to ask, confront, not something serious but the truth was out. She opened the old steel chest in the morning, found stack of papers—her parents' marriage certificate, old documents, his certificates, land title deed and others of important nature—some already eaten off by the termites, some torn at all corners, some with the writings already washed off and she did playfully without hurting him but in a jest and his phrase "I passed my matric in first division" stopped. Palmina understood why; A pure motivation to strive and achieve far outweighing him—an encouragement—his tactics for his children. She laughed it off; A smirk never left him alone but plastered well in his face.

CHAPTER 13

SELF DENIAL, A DREAM AND THE LOST.

The late afternoon bell rang, long and unattractive but welcomed by the famished children, eager for home; the wide gate of the corridor packed, jostling with the exit door letting students out at snails pace. The students with no patience too had no option; squeezed in between, Palmina made to the pitch road below, breathed relief, fresh air cooling and waited while Hilla left, said her good bye with Monica and company—the rich friends in school her parents had much encouraged to befriend and avoid the neighbors with the road opened. Jentilla pleaded headache and left half the day. Palmina was not friendless. Tina, her bench-mate in class came with hand in her shoulder length straight shiny hair in pony tail with much good shampooing that was what she bragged joined her on the road below; Lisha, too joined the duo, another of her seatmate in the long back bench where they sat, chosen more to talk but less interest in the teaching; Palmina much loved the topic her two seatmates chosen to talk-the boys—and tasted in imagination what she had not tasted in reality—love, emotion, smooching—Lisha was beautiful with silky locks, flawless skin on oval face, thick sexy lips smeared with lipstick and tall with perfect ten body. The former of the duo was the envy of every girl and the chase of every boy; moments often came to her with wishful longing for half her looks Palmina was never gifted; the latter of the duo was blessed with a pretty face, the only daughter of a class one contractor with an open display of their wealth, counted by the number of cars owned and envied by all, no less in look but often with inferior in thought yet unaware of the sparkling male eyes on her; with short curly hair, plump dark face and the body of the boy than girl she drove the boys ten feet away, she neither cared nor worry but her dream utmost in mind she scurried on towards it; but in her heart of hearts, a secret hope nurtured for a day unknown to be loved, cared, treat her like a princess and to feel like one too; the dream remained in the deep, waiting to be unlocked, the faceless nameless man waiting to sweep her off her feet like any other teenage girl; a horn blew in behind and the three girls turned their heads backwards and was greeted with the open topped modified jeep, stylish for the day and halted just behind the trio with few inches of gap; a handsome teenager with slanting eyes, dusky round face, straight black hair in levy jeans and black tee shirt with white letters across sheepishly smiled and with his magnetic charisma pulled one of them sat behind the wheel; Tina stepped aside and went near the jeep with a shy smile. Her two friends crossed the PWD pitch road to the other side and waited on the concrete footpath, impatiently; she watched the couple, their exchanged of words, their action, paired for two months in running with mixture of both happiness and envy; his elbow rested on the steering wheel, his eyes with a smile and eyes riveted on the love of his life at the moment, he asked her something out of their earshot; the whole day the topic centered on him but their friend looked right and left but not at him and her fingers arranged imaginary lock of hairs fallen on her face; her lips moved, inaudible but the smirk on his face satisfied their curiosity and her answers they well guessed were in affirmative; well matched couple, her friend remark, indeed with both painting the town red; she joined her friends back with unstoppable smile, floating in the clouds among angels. The whole picture was the picture people called 'love'; he started the ignition and zoomed off, date fixed; they needed not asked, both knew, their topic was open secret, still a teasing query of a fixed date got the affirmative answer, much to their delight; without a word all three went with understanding silence, the two with grim faces, purposeful, intent and the other with a permanent dent of a smile the other two are enviously looking; she too wished for that feeling in life and hoped it come sooner; a voice called out from behind for one among three, again but not for Tina, nor her; an old brown jeep halted on the other side of the street under the banyan tree, stood towering and bending protecting rows of shops from the tropical Summer heat, irritated and annoyed Lisha; she shouted rudely to the man behind the wheel with a strong message for him to go and let her walk home, not in it; the three walked with swift pace, left the jeep behind but to be called out again, the jeep a little ahead, stopped, waited; she threw a dirty look at the persistent driver once more and walked ahead; for the third calling she gave a rude marching order to the family driver sent the poor chap zooming in the opposite direction, frightened; a palatial house in sight, both had been in it a good numbers, the last, in the declaration of the Assembly election result with the big feast on, Tina stopped to bade good bye; with a good luck wish and a warning to swollen lips and with a remedy, a teasing remark, she turned; she gave a mock angry face, last; Lisha too warned to be back at night, her parting shot; the two in quicker pace walked in understanding silence broken by the delighted whooping sound from her friend, her eyes clearly few yards ahead; a myriad of college students headed towards, the source of pure delight and two small dents on her fair round cheeks; she scanned from the rows for her friend's heartthrob with a wonder how from a sea of faces one man stood out; with a discreet glance and a low tone, she pointed, she reacted with a swift glance at the far corner to the right side of the road, walking in a group of five, the three women, clad decently In salwar kameez and he stood out in average height with a lean body, his well-oiled short hair looked ready even for a fly to slip and he wore light blue shirt with a black pant, held securely at the waist with a black leather belt, not her choice and critically wondered in Lisha's choice; a sweet boyish face, an instant rejection but the thought she wrapped inside, respected her choice; he passed by with no glance in their direction and she muttered herself being lucky and assurance she'd sleep soundly; dent on her cheeks gave weight to her beauty, her eyes sparkled with happiness, she enjoyed the sight; with his name on her lips, she rolled her eyes upwards while her two palms joined in her heart as if she had just seen an angels, ecstatic, grateful for supernatural force above; she shook her head in open disbelief and laughed aloud; a non stop chatter with one man topic refused to sink inside her head as she too went into a dream of her own; a dream so far away yet near, looked easy to reach and with each step she made towards it every day she knew she'd reach it; a dream of name, fame, respect and admiration—a dream of tomorrow; a voice for the last called out; this time around she complied, went into a passenger seat and called her too inside; she knew why; he had gone.

The sight of the house somehow gave her relief in the hope her empty stomach would fill; a blazing afternoon sun had done nothing but thirst; coupled with thirst and hunger, she hurried down the steps to nothing but silence, absence of her mother; straight into the drawing room she took two three big strides, slid the school bag but the hunger and the thirst blocked her from stripping purple and white uniform and rushed out of the house towards the kitchen; a small steel bowl on top of the old round table survived the first generation, had a long way to go brightened her eyes; she opened the lid, took three pieces of boiled sweet potatoes and reached out for the cup; red tea with sweet potato tasted good for the mouth, perhaps it was the hunger overtook her decision; minutes later, a woman came, middle age, average height, her dry hair in a bun at the nape of her neck, her small face full of lines not of old age but of dryness, a bag full of groceries in her hand; with her burden on the corner an instruction came for her to fetch the evening water from the public tape; a refusal substituting to wash utensils drew dark anger in her eyes, larger with dilated pupils, she had no choice but to retract; 'itching to roam again? And go and sell yourself if you cannot stay at home' were her biting words, unkind, but common, she was accustomed to and hit not the intended mark; "the home is where heart is"; her feet itched every time she closeted herself at home, hated the sight of her angry mother, grumbling and cooking and the vile look given for some household questions she asked; the rude reply to her queries created uneasiness; she hated it all—household work, the angry face and uncomfortable beds; she wished for a good life, good room with a four poster bed, trendy clothes and shoes and to be admired and respected, someone to love and to be in love; but all these her wish nothing in reality; the thought in conflict with reality created frustration that drove her nearly mad; a need was there, unwritten, wordless, to escape from these all, a fresh air for a fresh thinking and to forget the reality; but yes, a day to turn it into reality would come, not today, nor tomorrow but someday in the future, indeed; she just needed to wait, take one step at the time forward, towards where she was going—to the future with one day at a time. A pink pant she wore was the only pant decent, bought with the money her uncle gave her for books. She had been an object of ridicule for it but just smiled and laughed along; a long brown shirt on top she wore along with it was hand picked from the second hand stall and had seen the better days; she owned not a matching pair of shoes but the idea seized her instantly; she peeped below the bed of her brother and the delighted at the sight; she brought the black pair out, dusted with piece of rag and slipped her toes into them, a little loose but fitted at the same; she went to the door, looked right, left and towards the step for the owner but no sign of him that served in her favor; the fear of bumping into him, her mother, she was sure of earful, made her tiptoe out of the house towards the steps and right into the road above the house, led to the pitch road; no one saw her and thought it was her lucky evening; with carefree mind and with a quick pace she started towards the main road from there to the pleasant cool evening of the town; fresh air and cool breeze blew around drying the sweat of the summer heat of the teenagers strewn, the street their favorite hang out; girl sat behind their boyfriends on the scooters and mo-bikes clinging tightly and zoomed off towards the Nehru Park, one or two of her classmates among them with it a sudden wishful longing; other group walked briskly with pen and long exercise book held on their chests meant they meant business and knew where they are going and what they are doing but detested, repugnant for the unglamorous thick big glasses they wore; the other group sat on the culverts in groups, made passing remarks on the passers-by, eve-teased and laughed for the discomfiture ones; but she neither fit to the first nor the second nor the third but a loner, a lone ranger with no group but a dream of her own, the only one without a purpose walking aimlessly like a ship without a rudder, doing work—releasing tension, stress and the stark reality hard to escape but an effort to do it away even for the evening; a familiar voice called out, her name in a woman's lips, she turned, her face behind and saw; Tina sat clinging like a limpet with her boyfriend in front, her hands clenched around his waists; the modified Yamaha black, the mo-bike he drove exuded class, style and sophistication but not surprised, his father was the minister in the government with him won the election last he could well afford one; she wore black jeans and red tee shirt with white bold letters across, her black straight silky hair tied on top of head in a pony tail, a total stunner, head turner; it was a passing wave she gave before zooming off towards Nehru Park; she just smiled at herself bitterly, in self pity.

Then she sat late at night. The books lay opened; her dream imprinted; the flags waving, on the summit. She kept her eyes fixed.

The rain receded, moved out, disappeared with no trace to and where, wordless, unexplained, suddenly; Ganol River shrinked, unfed, uncared, sadly depressed. The rocks once under water sprouted their black heads; three months for the year to end, the world took a sudden turn; wrens and robin deserted once when the rain began returned, flew to and fro, from one tree to another, enjoying, carefree with no sign of crow, she was delighted; black and yellow butterflies began mating in the air, oblivious to anyone with their love obvious and explicit yet delightful; an old amla tree with armies of green round fruits, huddled together stood still behind the house; a small vegetable garden sprung behind the kitchen; onion, tomato, cauliflower, potato graced it, delightful to the eyes; a young gourd sprouted from below, its stem tender green, and cared by; she took care of it, enjoyed, loved it and delighted; it was a pastime, a hobby, she chose for the season. November, the fifth, they all went to a L-style flat—roofed building, with separate sloppy green painted roof faintly receding with the age. The grill in the verandah with a little torn here and there but charmed all the way by the flower pots hanging warmed the girls. From the top to bottom printed curtain in the main door, impressively draped that seemed forbidden for the young girls for entering once before no longer they felt. Hilla stood on the door, smiled in welcome and asked them inside; they entered, hesitant at first shyly into the spacious living room. Two sets of sofa dominated the room with plump cushion on each exuding luxury and lavishness the girls never had experienced at home. The side tables stood in each corner on one of where mounted Indrajal Comics, her fascination and in the middle stood two big square tables. A well-furnished showcase, stood beside the door. It was a three storied, the top with a small portable black and white television in it beside the color photograph, she had taken with her parents on the beach in Goa with a sea on the backdrop and the coconut trees on the left side, standing side by side with her brother in the middle with the wind blowing away their hairs sideways. Phantom comics, his pictures, the stories each comic carried and his jungle adventure with Diana as a main focus riveted her eyes. Diana coming home and then got kidnapped with Rex jubilant with her rescue dragged her eyes away and her mind with the others glued to the old family album. A voice sounded loud, announced the new entry with all eyes on the door where on the threshold stood a beautiful woman, younger than her age and looked slightly elder than Hilla and almost like sisters with fair complexion, her hair cut short, smiled for a brief period and left them all, towards the bed room. A doctor for a mother, a doctor for a father Hilla, pampered and loved chose poor country neighbors for friends, not of their class they approved not but with no choice grudgingly allowed, they said once within Palmina's hearing and she revived within the words he callously said. Palmina shifted from side to side uncomfortably.

With the gap in between Palmina felt the curtain of class drawn, hurt, pierced deep inside that was kept well hidden but healed momentarily with a purpose in mind clear, the future counts and a determination to shape it lay ahead. The flag seemed frantically beckoning and she, eager to reach hurried forward.

The year nineteen eighty eight was an eventful year, something to forget but lots to remember, little to gain but many to lose, little to smile but many tears to shed; the month was the second in the year, neither too hot nor too cold but pleasantly warm, comfortable; January came and gone; the month too cold to bear with the morning and the evenings near the fire outside the kitchen, behind the house, with a small thatch roof, protecting the heaters from the dew drops; three dead big logs lighted the fire; the neighbors too came, sat around the fire, her father was the host and enjoyed the whole month as his full vacation, entertaining them with real events made into comedies; the neighbors talked about the politics, the number of men standing, personality of each, family members each, criticizing, rejecting each and accepting none; an old woman died on the second day of the year; it was a bad omen, Tochi-pa predicted, his face serious, lips compressed and his both palms opened towards the fire, warming; the dog in the neighborhood wailed in three nights of succession, pitiful and predicting something imminent ill in the neighborhood; the dogs, her mother said worriedly knew of the imminent ill or the incoming death; no one spoke but everyone considering the inevitable with each wrapped in serious thought and their faces expressionless in an ominous silence; all seemed to be thinking whose turn; or perhaps still from whose family. Palmina sat still on the *moorah* and pushed the dead logs for fire, blowing it with a pipe with her breath more pumping and brought the flame lighting in the darkness. The silence was daunting and her father felt it too. He cracked some jokes he collected in the village and made everybody laughed. Palmina who sat squatted listening also laughed and moved to the other side evading the white smoke came in her way; her mother a craggy thin woman her face unsmilingly serious, cut the green betel nuts, opening the hard green top with the nut inside out for the guests on the round small saucer with green betel leaves and small white container with lime in it; the white tea brimming in the long cups sweetened with more sugar with the melted sugar sweetened her saliva and still on her lips she licked; the late night saw her with old red quilt with cotton inside turned into many balls made the quilt somewhere thick, somewhere plain red *markin* cloth with cool air penetrating shivering but for the next body warm beside her, a lousy bed partner sharing it, but irritably unavoidable; Every night she got up in the middle unwillingly yet compelled with the cold overbearing and adjusted the quilt for them. But later at night she got up with weight above heavily and found half her body uncovered and pushed into right corner with anger. With a heavy leg on top she spent half the night furiously unloading, rudely pushing and aggressively pulling; one thin blanket and two shawls lay on top add weight to the quilt demand attention every night, three hourly for adjustment. With January gone, Palmina felt slight relief but with a little regret, the month a total rest from hectic school schedule but with new month the school reopens on the third week and she'd be in the higher class adding more books than the last, a whole lot of work load added; a second week came, a welcome diversion with the week of *bara sabha,* a gala event of a huge religious gathering yet less of it but more of a social, meeting people; she went in a church choir, a member in a group but she could neither sing in high pitch nor in low tune, neither in a soprano nor in alto but the shortage of members fixed an easy entry she was grateful for and grabbed, a God given chance; she sang in a group, her contribution in soprano croaky, voice barely audible for fear, enjoyed, met people from all over; when it was over after four days it was a tearful farewell to the throngs of people, she met, befriended and loved; Jentilla loved the river they bathed, washed and the hanging bridge above with the vast green vegetable garden they crossed every morning and afternoon, the sight of thick green cabbages with light green bundles inside, unopened, long green stems of onions, white cauliflowers hidden almost by the long green leaves and coriander leaves; Hilla loved the freedom. With her parents strict disciplinarians, overprotective, hesitated and asked hundred times their choir director to take care of her individually. They let her go with a worried frown, their hearts heavy and watched her till she boarded the bus; Chinche loved it most, found a new boyfriend on the second night, a tall man in black suit, carried guitar, strummed for the group he belonged which Chinche was proud of almost forgotten for the week the boyfriend she had back at home waiting eagerly before he go for his last year of engineering. Palmina skeptical of his skill yet said none. With his straight black hair above an oval face, red thick shawl around his neck, he sat near their choir group their choir director found irritating, lost his cool and said in general but none in particular to behave Chinche paid heed of; Saturday and Sunday thousands of devotees attended, a massive church *pandal* bursting, the loosely bamboo woven walls opened and who is who are expected, counted, and found; Monday morning came, a tearful farewell, Chinche to the guitarist; Hilla to her freedom; she the crowd, the river, vegetable garden but Jentilla laughed, a heartfelt chuckle; she mocked at them all and called them sentimental fools; they gladly accepted, wordlessly; the reserve bus dropped the party at place at the entry road to Bolchugri on Monday evening. With the beddings on the top, the women sitting and some men too lucky enough to sit even the little passage in between rows of seats on both sides with baggage loaded where some young men sat; a young man with a guitar strummed all the way back, entertained others and sang where all joined; Chinche took her best to sit near him and earned innuendoes from others she took lightly; she threw four times, and with the meal all out, the hunger took over; With a thick shawl around her neck, an air bag full slung across, a green polythene with her shoes inside, she struggled, heavily walked with the weight slowing her, pulling her back, on a narrow footpath that led towards home, winding; Jentilla found a man, sympathizer and with her light bag she happily strode ahead, smiling with baggage-less Hilla with a small man in behind with all her burden on, his hands both full, his shoulders not spared, the thoughtfulness of her parents she envied; with the women's bedding the men took care of she shared the light one she carried with Jentilla. A green holder and a thin yellow blanket were her contribution but a mattress and quilt as hers they spent the week in the tent and enjoyed; a narrow lane with pebbles strewn over, tricky to tread yet with caution and care, each step calculative, they walked, nearly lose balance at one point of minute. With the loose pebbles slippery half an hour later she sighted a sloppy thatch roof of the house she left four days back with relief, with it her burden turned lighter and their pace became slower; four men in front walking towards with a stretcher on their shoulders where a man lay still lying on it, his body covered from head to neck, his face uncovered but only his side was shown, hiding his identity; a woman, in late fifties, short in stature, face in pure concern and worry etched, briskly followed behind. Tochi-ma hurriedly kept pace, her face shockingly serious, accompanying with another neighbor, a woman—Milche—ma; the stretcher took left with direction to hospital with the women too tailing the stretcher. Their head on collision was evaded, with an identity of man lying on a stretcher a mystery to the girls but for the grasping sound.

"Father . . ." a familiar voice shouted from behind and footsteps echoed. Jentilla made a mad dash towards the stretcher, her luggage in the road, dumped unceremoniously, carelessly.

'Mother . . . What happened to father?' she shouted, voice full of concern and care with worry etched; a short stature woman answered hurriedly, kept her pace with the stretcher at the same and told her to go home without even a minutes stopping; Palmina knew not what to do; all rooted on the ground where they stood, stared at the grey haired man, his cheeks sunken, his thin lean body with eyes closed with mixed emotion—pity, sorrow, care—the last they saw of him; their mouths wide open with nothing coming out, not even a word of sympathy to the crying girl beside, nor a consolation. Two days later, the church bell chimed, three times, uncommon number and chilling and spoke something to the listeners; it was the number dreaded and brought worry and the hearers questioned wordlessly, in a simple yet heavy query, who's turn; the distance made it barely audible and her mother perked her ears for better hearing while combing her unruly hair flying in the air, her eyes, mind, ears all in full attention towards the church, worriedly tensed; a tinge of tension etched in her voice, a slight sound brought by the wind inside where she sat on *moorah*, sewing torn blouse brought her outside, apprehensive of the meaning; with needle in one hand and blouse in another, she too stood beside her mother, tuned her ears towards the church and the bell rand three times at one go, louder, clearly audible this time brought by the wind.

'Indeed, it is . . .' they both chorused, their uncertain worry and fear confirmed; two pairs of pupils widened; their hands stopped.

'Someone died.' It was her mother who said, unwilling to speak it out but with no choice but it was the truth.

A small compound in front of a long thatch roof thronged with close relative, neighbors and friends was crowded; an old bamboo woven wall showed signs of aging with the bottom part of it destroyed by white termites leaving the gap between the bottom edges of the wall and fresh smoothen earthen floor; it was the main house; the boys dormitory stood facing opposite, L-shaped in joined together with the main house, but smaller than the former, same with the thatch roof, bamboo woven walls and the mud floor with the gap in between for a small pathway for the kitchen behind both; in a small compound a tent was put up, a tattered plastic tarpaulin, supported by a mixture of slim tree trunks and in every corner by fresh bamboo poles with long wooden benches in it, brought from the primary school nearby, still bringing by the neighborhood boys for the entire gathering crowd to sit and to share their grief; a bamboo gate, only entrance to the compound, covered by blooming pink bougainvilleas, adorned by their enchanting beauties seemed welcoming the early comers as well as late comers, both exit and entry; Palmina looked up from the corner where she sat with Hilla, Chinche and Milche along with some neighborly girls, amidst loose fresh flowers sprawled, an evergreen leaves in more abundance, some already graced the round wreath yet unfinished, some on the round bamboo cross with loose fresh flowers in between, at the bougainvilleas and thought about the number of times she stood with Jentilla beside and took photographs amidst their blooming beauties; but today, the flowers looked dull, lifeless, pale with no charm as if sharing the grief; they seemed to know the man who went in and out in the morning and at night would no longer do so; wailing from inside broke in the murmuring of subdued voices outside, in the tent; but no one raised their eyebrows, nor did anybody craned their necks nor objected; the subdued voices and the expression on their faces a tell tale sign of anybody's feeling of sadness, grief, heavy heart; On an instant, Palmina felt the sudden need to be near Jentilla, share her grief, show she cared; she stood, strengthened the legs cramped with much sitting cross—legged, the low stools they were not spared not did they cared, the house like their second home, with an immense effort walked through the crowd, uneasy, with all eyes on her, focused; the narrow passageway between the boys' dormitory and the main house offered no way for the two, she nearly collided with the tall man, his sturdy body pushed blindly, his long neck bend evading the corner, the low roof, his eyes below, from the opposite side; his arms snaked out, steadied her, held her away from physical contact with him; she looked up, startled, eyes on instant recognition, her heart leapt at the sight of him, in total delight;

'Easy. Sister . . .' He threw his disarming smile, gave her heart a roller coaster ride, briskly walked away leaving a teenage girl with a violent heartbeat, he could not careless; the secret love for few months, nurtured, unseen nor felt by any, she termed it 'love', fuelled by one touch she longed for rose like a furnace from the flame. It no longer was a crush but the treatment he meted out to her as nothing but a small sister left her deflated; walking on the thin air, she reached an old kitchen, its walls festooned with black soot, the summer rain too unsparingly much damaged the thatch roof, thinning it with frequent and excessive rainfall; she stood on the threshold, barred from entering fully inside, unintentional, by a tall, hefty woman, her once long thick black hair thinned with the age sat on top of her head in round bun, a neighbor, comedian, entertained much in social gatherings, greeted her with understanding silence today, in respect of the sad occasion; she stood still, looked left and right inside, where few women sat on low stools, cleaning utensils, peeling pumpkin skin, onion, their eyes with tears rolling not with the occasion it came but the onion juice, garlic, cutting chilies, ginger; two *chulha* hearths in the corner stood, three stones in each, triangle, two big aluminum pots above, filled with the black tea boiling in one, water in another with the flame from below with dead firewood burning with Milche in front, stirring with the big round spoon, its long steel handle in her hand, took a drop of it into her palm and tasted, perhaps for the sugar, she guessed; she looked up, smiled, acknowledged, she with no response mouthed Jentilla's name, her face dead serious; she understood, pointed to the back of the kitchen; three men, their hands stained blood red, a slain pig in front, its head severed, its flesh above the banana leaves, its hair matted with the blood, head to the chest hollow, opened, with its two legs too severed, sat squatted; a granary stood next, a little small in size to kitchen, its floor made of wooden planks, the four cornered wall too, the roof of thick bamboo leaves, rested on six big stones below; behind sat Jentilla, on the bare ground, sad, morose, her slanting eyes with dried tears, swollen, neither smiled, nor welcomed, for her uncertain glance, hesitated; the swollen eyes returned, blank, the tall tamarind tree its focus, unwelcome attitude, discouraged others but her; they were friends,-childhood friends; the moment asked for her comfort, understanding, company, silently; she sat near, pulled a small wooden plank nearby, below the tamarind tree and let her full weight rest on top of it; no word passed in between for long but in companionable silent they sat, she, in respect of her decision, she too, she knew respected her company, deep down inside; the past sixteen years saw her with life uncomforted to anyone, now, in a sudden, she knew not to play this character demanded at that moment, the words stuck in her stomach;

'It is all right. Don't feel sad. God wanted him by His side that is why He took him away.'

She hesitated first, forced the words out later, waited for the response that never came; the words, she uttered, whether had any consolation, she never knew; there was no reaction but she heard, whether she registered was her query within; for sometime, silence stretched in between, both the girls, refused to look at each other, their eyes fixed steadfast on an old tall jackfruit tree, behind tamarind tree; a small branch of it swayed softly for the gentle breeze, felt by none, disinterested; she gave sideway glance, surprised; she knew she found an answer; she was touched, the words went deep, balm her wound; the tears, in stream, ran down, unrestrained, the pupils undilated, blank, but a good sign; she reached out, wiped them hastily with no avail, unbothered they flowed more freely down to the ground, wetting; she wiped them, sniffed loudly, from the front of her frock with pocket, she fished out, an old clean handkerchief, handed it; the momentary fear said her action would be rebuffed but not so; she wiped her tears, sniffed loudly, blew her nose so loudly but missed the disapproving glance the owner gave; 'why? God is so cruel to take my father away?" one question rankled still amidst hiccups, the streaming tears dried, the eyes more swollen red, small; she remained mute, unanswered, her knowledge of God limited, the Sunday Schools only her source of learning taught her less, not touched the topic only the miracles of Jesus.

'He loved us and died on the cross to save us from our sins.' The words of a lean woman taller than her average height, her light brown eyes on a small round face hidden by a square cut, framed glasses, their Sunday School Teacher rang; why her father was taken if He loved her? A small teenage girl found no answer.

"I hate Him. I hate God. He took my father away." While Palmina battled for an answer Jentilla shouted, wailed loudly; she perplexed, baffled, speechless, held her arms helpless, sooth her, looked up to the heaven asking but the answer was not found; God was silent. The wailing chorused, they stood, she with her hand tucked under her arm, led her friend, where in the *pandaal* the crowd stood, their eyes on the blue satin covered coffin, frilled on the edges with the white sewn cross in the middle, the loose flowers on top, laid on the long wooden bench; the ceremony began, the sobs, hiccups, sniffings, tears persisted, Jentilla too, her whole body shook. Amidst the wailing, shrieking, screaming cries, his body was taken when the funeral ended, the oversized leather shoes, loosely worn in the bag, slipped below to the soft red soil, covered, his footsteps stopped echoed in the night. Five kilometers graveyard took forever, the farewell party was huge, men, women, children, with him ahead on top of six men, still he lay, silent in his usual ways, but ready with the work done—for the society, for his family.

There he laid, below six feet ground beneath, the loose soil soft, below and above and everyone bade good bye.

A short cross stood above, flower decked.

R. I. P. on top in big bold letters. Rest in Peace.

His name was written.

His birth date; early twentieth century; born during British time at Biri Siri, read out in funeral service. Someone said it was Siri Biri and brought the chorus of laughter.

His date of death.

Nothing about his deeds.

Five months had gone, the neighborhood saw nothing but life came to normal. The schools went in full swing, regular with no mercy for the students, but Palmina cursed not. The year was her last and she dreamed of college, the life different from the school, dreamed of casting off the much fed up uniforms. It was joyless, the wearing of school uniforms and the disciplined it imposed but her dream of trendy clothes college going students paraded spurred her on and she strove. The dream hardened her work, a challenge; she took it up gladly, unflinchingly. The mornings are hard too, getting up early, fetching water from the public tape, stood in a long queued, a steel pot in hand, and even seldom fighting. Jentilla was missed, badly, way to school, in the evening playtime, even in the public tape. Sudden changed in her was noticed, people remarked and the negative comments flooded where it crowded most. She gave class long miss, sometime for a week, then appeared in the class like a Halley's Comet, disappeared again for another week, evaded questions, went unanswered, turned hostile to her friends in the neighborhood and even in the school. Her teachers complained, then scolded her but her utterance was benumbed. In the class she talked to none. She sat alone always, on the big pipeline, morose, her eyes with far away look, at times blindly stared at people, seeing nothing but as if probing into others' dark depths. Her mother said nothing, rubbed the green betel leaf, sliced, with the palm, put white dot of lime and with a slice of betel nut, chewed it, her mouth full and called her all the names for her disinterest in kitchen; her friends too noticed her strange behaviour; they thought she missed her father whom she loved dearly and left her alone, deep in her own world where she enjoyed thinking pensively, the subject none knew only her, unrevealing. Palmina asked her once in simple curiosity as well to help and sat beside her for long uneasy silence, ready with verbal help with the long big water pipeline as their seat, but she looked straight. Her slanting topaz eyes were blank, unregistered her query and her presence, turned her head to the other side staring straight at the hillock far distance, wordless, till dusk set in and she left leaving her all alone. She sat evening after evening, on the same pipeline, evading company, hostile to all, lest anyone dared to ask she burst, her eyes in angry slits, her lips tightly compressed, nostrils flared with the breath oozing out of it fast, heartbeat in swift rhythm, sent them all scurrying away. None dared later to broach. She had gone mad, they said in the neighborhood; spread it, with all avoiding her, their eyes narrowed at her sight. Her friends and elders, the children too, their whispered only for their ears alone, their palms shielding their voices yet the corners of their eyes straight at her pointing but she remained careless but in her own, in the world she had carved for herself. A group of neighborhood boys played football, and the poor ball fell near where she sat, below her feet, hit her first then bounced. Her temper flared and she threw the ball away and the children called her mad, mercilessly.

"Mad girl . . . mad girl . . . mad girl . . ." They shouted at her, relentlessly mercilessly infuriating her more. Her eyes glittered with anger. With her rage uncontrollable she shook trembling, took stones after stones, pelted one after another, nearly hit some but with no avail. They ran still shouting gleefully while their parents enjoyed the sight, the scene, their escape and smiled encouragingly and even cheering for their narrow escape. Palmina bruised inside.

"She had gone mad." Sarcastic.

'No. She is just pretending, not really mad.' Sceptic.

'She is plain lazy.' Assuming.

'Do you know she laugh alone, smile alone and suddenly angry.'

'The father loved her so much. She miss him.'

'The mother loved Nokam much, not her.'

'That old woman. Perhaps it was because of her the curse is on her daughter.'

'I told you no, those fought for land earn curse.'

'It is a family curse.' A scathing contempt.

Everyone playing God, all knowing, for what sin the curse was on and put the finger on for what deed, whether it was really a curse.

CHAPTER 14

<u>THE CONDEMNATION AND THE FIGHT.</u>

July came coupled with heavy rain and strong summer heat. The first was week laden with news, both hot and cold; the gossips were ripe, some indigestible, others expected. Chinche with her round belly, increasingly bulging monthly made the hottest news. The women stood, their dinner over, stood on the narrow path, cemented, a favour shown by the member, lost in the election last after winning for a term, designated PWD minister for three years with their backs towards the bamboo fencing and their faces towards each other, listening in rapt attention while the one speak, uncared of eavesdroppers, their voices rising, critical, in total condemning, playing God.

"She is pregnant." One spoke, announcing to the shocked audience.

"Six months already. Don't you know?" another added.

'She is a whore.' One spat.

'A promiscuous.' Another named.

'The relatives don't give a damn about her. She led a free life' Another reasoned.

'What example she would give her brothers.' A self righteous, self declared pious one.

'Her boyfriend sleep with her every night." Scornful.

"A bad influence for her friends. They should not be allowed to befriend her." Palmina's mother. Palmina smiled and thought of countless number of lectures given to her in mind, restraining their friendship yet carried on furtively, dreading the stick she always showed—a thick bamboo with the hard bottom.

'She is clever. Imagine getting engineer for a husband.'

'Did he get a job?' An envious.

'No. He already completed and got his degree. Very soon he'd get a job.'

'Would Jonty marry her?' Milche's mother, a little understanding.

'How would you know it was Jonty's? It could be of another.' Tochi-ma skeptical, condemning. Palmina listened, thought otherwise and disagreed, a teenager and remembered.

"They are going next month, on the first, to his parents." One announced, skeptical.

'I doubt, his parents would allow him. Even if the parents allow, the clan would not.'

'How did you know?' a sarcastic question.

'I met his aunty, last week and she told me. They all know of her character.' The poison injected already. Benta-ma

"I wanted to be loved and cared." Her tearful eyes with words echoed. The memory revived. Palmina thought with compassion and ugly rage for the self constituted judges.

The vile comments, the scathing, the scorns, a stigma attached, she smiled unaffected; unconcerned of all talks and not affected by it all with her belly protruding, she walked in gaiety, stitching woolen socks for the undelivered life yet with expectedly and walked past the gathering women who smiled not at her, spoke not a single word but looked at her stomach with open disgust she could not careless. Her father lived the destructive hell he still lived in. He never noticed her bulging stomach. He never knew. Nobody spoke. Nobody told him. The grapevine was whispering but not near his ears. His midnight routine home coming still going strong; he sang, he shouted, he laughed, he abused. His heaven and others hell; above all Chinche's. Every morning he awoke late for a brunch with red rimmed eyes reeking of stale alcohol. Chinche soaked his stench smell old bed-sheet in the blue plastic bucket, slapped it hundredth times and hanged them outside the house. Her eyes went sunken and she looked haggard and worn out. But she had no rest. She bought him new bedsheet after three months. They never lasted. Her grandmother came with grandfather missing conspicuously with their ears full of the tales somebody fed. They came not they cared for her but to save the embarrassment and the criticism they faced. He was too angry to come, his wife said later to Tochi—ma of Chinche's grandfather. She knew full well she'd overheard. He was too ashamed, Chinche guessed that hurt her not. The old man with old values he stuck fast, repulsed with the pre-marital consummation tarnishing the family's image more than hers. Tainted. Her grandmother brought not a long tail. Her cousin sister came, slim and pretty with her unmanageable wild curly hair tangled in between big black rubber band. Her ever caring husband was nowhere to be seen. He had an emergency meeting, his wife informed casually, hiding the truth. But Chinche knew better. Later her cousin revealed just as she thought. Disgusted. With her pregnancy, she told her scornfully. Derided. Yet Chinche smiled alone sarcastically. She knew another reason why. They sat outside the house and called the neighborhood elders. With five arm wooden chairs in the house *moorahs* are alternatives. The men sat on the chairs and the women on the *moorahs*. Her father abstained from office and sat at home once for a record. He was told to stay by his mother in law he dared not to brook. She was a tartar no one messed with. He never had inkling why and learnt much later when the topic began. He took it calmly, surprisingly. The headman began the heading and decided the future of a girl. Milche, Palmina and Salmina sat in Chinche's as kitchen maids and served the elders. Jentilla sat on the tree stump and balefully looked at Palmina when called her. The killer look; the freezing look and froze her on the spot she dared not melt again to call. Hilla absconded. Her parents saw the issue repulsive and tainted themselves not with it. Their daughter was given a strict warning never to involve. The date set, meeting ended early and benediction set with cup of red tea each and Marie biscuits on the plate full.

The long range, and the short range in left and right hands, the tall burly man went up, checked the big pipeline, steel hard with the joints as his main target and rested where their family private pipeline joint. He kept the bigger range aside, used the smaller range and loosened the smaller private pipeline, checked the inside and bent it with the bigger range, its steel hard teeth wide open, then closed, clamping on the joints. He went home unsatisfied. At home, the kitchen pots filled, the makeshift bathroom roofless with the bamboo walls covering their bathing nakedness with barrel in it filled, sufficient for the family of four and a servant with a stream flowing out of it, overflowing. The neighbors sat squatted in queue, bored chins resting on the open palms with their elbows on the aluminum pots, their eyes sleepy each waited half an hour for a pot of water. The two days later, early in the morning, a mini water pump was brought, fitted in the big pipeline on the joint where their private pipeline joint. The evening saw the commotion, the water stopped coming, the usual force of the water in the public tape lost its rigour and turned slow; Tochi-ma came up and a short woman too removing the imaginary dust from the betel leaf, her mouth full chewing red, watched the public tape where the crowd gathered, some washing, some bathing, the rest with their aluminum pots in a long queue waiting for their turn and loudly declared to all "the water stopped coming". The evening saw the verbal duel; the two women stood on the foot path, shouted at their top, their voices crossed Palmina's house, Milche's, Chinche's, Mittila's and rested in Hilla's.

'Greedy people salah.'

'Only few years back they came and now.'

'My husband brought the pipeline and now he act as if he own it.'

Few minutes silence. After half an hour, a man came, his face clouded in dark anger, his hand holding a short barrel *cartouse* rifle, his intention clear; the women ran but the men came out—Tochi-pa, short stout headman, Palmina's father, and the four young male bloods rushed out. Their timely intervention calmed the situation; they evaded the impending disaster. The fought ended in headman's courtyard; a peace treaty was signed and the situation with little tense was diffused.

The old pond water stood in perfect serenity, unused, reddish with iron filled.

"My father brought the pipeline"

Hilla claimed the other day, her eyes shone with pride and an open challenge. The neighborhood area fight saw a hot topic in the class, Hilla found the need for support and her rich friends her arm lifters, pounced on quietly sat Jentilla, in the corner alone, her eyes morose—a distant look on her face, disinterestedly.

"Hilla's daddy brought the pipeline . . ."

They all chorused.

She said nothing but they are like pack of wolves, pouncing, scorning then jeering and taunting. A few minutes later, a loud shriek and her instrument box, two books on the desk went flying towards them with its pages torn open. Pen, pencil, rectangle eraser, a transparent short ruler and compass hit them and closed their mouth but was thrown out later by the teacher, a stern woman, stood taller than all, her hair knotted tightly with hair pins all over it stuck to keep it in place, her thick eyebrows narrowed in anger but had a decency to ask the reason why and clearly sided with the group and made a pair of knees bruised with the pebbles crushed by them in the hot sunny day. She was baked hot. Her face red at first and turned deep brown later. They all giggled unrepentant and mercilessly. She closed her mouth with her smoldering eyes. Palmina could do nothing just spoke few words of comfort. Her words, Palmina noticed eased her anger. Jentilla softened.

The nail biting day came. Annual Result Day. Prize distribution was both exhilarating and disappointing. Exhilarating for prize winners and disappointing for losers with expectation. Palmina had over-expected. She nurtured a secret dream to receive the yellow wrapped prize for losing to the green. Her dream dashed. She lost the two and her heart sank. It was her father's face she saw. Grim and disappointed. They all folded the progress card in the classroom. When the lone huge bell rang, chiming in the old long building she ran eagerly. They all met on the road outside.

The long road ran endlessly, winding, sharp curves along, with few walkers even the day failed to bring saved for few students. Hilla, Milche, Palmina amongst, headed home after the year's harvest with incessant chatter, excited. Hilla failed in Maths pulled through, Milche in Science and Maths sent on mission mercy to the next higher class. Palmina with third, surpassed her and her eyes lit and her face creased in ceaseless smile and blamed not anyone but herself. She missed too much weekly tests and lost few crucial marks. Anyone met them needed no answer. The smiles on their faces were the tell tale sign, engrossed with themselves not on anything else incessantly chatting and saw nothing of morose Jentilla, behind. Her unsmiling face, said nothing neither sadness nor happiness but of darkly brooding, inscrutable. The trio looked behind, saw her, urged her upon, waved with no response but the shaking of her head, declining, threw neither smile nor words, discouraged the query of the result, they dared not asked but assumed the worst that proved true. She crossed wordlessly and walked ahead of them and they stared at her retreating back with understanding silence. Palmina was ecstatic but little disappointed. Her father came home for long winter break. In his hearts of heart he waited for her result eagerly. She saw it in the restless manner he sat, eat and talk nothing else but her incoming result. He was in the neighborhood when she reached home and called out her mother. The mother said nothing about the result. Just expressionless smile and one word good. Then she went to the makeshift pig sty with the big neck-less pot and fed her grunting pigs. Her father came later. He stepped down from the main road towards home. Palmina could not wait and told him while still half way, in the middle of the steps. He smiled asked for the second time, the third time and the fourth time to confirm. He stopped coming down, turned back up and headed towards neighbors. Minutes later, Palmina heard Tochipa's bellowed laughter and demand for a whole pig to kill. He came late but enjoyed the evening thoroughly. He had his balding head crowned; garlanded; his hopes on her soared. His dream for her higher. Her mother killed a fat rooster and saved the plump limb for her. Salmina bulged her pupils and pouted her mouth. Palmina showed her teeth gleefully. They had few neighborly visitors that night and enjoyed basking in Palmina's success. They all had good cups of tea and slept happily. In the near midnight hour when all are in deep slumber with their dreams good and bad and while the bad dreamers are screaming and crying and the good dreamers are laughing and smiling they all are disrupted rudely at the sound of the drumbeats and the group singing reverberating the cold night. The group danced in the neighbor's, collecting money for the new drum and the year's picnic with the youth as beneficiary and the adults as the patrons, indulging the youths grudgingly and some even willingly. They headed towards their house with the sound coming closer as its signal, and the noise and commotion as their symbol with balluk not barking but understandably silent. Palmina came out, her right hand holding lantern stood at the bottom of the stone steps leading down, tricky with loose pebbles and the stones too and lighted the steps for the group. The children came down first, a boy in average height followed, in his early teens with a stout body holding a small round drum, balanced by a belt around his neck and a lean stick in his hand, carefully lowered his feet in each step. The last of the group reached, squeezed in a small narrow courtyard, a tall boy led the song with the lyrics pleading for money or rice, the drummer began his job with the tune, the group followed the leader, in unison, singing, in the dark. She was drawn a little later to the steps, at the bottom to a lone body sat huddled with a white shawl around her body prominently showing. She went forward, recognized the huddled small body and pulled her out with no result. Jentilla stuck fast, alone, watching with sightless eyes wordlessly. She sat with her seeing nothing too but her. It took long time for the group but her mother lay wide awake on the bed, angry with her foul temper for disturbing her sleep, climbed down at her sight and rubbed her eyes.

'Mum, they are collecting money.' She pleaded.

'Give them a tin of rice.' It was a curt answer and her mother stifled a yawn, tying her disheveled hair to a knot and came out to watch. She stood at the threshold not amused but of courtesy. Palmina went to the kitchen, opened the round brown earthen cover of a big earthen pot, a storage, scooped out tin full of rice in an empty condensed milk tin, came out, put it in a plastic bag, half of it filled with rice, with a young boy holding it, opened wide enough for it. The group leader saw her action and his lyrics changed to that of gratitude, something somebody had rightly composed. The group thanked them for their generosity both in the lyrics they sang and also without singing when the drummer stopped and the leader too along with the group and bade goodnight both to them and made towards the steps. The lone body too stood up, went up the steps and disappeared in the dark, wordlessly. She held the lantern high and saw her departing back, the last person to climb the steps and said not even the courtesy good night she held no grudge of and let it go. She put the lantern down when her back disappeared into the darkness.

A short mini skirt worn with a long coat, its collars pointed below with a suit of ash teri cotton and a pair of black heels that added to her height and brought admiration and envy for Hilla but she basked in the new suit, a Christmas present given by the parents adored and carried it off well in the church service before Christmas that Chinche missed, busy breastfeeding the tiny bundle sucking greedily on her breasts with no one to company but for Hilla, Milche, Palmina short of Jentilla, remained seated on the giant pipeline staring at nothing, speechless. Palmina sat with her for a long time, spoke nothing.

"Don't you want to be magistrate anymore?"

It was timid.

Suddenly, she turned her way and gave her vile look.

Her eyes bloodshot. Rage.

'Who will pay for my studies?'

She shouted. Palmina rose and walked away.

Her father, Chinche said came in the morning, still with his eyes red and left the maternity ward of the government hospital with the scent of his breath he let out from the night last, much to the consternation of the other patients and to the scowling of the nurses tending that had her forcing him to leave the room. He too came, Chinche told her friends, the man who sired the bundle and left her few notes to buy fruits, she discarded carelessly on the stool, hating the man she thought loved once and said, she'd lived alone with her daughter. She had a story to tell but they knew the story well and clear, bit by bit, in detail right from when she went to his family, few months back along with her sister, brother-in-law, her father with a record sober for that day alone, her grandparents, few uncles and aunties. The whole obese pig with sagging white stomach nearly brushing the ground lay on the ground. It snorted its nose above two sprouting tusks. The whole swollen face hid his small eyes. It hardly could move its body and with two pairs of its legs tied it moved not. They killed it not and fed not the unwilling groom and his family. They left it there, behind the kitchen. They brought along too three fat roosters, few kilos of beef, kilos of fish, potato, plump orange pumpkin, chilies, onions, ginger and the best scented rice. A custom. The younger male relatives killed the pig and the women began cooking. Chinche's relatives served his with their culinary skills. They sat like being treated in a star restaurant. After their meal, the storm brew; his parents stopped at nothing but heavy downpour of hard words mingled with hail Chinche could hardly swallow and saw her temper the better of her. They were shamed with vehement rejection of her—she was pregnant with somebody's child not their son's, a prostitute, promiscuous, the words she knew well were put into their heads and mouth by somebody. She came from behind the kitchen where a temporary kitchen was set up. She left her cooking and stood behind the circle of elders—his parents, relatives, uncles and aunties with disparaging glance at her and her grandparents and few uncles and aunties close enough and came to set the date for wedding. She stood ramrod straight; her eyes blurred with angry tears she wiped angrily and blasted—first at him, then his mother with the piece of her mind. They stared at her dumbstruck. Her cousin sister with her cooking and few of her closest young relatives rushed forward to restrain just not fast enough and watched her in open mouthed silence. They hanged their heads in shame and she decided then, a life to live alone, to raise the child single handedly. With her pride salvaged, she remained stubbornly not to backtrack and dumped him where he belonged—in the gutter. Well, she certainly needed not a mama's boy. She needed a man; a man who'd stood by her and believed not the slander. She needed a man who'd judged between jealous neighbors severing them and love her, care for her, defend her. Speculation was rife of the messenger—it could be either of the two woman neighbors, Chinche told Palmina bitterly, without literally naming but she knew just the same—two tale bearers. The son too said nothing, neither defended her nor acknowledged the child in her womb but meekly submitted to the decision his mother imposed on him, Chinche added bitterly, recounting every bit with no omission and lost her respect completely. It was a trap, he accused her later, to tie him down to her and proposed abortion she flatly refused. Still he denied impregnating her and accused her of cheating on him. It was an effort to escape from the blame, Palmina comforted, bitter with him at the same. The man was not a man—not a man enough Palmina consoled not knowing how to console yet trying with no effect at all. With each passing month her belly swelled in bigger rounds till it looked like a big round balloon tied in the middle of a tree. She walked heavily, slowly and smiled at all. Nobody smiled back. They stared hard at her stomach then whispered in each others' ears. Palmina knew not the contents. Jentilla too. Chinche could not careless but held her head high. They well must be curious of the latest month, Palmina assumed. Palmina—ma was scornful yet sympathetic at times. Tochi—ma was openly derisive. She went door to door in the neighborhood, sat on every moorah she could find outside each house and took the super fast minutes to spread her misfortune. If somebody showed sympathy to Chinche she showed open disgust and dig her past spicing them and painting her as somebody black to enjoy happy married life. She had an ally. Benta—ma. Jentilla—ma spoke to herself with the betel nut in her hand peeling the hard skin. Milche—ma felt her as contamination to the neighborhood and a bad example. She glowered at her if came ten feet towards Milche. She stepped back.

Three months she waited for the exam. It was slated to be in February. It was a final year for her to cross the school life, to enter the life she desperately wanted; for her life in the college meant—freedom, less books, she saw the college students with just one notebook and a pen. She wished to go to college in trendy clothes, jeans, shirts, shoes of variety except black she wore to school, the boyfriends. But something nagged her, a flag on the summit above all, a success, a battle to win, slap to poverty, pull down the class barrier and to prove, not only to the world but herself. It scurried on. She lit the midnight lamp; minutes are not wasted; the hours are precious; to the mornings and evenings too she attached herself like a glue; her eyes riveted on nothing but books, her only obsession; the friends are ignored; the shrieking and screaming in the playfield was an irritant, an itch she wished to scratch but could not; books became her pals, her focus clear like a crystal ball, her dream was her goal, a hurdles to cross but her steely determination, will, desire bull dozed and when the three months end, nothing was left but everything ready, a track towards her goal, clear. She had checkmated the questions to come from every corner and every angle.

Deep in the night when all are in deep slumber with nothing but dreams captivated every sane person when she could hear nothing but the occasional barking of the dogs somewhere in the neighborhood, the cry of the babies from somewhere nearby, Palmina stayed awake; The dim kerosene lamp light barely enough for small letters of Indian History, her strained eyes tuned in; History was her favorite subject, Akbar, her favorite king; An old woman, few months for retirement pushed her unglamorous square glasses back, looked sternly and hinted for the exam, Aurangzeb as the chapter likely to come as the exam; the character she detested, deterred; the fanatic she thought of the cruel man and hated; with the final exam just three months away, she had lots to browse, cover, memorise with no hour to spare but to value each; The March and Mathematics, dreaded Ms but for the determination within, with it the strength, the hope, the will kindled. Maths was her weakness and filled all blank papers with the mathematic equations and blocked all the escape routes and mastered it in few months. The malicious neighbors and gossip mongers, their sarcastic\ and insulting comments they hurled at she took right in. They were her driving force and her smile with their jeer; a would be mother, a single, they scorned on her routine outing for fresh air that never hit the mark but returned with an adverse affect, a challenge to disprove and to proof; nobody saw a smile sarcastic for self encouragement with satisfaction, a desire so strong to prove not in March alone but in the months and the years ahead—in the future; what the world thought was never true, her only thought and focus nobody knew—to hit the bulls eyes come what may; midnight came, the small round table clock warned but she had lots to cover. It was her brain that protested but with the afternoon stretched to evening, evening to night, night to mid night and midnight into earning morning she worked nonstop with steely determination to success. But she closed the book when the cock crowed first, put off the tiny flames, shoved herself into the blanket with her sister in open mouthed deep sleep, an open invitation for the night insects interested with no takers; it took minutes but she too joined but repelling sound of roaring snoring of her sister much in her deep sleep, munching something in her sleep with nothing in her mouth she was chuckled at. Sleep came instantly and she too snored heard by her mother not by herself.

A narrow street lay in the middle with both sides with thatch roofs, their playground; four piled up flat stones with three flat stones on either side; she tiptoed towards the pile; someone guarded it with her back towards, a ball in hand; she turned her face, half, her shock; a menacing smile and who—dear old friend Milla; she shouted, screamed the truth with futility; it sank no in but simply with an evil smile she advanced menacingly more towards her till she ran for dear life; she screamed, she shouted, unheard till hoarse but nobody came and no rescuer but alone; Her body shook, a voice in the background; it took time but senses came, she opened here eyes, relieved, the chase just a bad dream; her mother stood near; concern etched her voice, she asked; she told, shivered, a stark fear in her eyes, the dream and her dead friend; she consoled, soothed, patted and left; sleep eluded her; she lay awoke for a long time, thinking, the dream rudely took her sleep, slept at the first cock crow rudely awakened at the first light.

CHAPTER 15

<u>THE FLAG AND ITS HOLDING.</u>

"Balluk . . . balluk . . . balluk . . ." her mother stood, left over food of the dinner last in her hand, an old dirty plate, unwashed for years beside her foot, dried rice stuck hard on it but balluk never come. He came not the night before, the night barren without him, his usual barking, snorting and wagging missed, an animal more attached than a friend, served faithful for twelve years than a son, parted from the mother in the village where her father work, reared from a month old with the milk; neighborhood was searched—Tochi-ma's, Benta-pa's, headman's, Chinche-pa's, Hilla-pa's, Jentilla-ma's, Milche-ma's but nowhere found, vanished without a trace; many theories are given—dog theft was ridiculous, a feast with his old body was probable but ruled out—he left the world was the last and the most probable, even without a proof, their belief proved; the dogs well ahead knew of their death and ran away from the house, somewhere deep, nowhere to be found, to die quietly, somebody said, Palmina could hardly accept; a proper burial for him was respect for the service rendered he not allowed them; "clang . . . clang . . . clang . . ." a rice-full of plate fell, bounced on the ground twice, rice fully strewn, not an accident but an action of grief, heart broken while she sat numbed on the moorah below, speechless but her mind too conjured with the exam she had on the afternoon, Palmina left the grieving anxious family and left with a long transparent ruler, an instrument box, a hanky and two books far ahead of the time slated for the exam and with enough time for brushing up the topic, browsed over them the whole morning with a luck. The exam resumed and her studies too—she missed the neighborhood, the evening outings, the friends but her goal drove her on and on and after one month of exam it was over with her a freedom to enjoy. The result declared four months later brought the result expected by her and her family but to the shock of the neighbors, undermining her—First Division with three letter marks; History, Science and English. Her father saw a white cloak and a stethoscope around her neck, she never wished to disappoint. Her father's wrinkled nose pointed up irritating the neighbors yet silencing and her mother showed endless smile—in the kitchen, on the roadside with neighbors, while cutting vegetables and also in cooking. The first year of early nineteen ninety, in the month eight saw her in the college, in a town bigger with a reputation for good education. The college life began, new and different with it the freedom too she desperately waited both in the hostel and in the classes too and saw the change something unlike school life but one thing remained unchanged—her struggle; her father sent her money, one thousand and two hundred, five hundred for mess fees and seven hundred for books, she used for clothes and third meal for the two she had in the hostel; her friends received two thousand and five hundred each, much in excess than was necessity, bought bulky books they left on the three storied racks for hatch that never did for them but for her; they smoke, party, drink both hard and soft and the boyfriends too they changed like socks off the feet; she wished she too could like them all, the city girls but the values imbibed and the foundation it laid stuck hard and formidable she felt instantly alone and lonely but struggled with her aim one and goal ahead she pursued steadfast. She thought she had seen all, at home where she grew, in her surrounding but not all; the life waited for her to show all—everything. The small square table clock struck ten, early for the hostellers, sat in groups in a room, chatting, talking almost about everything—boyfriends, family members, parents, the movies they watched—Palmina sat, her bottom on the head of her bed, two of her pillows propped up where her back rested comfortably, her eyes on the black lines on the opened book in front, borrowed from the College Library when the door that stood ajar opened slowly with care and a head popped in with a finger on her lips, silencing and called her out. Three girls were out, stood in the verandah on the wooden floor, one pair of eye on the small hole to the room next to her and the other two fought for the hole noiselessly with actions and extreme care and caution. It took minutes for her chance with the girl with a chance to the hole backed out with a stifled giggle arousing her interest and curiosity, prompting her instantly towards the hole once the other girl backed out straight to see something unimaginable she thought not possible that refused to register inside her innocent brain. Two bodies of room-mates, their total naked bodies romped on the bed, on top of the other, entwined, licking and sucking, moaning with pleasure totally engrossed with each other. Everything came clear now—the innuendoes, the jealousy, possessiveness and constant attention one of them demanded in the open water tape, in the television room, in the classroom, dining room. The hostel life and the hostel romance—girl to girl—woman to woman—two liberated women. The next day began as usual, no fuss, no giggle, just normal like any other day as if nothing happened the night before, easily forgotten—the morning tea, breakfast with red tea from the hostel and bread and butter of her own but the early lunch of yellow dhal and yellow fried cabbage with potato made up for the light breakfast. The years passed—one, two, three, four, five years gone. It was the sixth year. The year bygone she revived lay alone on her single bed staring at nothing but the white ceiling fan fanning away her sweat. She took minutes off, halted her brain rejuvenating, cooling after hours of staring at the thick book that strained her brain more than anything else. She easily could count the number of days she had a hearty slept and hardly could count the number she lose her sleep. The hostel food tasted like a saw dust and she ate in the canteen mostly then lavishly enjoyed the self cook food in the heater in their room when relaxed from books. The white cloak much used hanged in the wall. She had what the world called degree, attached to her name and became a tail not to be cut off. Her friends are there, with their degrees all tagged, excited, ready with the intern for a year and then a work; staying in a real village squirmed them but with no choice for the payment rendered by the government for their quota. All began with the thought for higher studies, not some really wanted it but for the escape—escape from the village, serving for the villagers and the dirty backward villagers that was what her friends had discussed and she listened not deciding and content with what she had that moment.

Now after her degree in tag, she lay in bed, watched the ceiling above counting the numbers traveled from Tura to Guwahati, for holidays—yearly Puja holidays, summer vacation, winter vacation, semester break. She loved night traveling in night buses, it simply made her journey shorter, seen her slept throughout the journey up and down, knew only when he got in and when he got out unlike day traveling when the bus stopped at every two three kilometers with the passengers coming in and going out and the conductor shouted loudly.

'Jaaoo . . .' Then hit the door hard three times, emphasizing his word.

The halfway of her study marred her night travel. The newspaper carried items of dacoity, armed robbery of the night buses, saw with her own eyes the shattered front glasses of the Night Super, then stopping bus halfway at Dhupdhara and Dudhnai. The names were mismatched, her friend once remarked on their way to Tura for Christmas.

They pronounced Duphdara as Dudhdara. The latter name had relation to milk. They sat in tea stalls, left opened at night for night bus passengers and asked for tea.

At Dudhnai, they got, much for their joy—milk tea. At Dhupdhara, all three stalls had no milk tea but red tea. It irked Palmina and her friend.

"How can this place be called Dudhdara? This place should be called Dudhnai. There is no milk here."

"Dudnai should be called Dudhdara."

'Dudhnai means 'no milk' but there is milk.'

She had the knack of entertaining. She had entertained them all with a treat of hearty laugh. Her father was overjoyed; he left for the neighbors in her mother's latest *gana,* tying a big knot in front of his protruding belly and smiles seemed permanently attached; he vied for praise; he vied for appreciation; thirst for their show of envy; his daughter had come back; the only qualified doctor in the neighborhood and his pride; his achievement as a father, not the daughter's and called for thanks giving service, not really meaning it but for the appreciation of the others; her mother was happy too but with no expression, showed her modesty but still fed her two plump pigs in a sty, busied herself cooking yum leaves and stems for the hairy pampered fatsos with their once bulging eyes well inside the two high lids-upper and lower and their four pairs of short legs lifting drooping abdomens and circling the small sty in hunger demanding what they thought they deserved—their dinner. But her thoughts are interrupted; she was troubled. What she saw the evening earlier was disturbing, completely agitating her mind, heart, soul and body and the sleep was eluding. Life changed; people changed; world changed; world was cruel; people are cruel; for her it was kind; for her parents it was kind but not for all. Someone shouted from behind earlier in the evening and she stopped to look and the cause of commotion. There are many onlookers, all stopped and gaping, their mouths open, staring at the girl with a disheveled hair running behind her with a small babies' clothes in her hand dangling.

'Catch that mad girl . . .' A woman with a curly hair, her hair tumbled out of the big black rubber band she wore that gave her of the picture of mad woman rather than about the other; it was the shopkeeper of the babies garment shop who ran chasing her, she learned much later.

'Catch her. She is running away with my cloth.'

She cried hoarsely after her again, unable to keep pace with her and stopped to catch her breath. No one seemed to be in a helping mood though packed with onlookers. Some are openly gleefully watching with help last thing in their mind; Some with open curiosity not able to understand the cause. Aghast. They just got the whiff of her running fast. Swiftly. Her hair swing from side to side. It was opened, the original silky dark brown hair she was gifted with and not the product of any hair lotion. The streak of white on her forehead still at the roots was never due to old age. But what they called premature graying Palmina had a glimpse of. Palmina watched her with curious interest at the thin woman running behind, openly flabbergasted when she saw the thin lean face, sunken eyes and cheeks for the strong familiarity when her straight deep brown hair parted to reveal her face. She stopped not nor looked at her but ran past her with an intent to outrun whoever was behind her running. Jentilla. Palmina rooted to the spot with her breath stopping for few seconds, her capacity to believe leaving her completely. She was not insane; she could not be; the world made her believe that. She believed what the world made her to believe; it was imposing on her by the people and she steadfastly refused it. It pained her deeply. The wound was bleeding and no one saw but she felt it—for her friend. Jentilla and Chinche. Chinche with her son, Jasper. She was an outcast. He was an outcast, literally and socially, both the mother and the son. In Hilla's wedding, Chinche sat in the corner wrapping rice in a plantain leaves unsure of herself and her acceptance in the community, her first socializing after her labour; Palmina came for the Semester break, a God sent for her and attended and saw all. She sat with her with little Jasper hanging onto her. The corners of each eyes directed at her with their palms covering half of their mouths while the other corners in other's ears and at the end both the mouths twitched with scorn. Palmina saw it; Chinche too. Palmina felt the pain. Chinche was humiliated and shamed silently of course; she lowered her eyes. A scarlet woman she was painted and learned to live with it. She noticed one thing too for Hilla's pre-wedding preparation—silent Benta—ma and learnt of the reason later. Benta disappeared on one night and learnt she eloped with a much married man, a father of four children, a forest range officer she met somewhere. Her mother went to bring her back but she refused with the word she'd escape from her leery stepfather. She returned home alone and the neighborhood saw her change for the better. The wedding went off well. Hilla was married happily with the man of her choice, an engineer her parents well approved of and excitedly brought home. A short man with sparse hair, fair skin, a man who laughed bellowing all the time with a real show off; nothing interesting in man saved his status but for that her parents approved him off, nothing else; building a family status through marriage and for Hilla, the money his status brought and the luxury that came with the package and the lavishness it promised. For him, pretty wife to parade before his friends and walking tall with pride, soft hands to tug under his arms and to smile standing beside him, a toast amidst his colleagues he so much would be proud of. To cloth. To breed his child. Nothing else. The life still seemed curse to Chinche. Her father fell ill. Liver Cirrhosis, the doctors diagnosed him. The diagnose was few years back. Now he lay in bed, ridden, sleeping. His face shrunken thinly; his cheek sunk deeply; the flesh in his arms and legs drooped hanging and lay on each side of his bed. His skeletal was covered by his mere skin. His illness chained Chinche at home, busy. He needed constant attention and care. Under his bed lay a permanent bed pan her cousin sister sent. It was an old rusted steel Chinche took pains to change morning, noon and evening. He received few visitors—the headman, Palmina—pa, Tochi—pa and Benta—pa with his mouthful of betel nut and his right thumb grinding tobacco in his left palm. When he spoke few red betel nut particles landed on Chinche's face. Her father opened his eyes, looked at them complained of pain and closed his eyes again. Chinche knew why they came—to assess his time. He stood no chance. Her cousin brother in law came and injected pain killer. Her grandparents came and took him to hospital. They had no sympathy in mind but more of duty. The doctor shook his head and said sorry. Few days later, he stopped his breath in his sleep. When Chinche went to feed him soup his body was hard and his mouth open. The nearest neighbor came running when they heard the loud wail came from their house.

With years bygone she had changed—from girl to woman, duckling to swan, ugly to beautiful, in heights, looks and manner; blossomed; bloomed; awakened; thoughtful; considerate; sensitive. She lay in bed awoke late at night; her degree completed; her toil paid in full; the first doctor in the neighborhood and the locality everybody's talk zeroed in; her parents are happy; her father grinned from ear to ear; he went to the neighbors, sat in each house; he was respected; he was honoured; 'Doctors are plenty' remarked Milche—ma; her scorn and bitterness seen in it; but Palmina smiled, a smile of understanding; she knew why, her daughter climbed not the ladder she climbed and she wore not the crown her parents wore; her mother killed the fattest rooster and saved the limbs for her. Samina showed her full round pupils un-dilated; She chuckled contented. It was her day. A week later, her father called the church elders, the members both the elders and the youth. He killed the fat swine his wife had fed for one and half years. All neighborhood came. The male youth killed the swine, immersed the whole body in the boiling hot water, removed the hairs, burned the skin, cut the meat into tiny pieces and made it ready to cook. The male elders cooked with pumpkin, powdered rice, with the intestines and other inner parts cooked apart. The women cooked rice, struggled with the wet firewood that saw more of the white billowing smoke rather than the orange flame and spoiled one pot full of rice Palmina's mother had cooked again later with extra water and overcooked it. Her mother amassed a mountain pile of rolled plantain leaves the girls had heated ready to wrap rice and wrapped in small square packets stocked in three tall bamboo baskets. Later when the food was ready, the thanksgiving service began and the oldest man delivered the message apt for the occasion. They all ate, enjoyed the chicken and fish for those allergic to pork and slept the night with their stomach full. Her mother laughed the whole day round, cracking jokes, bantering with witticism. Her father never stopped grinning from ear to ear, his sagging skin prominent with wrinkles hiding his eyes between two lids. Palmina watched with her joy in their happiness, her smile in their laughter and her success as their garland bedecked with beautiful flowers. They were garlanded. They were crowned. It was there in their eyes, laughter and happiness. Her hard toil vanished. Her pain disappeared. Her future secured. She had reached the summit where the flag waved at her. She had it in between her palm holding it and written her name.—Proudly for herself and her parents; then her friends. They came—Hilla came with her toddler son and sat the whole day. Milche too with a daughter of five and a three year old son with a body guard of a husband. Chinche came with her son and sat with her friends. All glanced her way, some whispering and from the way they look at her, their derisive eyes and scornful looks and kept themselves at bay from in talking with her that was scarcely decorous in her eyes said what she hated to know. She was pariah, someone tainted. But she could not careless but carried her smile in every step she took and every eye she met. She met somebody, someone she cared not but somebody who cared for her—a fine gentleman ready to give a name to her son, Palmina felt nothing but happiness for her. She thought she deserved that much after a long years of suffering and social boycott. He came that gentleman to visit her father lying sick at home; a young officer, a colleague of her father who came more of a courtesy than real desire. She fluttered her lashes in simple lure, smiled gently and looked at him with soft sad eyes across her father's bed. She had him smitten in her simple mystic way. Few small drops of tears in her lashes had his heart softer and he came the next day again. He ordered a fine teak coffin sleekly burnished for her father and held her tight to comfort her. He stayed on the funeral night, went home the next night and made it his duty to visit her often. Her grandparents thought it was God-sent and betrothed them in a hurry. Jentilla hardly cared the importance of the thanksgiving service nor did she bother of her old friend. She was missed. She sat the day long the day before on the footpath near their house, went wild with frenzy suddenly for nothing and at nobody then cried profusely, wailing like a little child, she was told of her childhood friend, her heart shook. Her happiness marred by what was become of her and stirred in her thought she never thought possible. Jentilla with a child, a fatherless child—a bastard with none claiming as his siring she thought inhuman. Her heart rendered, hated him, the swine of a man. The nameless son of a bitch.

Then she decided her something she never thought, never occurred in her mind, not even a single cross of word. She'd be Psychiatrist. She'd try to help. She'd help her back to live life like they had spent in their childhood. Carefree. Full of joy. Full of laughter.

The freshly painted smell of the two storied building gladdened Palmina. She had chosen the colour well. Pink. It was her favourite colour, something she thought feminine and well suited for the building. She had built it with loan from the government and had the words of appreciation from all corners pouring in. She had received donations too from well meaning people, from well wishers. Her salary in the government hospital looked after her. She had no need of looking after her family. Her parents lived on her father's pension. They too earned from the areca nuts her father planted long years back. He sold them every year to the traders and earned well out of it too. She stood outside looking at it over and over again with the thought the building looked new again. It was two years old only but the incessant rain had done much damage to it outer painting making it dull and lifeless. Her loan of it would be completed in another one year, she calculated. Then it would be hers, completely. She was satisfied now and satisfied with the signboard with big bold letters. MENTAL CARE HOME. She avoided both the name clinic and the hospital but rather chose it to call it home. She wished the inmates to feel rather like a family not the patients. She had every kind of patients of all mental sicknesses she found challenging treating them. For her, their sicknesses are like any other sickness—malaria, jaundice, influenza, cough and cold, diarrhoea, dysentery and simple fever. In her mental care home, she had cared and treated many with mental sicknesses and sent home. When she started it, she had herself to counseling her patients and made in depth study into their psychology. She knew much, learnt much and it became her passion. Her sister came once to visit and complained later that she thought her as a mental patient with her sister just merely looking at her intensely and not talking. Now sat in the air conditioned room of her small chamber, she relaxed and thought of her mental care home. She had herself fully occupied with an engineer kidnapped by the extremists group operating in the area for huge ransom and was rescued by the police even before his family could pay the ransom demanded. He was not beside himself but there was stark terror in his eyes and he sat not still even in his chamber even for few minutes but looked at sideways and said they are coming to kill him. His brother said he had been behaving like that after he was rescued. Fear psychosis. It would take time, she told his family but their understanding, love, care and above all patience mattered much and written some prescription in the paper. It would take time to recover, to cast aside his fear he said but he'd be well again and the family thanked him profusely. She told them to give him much needed support. She smiled in their relief and it was her satisfaction in their happiness. She opened the brown envelope addressed to her and went perusing and went into deep thought considering. It was from the head of some

Non Government Organisation creating social awareness wanting her to give a lecture on the 'Mental health in relation to environment.' she was not averse to the subject and had given much of its kind in the past two years, the last was for the police department who invited over her to give a lecture on 'Alcohol abuse and its addiction.' She had policemen as her patients too with majority with alcohol abuse and addiction to it that was self destructive in itself. They ruined along with their career and life, their families and children who too chose the path their fathers have chosen and became a menace to the society. She made them talked from the beginning till they were as they were and listened when they talked and linked all the jumbled up and understood their frustration and depression and the final flung they took with no outlet to their frustration. She had a new counseling assistant, someone invaluable to her. He was fresh out of the university with Post Graduate degree in Psychology. He though new was eager to learn and was as passionate as her and learnt much in a short time she had appreciated of. She had few trained nurses yet still needed to be trained fully she was satisfied not of and fifteen beds fitted in the building. For some patients, the relatives brought them from a long time and never bothered to visit or to know whether they are dead of alive. She made them worked in the kitchen fully after their recovery. She had a beautiful young girl for a patient depressed after her boyfriend left her came to her and consulted her and counseled her for more than an hour. She had a big empty space inside nothing could fill up she said. She had a permanent patient too—Jentilla. With love, care, understanding and much treatment she saw a recovery in her she was delighted of. She should have been treated from the beginning but she was left careless. She was busy, much too busy to give time to her fiancée. Only in the morning he received the message in her mobile with the mock hurt. She missed the dinner he hosted the evening before but she had a serious patient with violent bouts of temper she took care of. With the evening well near the dusk she left for home, exhausted after a hectic day and relieved when her mother brought a hot strong tea with a mouth watering slice of cake and placed the tray before her. Her father, retired from the school he taught sat in the verandah had his mind busy engrossed in the book he was reading. He went to the treasury her mother informed to withdraw his pension he collected monthly and brought the cake. Basked in the respect her name brought her father was happy and contented. So also her mother. Everyone recognized her as her father through her identity and respected well he enjoyed no end. She felt complete as human now and enjoyed the job she had chosen for herself. She reached out for her new album and flipped through one by one straight into the black and white photographs of five girls tensely sat on the wooden bench with the black and white plastic flowers in the middle and plastic wrist watches the five girls showed proudly at no one but to the photographer. The photos are much faded and partly damaged with the time but awoke in her bygone days but held a place of honour in it. Her mind journeyed back to the past.

Laughter.

Tears.

The valley beyond.

Her struggle step by step.

Every rung of the ladder.

She had achieved.

She had reached to the summit, climbed from the lowest step.

She was satisfied looking down from the summit.